D1448727

NIGHT TRAIN BLUES

by

Edward Hower

THE PERMANENT PRESS
SAG HARBOR, NY 11963

Library of Congress Cataloging-in-Publication Data

Hower, Edward.
Night Train Blues/Edward Hower
p. cm.
ISBN 1-877946-71-0
I. Title.
PS3558.0913N54   95-19559
813'.54--dc20   CIP

First Edition, June 1996 --- 1600 copies

Manufactured in the United States of America

THE PERMANENT PRESS
Noyac Road
Sag Harbor, NY 11963

I wish to thank the Ingram Merrill Foundation for a generous writing grant. I am grateful, also, to Yaddo, in Saratoga Springs, New York, for a Curtis Harnack residency fellowship.

Several chapters of this book have previously apeared in slightly different forms, in *Southern Review*, *Greensboro Review*, *Mississippi Valley Review*, and the *Ithaca Times*.

For
Jim McConkey

The tidal wave devours the shore
There are no islands anymore.

--Edna St. Vincent Millay

- ONE -

I picture an ocean liner floating beneath a black and silver sky. Carnival lights outline the tall smokestacks, pastel paper lanterns sway along the railings, and the portholes gleam like rows of gold buttons. The moon drifts on the wake of the ship, slipping up and down the waves.

I hear dance music splashing onto the decks from the ballroom, where a 1920s theme party is in full swing. Cutouts of flappers and Stutz Bearcats are hung at crazy angles on the walls. Over the dance floor a revolving mirrored globe releases swarms of sparkling butterflies. Men in white dinner jackets dip and glide; women in ball gowns throw their heads back and click their heels on the parquet.

I picture myself as the band leader in a smart blue uniform and a cap with a shiny black bill. When I croon into the microphone, *Yes sir, that's my baby,* waves of gaiety wash back and forth across the floor.

The dance contest is beginning. Smiling, I step down off the bandstand and dart among the couples. Whenever I tap a man's shoulder with my baton, the couple has to stop dancing and leave the floor. The young ones go first. Then I search out the middle-aged men who have kept themselves trim with lifetimes of polo and golf, and women whose breakfasts of mare's milk or whatever they drink has kept them willowy. These couples I cut down with flourishes of my wand, bringing it to rest on the backs of necks like the tip of a sword blade.

The captain has given me strict orders about which couple is to win: a beaming bald tycoon and a young blonde woman with a face like painted china. I have other ideas.

Only one other couple remains on the floor now. They're good, especially him, a tall, hawk-nosed man with a shock of gray hair rising from his forehead. The woman, fortyish, slender, bespectacled, seems to be fueled by champagne and a kind of ecstacy. What can be getting into her tonight?

It must be the cruise: finally being here among the sort of elegant people she could only have dreamed of during her grim

7

childhood. Even her best friend from the 1920s, a woman who writes to her about holidays on exotic islands and nights at the opera—even she would envy her now.

As the band goes into a final Charleston, I strut around the dance floor, my baton bobbing in the air before me. All eyes follow me. Ladies squeal behind gloved fingers; men stomp their feet like a crowd at a public execution.

Who is to be slashed and who spared? I half-shut my eyes, spin in place, and bring my baton down on the nearest shoulder.

Did fate decide? No, that spin was just to please the audience and to deceive the captain, who glowers at me now like God in epaulets from the shadows behind the bandstand.

The deadly wand has touched the tycoon. Holding his drooping partner, he shuffles to a halt and bows briefly toward the winners.

The lucky couple freezes for the camera. Its flash turns them incandescent—hands touching at arm's length, knees bent, heads back. The man looks as smug as I knew he would. But the woman's face amazes me with its beauty. I snatch up the tall winner's cup and run with it across the floor, pumping it high into the air to make the applause flutter down like cascades of silver leaves.

Later, I roam the decks watching the phosphorescent waves roll past the ship. The captain, undeceived by my act, has fired me, and now my baton floats somewhere on the ship's wake.

I hear voices nearby and duck behind a funnel. The winners pass by. The woman holds her husband's arm and hums something in a high, small voice. A champagne bottle swings in her free hand. She raises her face, bathing it in the glow from the paper lanterns that bob on strings overhead. The deck tilts gently; snatches of dance music fly on the breeze with the scent of salt spray. She pulls the tall cup from under her husband's arm and gazes at it. Though it is only tin—I've given away dozens of the things—it seems to gleam like a grail. Now she sloshes champagne into it, raises it to his lips, then to hers.

They stagger off down a corridor. I perch precariously on a railing as they rush into their stateroom. The porthole's round glass turns them into contorted, enchanted figures in a fish-eye camera lens. They fall onto the bunk, and the whole ship seems to rock with the impact. My stomach tilts; I clutch the railing to keep from tumbling off. One lantern remains stationary as the others sway around it: the moon.

The woman in the lens turns onto her back, her gown and petticoats rising above her white thighs. She spreads her knees as if to absorb moonbeams into her womb. The man kneels over her, his suspenders fallen. He raises the bottle. Champagne splashes over her. She screams, laughs, the bubbles sizzling on her bare skin.

I turn away quickly—I lose my balance on the railing—I tilt backwards—and plunge toward the waves. The spray rises fast. As the phosphorescence closes around me, I hear a woman's voice singing: "*Yes, sir, that's my baby, that's my baby now.*"

The next morning, my parents go for a walk on deck, feeling sheepish, blurry, amazed. When couples from the dance nod at them, they smile back, shivering with the thrill of their social success. Someone raises a camera and click! they're frozen in a strange lock-stepped stroll.

Do they know that what they have done the night before will keep them locked to each other for another twenty years? No, no. In the brilliant sunlight of a cloudless day on the open sea, the notion that a child might have been conceived on moonbeams and champagne cannot have occurred to them.

Years later, fascinated by old photos I found in the attic, I began to make up stories about the people in them. I pictured myself among them, and we all took on lives of our own.

Some of the photos I remember most vividly may never have existed; what I'm recalling are sepia-toned scenes I made up out of scraps of information that fell my way. Notes found scribbled on envelopes, old postcards, ends of overheard conversations, snatches of songs that stuck in my mind—they all helped me to fill in the blank pages in my family's life, past and present.

I jumped into those gaps, too, picturing myself in important roles. I think I wanted to do more than fill in the dark, empty places in my family's life; I wanted to change it. Of course I didn't succeed.

But anything is better than a blank page.

I remember looking for photos of my arrival in Connecticut as a new-born baby. Miss Gilly, the English nanny my mother had hired in a panic a week before my birth, told me that I rode home in a laundry basket in the back of a station wagon. The basket was packed with soft towels to keep me cushioned from the bumps in the road. She said that when the car stopped in front of the big white house, my mother, sitting beside the driver, opened her eyes slowly and squinted around the yard as if she expected my father to rush out to meet her from behind a tree or a rock. "He's not even here," she said, finally. "I need a drink."

Years later, at a cocktail party, I heard my mother say to a woman in a white fur stole, "Of course, when Jerrett arrived home, his father was there with his camera."

I found no photos of this event. But I could picture Robert, my nine-year-old brother, waiting all day for me to arrive from the hospital in New York. Now he lifted the back of the station wagon and found me lying in my basket. The bill of his blue baseball cap shaded me from the pale winter sun. Giving off a scent of soap flakes, I smiled up peacefully at him.

My mother leaned against the car door, looking exhausted. Well-to-do women of her age—42—didn't have babies; she'd never dreamed anything like this could happen to her. Her cheeks were caved in; tangled hair made a blur in front of her glasses. When she saw my brother thrusting an orangish-colored teddy bear into my face, she cried, "No, Robert! I just got him quiet!"

"I won't hurt him!" Robert blinked fast, his facial tic acting up. He saw me waving my arms as if to reach out for his present, and the worried look on his round face turned into a grin.

My mother tried to push the bear away. I groped for it and started to screech.

Then Miss Gilly intervened. She lifted me expertly from the basket and squashed me against her soft chest. I rose to what must have seemed like a great height, though she was actually short and squat. She smelled of peppermints. I liked the soft hair on her forearms; her white uniform felt like tissue paper against my face. With her smiling poppy eyes, she looked like a red-cheeked frog.

Dropping the orange bear, Robert rushed away. He ran past

the house and into the woods at the bottom of the hill. I stared after him as he vanished among the trees.

My mother walked slowly through the front door. Her footsteps echoed on the stairs. Her bedroom door shut behind her with a thud. She stayed in her room for a month. Miss Gilly had to bring her meals, cigarettes, and ice cubes three times a day.

"When you arrived, that woman handed over the house to me," Miss Gilly told me years later. "I might have known that one day she'd want it back."

"Where did Robert go?" I asked Miss Gilly, as we watched cocktail party guests arrive from behind my window. I was intrigued that I was now nearly the same age my brother had been when I was born.

Miss Gilly shook her head. My brother's movements were as much a mystery to her as to everyone else.

We were having our afternoon tea in the little room off the kitchen where, with Miss Gilly in the room next to mine, I'd spent the first eight years of my life. I loved the cluttered, barricaded feeling of our rooms, which had once been the servants' quarters. Remembering a story Miss Gilly had read me, I'd pictured our wing of the house as a thatched peasant cottage tucked under the high battlements of a haunted castle. At night, the castle filled with muffled reverberations, as if my parents were stamping around, bumping into furniture and each other.

More cars rolled up the driveway. My mother's preparations for this particular party had been even more elaborate than usual. Caterers and butlers were hired. The piano was polished until it glowed. The grass was mowed so that the lawn was laid out in formal green stripes from the terrace down to the edge of the woods. Along the driveway, petals were raked from around the flowering dogwood trees that shone in the sun like red and purple parasols.

The cars that passed my window were boxy four-door sedans, no convertibles, no flashy colors. They parked side by side on the lawn. Out of them stepped men in light summer slacks and sports jackets to open women's doors. The women walked precariously in long dresses and high-heeled shoes across the grass. My parents greeted them at the front door. My mother laughed determinedly. My father smiled, holding a man's elbow to steer him inside.

11

I sipped my tea as slowly as possible. On my table a minia-ture turtle floated in a glass bowl, its legs and head motionless in the water. Miss Gilly had recently given it to me. Each week after her day off, she brought home small gifts to make up for having left me "alone in the house." On the turtle's back was a painting of a boat, some sort of river barge. My mother said that the turtle was going to suffocate because of the painting. Miss Gilly promised me, though, that the picture wouldn't hurt it—why else were they called "painted turtles"? I worried about this, though, and often poked it with my finger to make sure that it could still move.

Sitting at the window beside me in a lumpy old housecoat, Miss Gilly sipped her tea slowly, too. The clicking of her knit-ting needles kept a steady, quiet rhythm. She was making me a sweater; her chins quivered as she moved her lips to count stitches. Suddenly she heard my mother's voice in the kitchen next door, and dropped a stitch.

"You'd better go change now, Jerry," she sighed, and glanced at my dungarees. I'd been picking dried mud from them under the table.

"I haven't finished my tea." I pushed my tongue deep inside the cup to get at the melted sugar at the bottom. "Why do I always have to go meet the guests? Robert doesn't have to!" A few moments ago, I'd seen my brother headed out toward the toolshed, pounding a tennis ball into his baseball glove. He played games of catch with himself against the side of the shed for hours at a time.

"Listen, dear, d'you think *I* like going out there with all those people? I have to stand there until your mother comes and takes you away." Miss Gilly pressed her lips together. "Right, and then I'm supposed to come creeping back to the scullery. Like I was a servant!"

"Aren't you a servant?"

"Certainly not!" Her cheeks went dark pink. "A nanny isn't a servant! When I was in Europe with the embassy family, they invited me to meet the guests at their parties. I mingled, I did. I went on trips with them too." She filled her mouth with a party canapé and chewed it slowly. "In Egypt, we drove out to look at the pyramids in a car with the British ambassador himself. That car had cut-glass vases next to the windows, with real flowers in them."

"Is that where you went up in a balloon?"

"No, dear. That was Paris, France."

"I want to go to those places."

"I dare say you will, one day." She sighed.

"What else did you see in Egypt?" I asked, hoping to hear the story about her trip down the Nile.

"You're stalling, Jerry."

I glanced outdoors, then suddenly leaned forward, my forehead touching the window. "What's *that*?"

A cream-colored whale was heading up the driveway toward the house. I'd never seen such a huge car. Its windows were so dark that whoever was inside was hidden from view. The silver spokes of the wheels blurred like pinwheels. The huge gleaming tail-fins were studded in back with lights that glowed and tinted the air red.

The car stopped. A man in a uniform and black-billed cap walked quickly around the nose of the car. He pulled open the back door, gazing straight ahead as if forbidden to look upon whoever might emerge. I wanted to wear a uniform and drive a car like that.

A small, plump, ordinary-looking man stepped out.

Then a woman emerged in a blur of colors. She wore a silky green dress with a white fur stole over her shoulders. Her hair, which she shook away from her face with a toss of her head, was as red as the car's taillights. She put a cigarette in an ivory holder between her lips. The man reached up—the woman was taller than he was—and produced a flame right out of his fist like a magician. Her head tilted back. She exhaled a thin stream of smoke. I waited to see what she would do next. Her face broke into a wide red-lipped smile as she saw my father coming down the walk toward her.

"Fancy her being here," Miss Gilly said from behind me.

"Why shouldn't she be?" I asked.

Miss Gilly rolled her eyes: another secret. The house was full of secrets. They collected along the clean white ceilings of the rooms like cobwebs which everyone pretended not to notice and which I was too small to reach.

I watched my mother take my father's arm. Then she did something even more unusual—she suddenly embraced the woman. Her eyes were closed tight on the woman's shoulder as if she were about to cry. Then for a moment they stood staring at each other. As the woman glided through the front door, I pushed my forehead against the glass. Miss Gilly yanked me back by my shirt collar.

"Who *is* she?" I asked.

"Laura Miller. . .the husband used to be a business partner of your father's in New York. That was years ago, before your parents moved out here." Miss Gilly narrowed her eyes. "The four of them used to be thick as thieves, the way I heard it."

"Don't you like her?" I asked.

"It's nothing to do with me, I'm sure." Miss Gilly steered me toward the door, her hand warm on my neck. "Go on upstairs, now. You can bring your turtle with you," she said. "Don't let your mother see you in those filthy trousers. We don't want a row this evening."

Walking stiffly in her too-tight beige suit, Miss Gilly led me onto the terrace. I wore my white pants and blue Sunday school blazer. My combed wet hair dripped under my collar.

Marbled clouds fanned over the sky toward a sunset that was singeing the far hillside a dusty purple and scarlet. The flower beds along the terrace reflected the brilliant colors overhead, and I heard guests complimenting my mother on the heavenliness of the view. Clusters of them talked about tennis, crab grass, the Historical Society—just as, my mother always complained, they did at parties week after week, year after year.

As she started moving toward me, I expected Miss Gilly to slip back into the house, but she didn't. Her eyes narrowed, as if she'd just decided something. Hunching her shoulders forward, she lumbered across the side lawn toward the toolshed, where I could hear Robert slamming the tennis ball against its side. What did she want with him? I stood on tiptoe to watch her go, but some guests blocked my view.

My mother, still headed in my direction, circulated among the guests, trailing a clink of ice cubes. The pewter-colored dress she wore rustled at her ankles. Her frosted hair seemed to need a lot of patting down. As she paused to talk to people, her eyebrows flew up in exclamation, but her eyes rarely focused on anyone. She looked as if she had what she called one of her "boring headaches."

"Where have you *been,* darling?" she asked, leaning over me. Faint blue veins were visible in the pale skin of her chest.

A circle of women formed around us. The air went blurry with the scent of martinis. I staggered back. Faces dipped down to my level; high-pitched greetings sprayed out of smiles. A lady with large nostrils breathed anchovy paste into my face. I scowled at her and tried to tune out what my mother was saying—something about my music lessons.

"Would you like to play the piano now?" someone whispered. I looked up. The woman with the white fur was smiling at me.

It occurred to me that music might stop all the embarrassing talk. I nodded. My mother, delighted, led me into the living room and waved her hands to hush the guests. I put my head down and cranked out "Country Gardens." The gardens' flowers—I pictured them with wire stems and jagged steel petals—formed a shield around me. Finishing, I glared around at my audience. A man with a bald dome stopped whispering to a woman with painted pink and beige cheeks. The crowd of faces watched me like the row of china Toby mugs on the dining room shelf whose contorted smiles I always ducked when I passed them. I pictured myself knocking them off the shelf one by one with a stick.

Then the woman in the fur leaned over the end of the piano. "How about something a little livelier?" she asked. Her voice was quiet, almost a whisper. She seemed to know my secret—that I'd been learning to play by ear. I played something I'd heard my mother humming behind her bedroom door: *Yes, sir, that's my baby.*

Most of the guests seemed to recede into the distance. Mrs. Miller, in my peripheral vision, was a fuzzy white blur nodding in time to the music. A silver vase rocked on the piano. My mother, holding her glass close to her face, began to dance in place. She looked amazingly graceful. I'd never seen her do anything like this, and almost lost the beat. Then my father appeared—to dance with her or to stop her from dancing I couldn't tell, for just then I came to the end of the song. The applause exploded in my ears. I fled into the kitchen, my face burning.

"Why did you go talk with Robert?" I asked Miss Gilly.

"When was that?" Holding two plates, she shut the kitchen door with her foot. The caterers' voices and the clat-

15

tering of dishes suddenly ceased; the room went quiet.

"When you—you went out to the toolshed," I said, stammering for some reason. "Robert was playing ball."

"Oh. I just needed to find something." Red splotches appeared on her cheeks. She set the plates down on the table. "I got you all white meat, the way you like it. Now eat and don't talk so much, dear."

After dinner, I started upstairs to my new room—the attic where I'd moved just that week. I felt a hand on my shoulder. Cold bracelets clinked against my neck. My mother was walking unsteadily behind me with a glass in her hand. She said something about the bedtime prayers I'd been learning. Her face dipped close to mine. "Just as you always do," she whispered into my face. "Just pretend we're not even there."

I went to my bed and knelt beside it. Several women were clustered behind my mother at the top of the stairs, but I didn't see Mrs. Miller. The women smiled encouragingly at me, holding glasses close to the folds of their dresses as if to hide them. My mother switched on the overhead light. I clasped my hands on the pillow, my forehead prickling.

"Our Father, Who art in Heaven...." My mouth stuck shut.

"That's lovely," my mother whispered, the ice swirling slowly in her glass. "Go on, darling."

"Hallow-ed be thy name. Thykingdomcomethywillbedone."

"_Jerrett!_"

I ground my teeth.

"You're rushing it badly." She sat down hard on the edge of the bed, causing my chin to bounce on my folded hands. A stain appeared in the sheet, smelling of gin.

"You spilled your drink," I said.

"You didn't rush the pieces you played on the piano, darling. I know you can say your prayers just as beautifully." Her fingers gripped my shoulder.

I began more slowly. Dresses rustled behind me. Someone whispered, "Lovely!" Someone sniffled.

"Amen," I said, finally finishing. Silence settled over the room like snowflakes in a glass globe. "AND GOD BLESS MISS GILLY!" I screamed, "AND MY TURTLE!"

Someone coughed. From far downstairs, I heard a burst of laughter.

My mother stood up and gripped the bedpost for support,

breathing through her teeth. She squinted down at me. Then she wandered slowly from the room, holding her forehead.

One by one, the women glided out, their dresses whispering on the stairs. In the hallway below, I heard my mother's voice rising, scraping my eardrums like a fingernail. Then it fell away. I scrambled to my feet.

The turtle was floating motionlessly in its bowl on the bureau. The picture on its back reflected the overhead light; the paint looked hard and thick. I scrubbed at it with my fingers, but the colors seemed to be baked into the shell.

The attic room was long and cavernous. I missed my little room downstairs next to Miss Gilly's. My mother had had the attic painted in cheerful colors and furnished with a new desk and bed and shelves for my toys. She'd insisted that I was too old to be crowded in with Miss Gilly downstairs, and that I would enjoy having the space to spread out in. I'd kept my outrage to myself, having often been warned by Miss Gilly about making scenes that might endanger her job.

I put on my pajamas and, keeping the reading lamp on, crawled into my new bed. The pillowcase felt starchy and the blanket smelled like a department store. After a while, I seemed to be sleeping. I dreamed that I lay buried beneath layers of sticky sheets. They tightened around me, hardening like paint. I couldn't move my legs or my arms. I couldn't breathe. Crying out, I jerked my head up hard. I was sitting, awake, gulping in air. My sheet was snarled in a heap at the foot of the bed.

The walls faded into the darkness at the far end of the room, contiguous with the night outdoors. Was I really awake? My clock said 2:00, later than I'd ever been up. The turtle was still on the bureau. I lifted it out of its bowl, water dripping from my fingers. It looked lifeless in my hand. Finally its head poked out of its shell, and the hard little feet began paddling weakly against my palm. I started breathing again.

The party downstairs made the house reverberate. I wasn't used to so much activity there.

During the war, when I'd been smaller, the main house had sometimes been entirely empty. My father, who had flown in the Army Air Corps during the First World War but was too old for the Second, spent months at a time away from home working, like many senior business executives, as a dollar-a-year man in Washington. My mother served with the Red Cross Motor Corps, driving soldiers to hospitals around Connecticut. She often stayed over-night and arrived home too exhausted to come out of her room for days. When I was five, my brother was sent away to prep school—as punishment for something bad he'd done, I thought, though my mother had tried to reassure me that this wasn't so.

On a rare night when my father had come home from Washington, I had tiptoed upstairs to find him poring over papers on the desk in his bedroom, which was across the landing from my mother's bedroom. When he finally saw me standing in the doorway, he said I could come in for a little while if I was quiet. But there was nothing in the room to interest me—all surfaces were neat and bare. He took off his half-glasses and smiled down at me. "Here," he said. From deep in a desk drawer he pulled out a small airplane. He said I had to be careful with it. I nodded, taking it in my hand. The cloth on the double wings was translucent like the wings of a dragonfly. As my father filled in columns of figures with his gold pen, I lay on the carpet and swooped the plane beneath his chair as if it were flying under a tall bridge.

Now, listening to the party at the top of the attic stairs, I put on my bathrobe and dropped the turtle into the pocket for company. I tiptoed down to the second floor landing and stood very still outside my father's room, rubbing my eyes. Voices buzzed from the rooms below the banisters. Footsteps clicked on hardwood floors. Treble notes from the piano bounced like handfuls of Ping-Pong balls on glass.

My father's door was ajar. A light was on in his room. Stepping closer, I heard someone wandering slowly back and forth. It wasn't my father. Smelling perfume, I tiptoed up to the door.

Mrs. Miller, her back to me, stood over my father's desk. Her shoulders were bare; on the bed lay a heap of dazzling white fur. Her green silk dress said "shhh" as she turned toward me.

"Hello again!" She smiled, and lines fanned out into her cheeks. Her mouth was the color of raspberry sherbet. "Jerrett, the musician," she said, her voice slightly slurred. "I've heard...so much about you." She reached out her hand. Her gloved

18

fingers felt as if they were made of velvet. "I'm Mrs. Miller and...I'm very pleased to meet you."

I pushed my bare toes into the carpet. "Hello," I said. No one had ever called me a musician before. I liked it.

She sat down on my father's bed. "You know, I came up to find you," she said, piling the fur stole in her lap. It squirmed like a white animal. "He said you were upstairs. But once I found his room...I got distracted."

"My room's in the attic."

"Oh..." She gazed at the ceiling. "Isn't it lonely up there?"

I stared at her and nodded.

"I'll bet it is," she said. "Would you...like to sit down?" She patted my father's desk chair. Her hand moved up and down gaily, as if her palm were resting on an invisible spring. The movement made me smile, and this made her laugh, her eyes widening.

I could see that she was drunk. I knew that my mother got drunk sometimes, but she did it quietly, ashamedly, as if her gin was a medicine she had to drink to keep her headaches away. Mrs. Miller seemed to have done it just to make herself laugh. Her hair glowed red in the lamplight; watching it brush against her neck, I felt my own skin go faintly warm. It was rude to stare at her, I knew, but at this strange late hour, all the rules were different. I climbed onto the chair and sat down.

"I heard that some ladies got to hear you say your prayers," she said. "I'd have loved to have heard that."

"I hated it." I squeezed the knot of my bathrobe cord.

"I suppose it couldn't have been much fun for you," she said. "Isn't it silly—when I wasn't invited to your prayers, an awful sorrow went...stabbing through me." She touched her chest.

"Why?"

"I felt like...the woman in the fairy tale who wasn't invited to the child's christening. The one who cast a spell..." She wiggled her fingers in the air, smiling. "But I thought...I'll just go upstairs and see him by myself. I'll probably never...get another chance. Oh, you do look like your father! I'm so glad you came to see me."

"I heard you in here. I was curious."

"I like curious people. Brave people," she said. "Tell me about yourself. What do you do...up there in your attic?"

19

"I explore under the eaves sometimes," I said.

"If I had a wonderful little boy like you, I surely wouldn't keep him in the attic..." Her voice faded out.

"Don't you have any children?" I asked.

She shook her head slowly.

"Maybe you will," I said.

"That's sweet." Her hand lighted on my wrist. I felt my face flush. Then she turned and picked something up from the desk.

"What were you looking for?" I asked her.

Her lips sank at the corners. "I've always wanted to see the house he'd gotten out here, and his room..." Her fingers opened slowly. She was holding my father's tiny model biplane. The cloth on the wings had almost disintegrated in its wire skeleton.

"You have to be careful with that," I said. "It's old."

"Old...yes." She nodded slowly. "I'll put it back. I just wanted to...hold it." When she set it on the desk, she had to push her other hand down on the bed, as if the plane had been giving her ballast.

"My father was an aviator," I said. "I think his plane looked like that one."

"He used to tell such exciting stories. Has he told you some?"

"No." I stood up to have another look at the plane.

Her brow rippled with lines. "He doesn't talk much any more, does he?"

I shook my head, pushing the plane across the desk top. I left it there and sat down on the edge of the bed. The fur shifted. My toes were restless on the carpet. Suddenly I felt something move against my thigh. It startled me so much that I almost slapped at it. Then I remembered my turtle and reached into my bathrobe pocket.

Her eyes followed my every movement. "What've you got?"

"It's just my turtle." I rested it on the palm of my hand so that the light shone on it. Its head ducked back into the shell.

"Oh, can I see?" She pulled off one glove and picked up the turtle from my hand with her thumb and forefinger. The skin around her knuckles was wrinkled. "He's got a pretty picture on his back," she said.

20

"I wish he didn't. The picture's going to kill him."

She dropped her eyes. "I used to have turtles like these when I was a girl. Grown-ups used to give them to me. The poor turtles always... died, I'm afraid. Eventually. The truth is, Jerrett..." She leaned forward and gazed at me. "It had nothing at all to do with the paintings on them."

"It didn't?" I sat up straight in my chair.

"I think..." She raised her hand slowly until the turtle was inches from her lips. "I think they're just not made to...to live in captivity. It's their nature."

"Oh," I said. "I never knew that."

She nodded, gazing at the turtle. The tip of its nose appeared, then slowly its head stretched out toward her, rising in the air.

"That's amazing. He hardly ever comes out if somebody new is holding him," I said.

"Maybe he knows he's among friends."

She set the turtle down and we watched it explore the blue bedspread. We were both smiling, as if we were discovering the huge blue territory ourselves for the first time. The room was warm and smelled sweet like her perfume. Her fingers pushed down the spread, creating a hill for the turtle to crawl down. I noticed that her glossy red fingernails were bitten down, the way my nails were.

Suddenly her hand rose fast from the bed. The turtle flipped over onto its back, its legs paddling in the air. "Damn!" she whispered.

"What's the matter?" I asked. Then I heard.

My mother's slow, tired footsteps approached along the landing outside. I slipped the turtle into my bathrobe pocket. Mrs. Miller clutched her white fur against her chest. She tiptoed to the door.

I went with her to look out. Robert stood beside my mother, talking to her in a low voice. I couldn't hear either of them through the party noise. Robert's face was a dark red, as if he'd been holding his breath. He blinked fast as he spoke—I'd never seen his tic so out of control.

My mother's mouth opened as if she were screaming. Raising her hand in the air, she gave Robert's shoulder an awkward push. He tilted backwards, off balance. She rushed away from him and fled into her room. Her door slammed with a

21

loud crack. Robert rushed downstairs, vanishing into the noise.

Mrs. Miller let out all her breath. The lines around her eyes deepened. "The party seems to be over." She sighed.

"I guess so," I said, still staring at my mother's door.

Mrs. Miller leaned forward, her face level with mine. "Are you going to tell anyone I was. . . here?" she whispered.

I stared back at her. Something in her face both calmed me and agitated me at the same time. "I won't tell," I said.

"Good!" She held my chin lightly in her hand. Her sherbet lips were cool and wet against the corner of my mouth. "It'll be our secret." Hugging the white fur to her chest, she lurched out of the room.

In the morning, I awoke feeling strangely uneasy. I seemed to be part of a conspiracy against my mother, one it was too late to get out of now. I began pacing the attic floor. My turtle distracted me. It was swimming in place, butting its head against the glass side of the bowl. I remembered what Mrs. Miller had told me about it.

When I walked outdoors, dew was glistening in the rows of tire indentations in the grass. The terrace was strewn with cocktail napkins. Sunlight ignited the yellow forsythia bushes and bleached the sky light blue. The turtle moved in the pocket of my shirt. Holding my hand gently over it, I rushed down the lawn and into the woods. The air was shadowy and cool. Branches brushed against me as I ran.

Arriving at the brook, I sat on the bank. Light flickered through the trees onto the water; I could see the current sliding between the smooth rocks. I set the turtle down and watched it for a long time. Its feet made tiny tracks in the dirt.

Finally, I gave the turtle a nudge. It paddled away and sank below the surface, glided along the sandy bottom between the rocks. I closed my eyes, and in that moment, I knew just how it felt to swim along the sand and out into the current.

22

- TWO -

Remembered photographs and remembered images blend together:

I picture Robert walking with me along a brook. The warm summer air smells of trodden leaves. We come out of the woods into a cornfield. The air turns a hazy sepia tint around us.

My mother, a girl named Marian who is about 12—my age in this picture—sits on a horse-drawn wagon leaning back into a pile of hay. She wears a yellow calico dress and round spectacles that glint in the light. When she sees Robert and me, she smiles and waves.

We jump on the wagon. The horse begins to plod forward. Robert sits up front, holding the reins. As we bump along the dirt road, Marian points out her old home, a tall farmhouse leaning into the gray Nebraska sky. The seasons have stripped off its paint. A rusted hay rake lies in the yard like the rib cage of a huge extinct animal. Noisy blackbirds swoop overhead.

Several years before, Marian's father walked away from the place and never came back. To keep the farm going, her mother worked herself to death; one morning, Marian saw her legs buckle under her in the barn as if she'd been struck down by an invisible sledgehammer. Marian went to live with an aunt and uncle who had nine children. Like Cinderella, she had to clean ashes from the kitchen stove every morning, and her chores never ended until she went to bed.

The hardest thing, she tells me as we ride along in the wagon, is that she has almost no time to read. There are cousins to care for, many farm animals and fowl to feed. They're all so boring! She gazes up at the small white clouds spattered like chicken droppings across the sky. Lying back with her head close to mine, she tells me about places she's read about where girls ride *on* horses, not behind them.

"In my books, people get to live in castles," she whispers. "I want to live in one—on an island in a lake, surrounded by high, high forests. With no little children or animals around. Maybe one dog, a graceful greyhound, but no more." Her breath is warm against my skin. "I'll have nothing to do all day but go for long walks and stare off into the mist and listen to the lake lapping at the shore."

"You'll live in a place like that," I tell her. "There'll be beautiful cedar trees, and a driveway lined with dogwoods...." I look to see if she's heard this—I can never tell if she's even aware that I've spoken. Her eyes are closed, her arms spread in the straw, pale sleeves turned to dusty angel wings. Twilight falls around us like soft summer blankets. Waves of high corn lap at the wagon's sides. The wheels squeak in rhythm beneath us. She recites verses from *The Lady of the Lake*, by Sir Walter Scott: "Harp of the North... the wizard note has not been touched in vain... silent be no more...."

We arrive at a weathered four-room schoolhouse. Winter has come; the fields are hard and stubbly with corn-stalks. The furrows' stripes barely pause for the schoolhouse yard on their way to the flat horizon.

Marian is older now, about seventeen, and Robert and I are older, too— about her age. Dressed in a middy blouse and long skirt, she holds a stack of books against her chest. Her future adult features are starting to show—clenched determined smile, quizzical eyebrows, drawn-in cheeks.

At high school, she has been constantly busy: historical society, poetry society, literary magazine, yearbook. She's sure that all these activities, along with top grades, will win her a college scholarship.

Marian and I wait in an empty classroom while Robert goes to get the news about the scholarship. She gazes out the window, seeing past the frozen fields all the way to the skyline of New York City, where the streets are strewn with gay confetti, where poets create great works in garrets, where couples in furs and top hats step out of limousines to attend the opera, where a ship glides out of the harbor onto a moonlit ocean....

Robert appears in the classroom doorway, out of breath. Marian rushes to him to hear the decision. He speaks in a low, halting voice.

"*Rejected?*" she gasps.

She glares at him mutely. Her lips still form that horrific word. They part, and I feel a silent screech reverberating up the walls like the fast-beating wings of a trapped bird. Her fist strikes Robert's shoulder. As if hit by something much harder, he staggers backwards. Then he flees out the door.

I search for him, but he's nowhere to be found. Marian and I wait in the schoolroom for him to come back. She rests her forehead on a desk top, moaning quietly. I tell her she can still go to college—she can work her way through a school where she can live in a sorority.

"You'll have your picture taken on the steps of the house with the other girls," I tell her. "You'll all wear white gloves and long elegant dresses."

"God, how I want to wear clothes like that!" she says, wiping the tears from her cheeks.

I don't describe the rest of the college to her—a provincial place where, her poverty showing like a rash, she has to wait on tables at the sorority and share a basement room with the cook. I want to tell her that though she'll never get her degree, she'll meet a bold young man who will become an aviator in the war and return to begin a business career in New York and buy a beautiful big house in the Connecticut suburbs.

"There'll be wide green lawns and cedar trees," I tell her. "You'll have nothing to do all day but...."

Robert appears in the doorway behind her. He is shaking his head hard at me—signaling me not to tell her what comes next—as if our lives depended on it.

My father missed a lot of trains, sometimes arriving home from work very late or not until the next evening. Sometimes the phone would ring around supper time, and my mother would go into her bedroom to answer it. I'd hear her voice rise, then drop off into silence behind her door. Miss Gilly would give me a look, and we'd sit down together in my old room to eat the meal she'd prepared for four people. On Tuesdays— Miss Gilly's dreaded days off—my mother would have to cook supper. After putting a roast in the oven, she would usually wait for my father at the kitchen window, clinking ice cubes round and round in her highball glass.

On the Tuesday evening after the cocktail party where I'd met Mrs. Miller, she waited for my father on the flagstone walk in front of the house. The sunset cast long shadows across the lawn and turned the pines to jagged black spikes around her. Her eyes were darkly rimmed—I'd never seen her wearing so much make-up. The pink splotches on her cheeks didn't go with her brushed-down gray hair. Glancing at her wristwatch, squinting down the hill, she talked to me whether I was nearby or not.

I changed my hiding place, moving from beneath the flowering dogwoods to spots behind the two cedars that guarded the driveway like tall green Buckingham Palace soldiers. I liked to jump out of hiding into the driveway to make my father stop his car and let me ride with him to the garage.

The sky darkened. My mother walked down the drive holding her glass against her chest. Crickets raised a scraping noise around her like a glare from which she couldn't turn her face.

"Come up, Jerrett!" she called, her eyes nearly shut.

"I don't want to!" I shouted.

"Please, Jerrett!"

I crouched lower behind the cedar.

"He's not coming!" she shouted into the dark.

"He isn't?"

"No!"

"Why?"

She clapped her hand over her mouth and turned back up the hill.

Sitting in the grass, I tried to make sense of everything that had happened lately. After the party, my parents had wakened me with their shouting across the landing.

"If only you hadn't involved Robert!"

"I never said a word to him, Marian!"

"Then who did, Dean?"

That was all I could remember. On Monday morning Robert left for prep school in a taxi, though his classes weren't scheduled to start for a week. When my parents called the school the next day, he hadn't arrived there, and no one knew where he'd gone.

I heard no voices on the landing that night. I tiptoed downstairs. My father's door was ajar. A slice of light lay along the carpet on the landing. I stood with my toes touching the edge of it, thinking he might let me come in to play with the plane again. Suddenly, behind me, glass shattered in my mother's room. I flattened myself against the wall, my heart pounding, sure that my father would come out to see what had happened. But his crack of light on the landing

26

grew narrower, not wider. I took a step toward it.

I hung back a second too long. The door shut with a loud click.

Could I have changed everything if only I'd moved faster toward that light?

The house rang with silence. Finally I tiptoed back upstairs to my room. I lay very still biting on my sheet until I felt myself tilting into drowsiness. Footsteps stomped into my sleep. I sat up. My father was on his way down the stairs into the hall. I heard him walk quickly through the dining room and into the corridor that led to the garage.

I rushed downstairs. The house was dark. His room was empty. I opened the drawers of his desk. All the papers were gone. Nothing remained but the model airplane.

Did he forget it, or did he leave it for me?

I stepped out from behind the tree and walked down the driveway to the mailbox. I knew that it was too soon for any mail to come from Robert, but I wanted to check, just in case. He'd sent me postcards from prep school before, and from several places he'd gone when he'd run away from school. I remembered the first card I'd received, while I was still in kindergarten. It had a picture of an old-fashioned locomotive on it.

I brought it with me one afternoon when I went to Robert's room to listen to his boogie woogie records. Suddenly the door opened and my mother stepped inside. "Oh, God!" She pressed her hand to her chest. "I thought your brother'd come home!"

I took the record off the turntable and waited for her to leave. She was wearing her bathrobe; her hair was flattened on one side of her face as if she'd just been lying on it. "Jerrett, you know he never lets anyone touch his records," she said.

"*I* can." I showed her the postcard. On the back it clearly read, *Go ahead and play my records, but not too loud—you know why.*

She squinted down at the card. "When did you *get* this?"

"A few weeks ago."

"It's more news from him than I've had." She lit a cigarette. "I miss him. Do you?"

I nodded. As she held the postcard in her hand, she looked so sad that I had the impulse to give it to her. Instead I showed

27

her the record I'd been playing. "Do you want to hear it?" I asked.

"I've got such a headache...."

I came closer to her, holding up the record. "It's called 'Night Train Blues.'" I ran my fingers several times beneath the words on the record's round label. "It's by Pinetop Smith."

"Yes, I see."

But she didn't. "I can *read* now," I said.

She squinted at the label. Suddenly she sat up, facing me, the ash dropping from her cigarette into her lap. "Jerrett— that's wonderful! How did you learn?"

"Robert taught me," I said, staring straight back at her. "From the records." This statement wasn't exactly the truth. But it was something better. I was amazed at the result it got.

She reached her hand out and rested it on my arm. "You can play that song if you like," she said.

"Won't it hurt your head?"

She shut her eyes. I felt her fingers holding me gently. "No," she whispered. "Play it."

I finally walked up the driveway, without any mail, of course, and went into the house. In the kitchen, my mother leaned over the stove, wisps of loose hair falling into her eyes. She pulled open the oven door. The chicken inside was charred black. Sitting at the table, I watched it wave in the air on the end of her fork.

"It'll be okay," I said.

"It won't." Her voice was choked. She flung the chicken toward the garbage bag in the corner. It bounced off the wall, skidded along the linoleum.

I picked it up and dropped it into the bag, my fingers feeling trembly. The room went still. A glowing liquid like clear yellow glue flowed out of the overhead light fixture and flooded the room, slowing her movements.

"I'll find something for you, I promise," she said, opening the refrigerator door. She squinted inside for such a long time that I thought she'd forgotten what she was looking for. "Oh hell! There's nothing but eggs. I'm sorry."

Both yokes broke in the frying pan. I scraped the butter knife across the toast, a sound that made her dig her fingers into her scalp. Sitting across from me at the table, she pulled her

28

highball glass and her pack of cigarettes in front of her.
"Is that your supper?" I smiled at her.
"That's just a joke, isn't it?" she asked.
"Yes. Why don't you laugh?"
"My face would explode," she said.
I ate very carefully.

There was something strange about my father's absence.
He'd gone away on business trips before, but this time my
mother began to spend all day in bed with the curtains drawn.
Miss Gilly said I needn't concern myself; she and I could man-
age just fine on our own. The following Tuesday, though, she
decided not to take a day off. Just to make sure I got fed, she
said.

As I woke that morning, I thought I remembered a motor's
hum hovering over my bed during the night, and red lights spinning through my room like the long blades of a fan. Miss Gilly,
who didn't usually climb the steep stairs to my room, was sitting on the edge of my bed. I asked her if I'd been dreaming
about the hum and the lights.

"No, dear." Her jowls quivered. "An ambulance came last
night. It took your mother to the hospital."

"*Why?*" I sat up.

"She's all right now, Jerry. It's nothing to worry about."
Miss Gilly pressed my face into her woolly housecoat.
"They're bringing her home today. She just got sick from swal-
lowing too many pills. The doctor pumped out her stomach."

I pictured a man pushing a bicycle pump's long black tube
down my mother's throat, and felt my throat constricting.
"Why did she swallow the pills?"

Miss Gilly glared in the direction of my mother's room, her
eyes growing small in her pudgy face. "I never understand why
that woman does anything," she said.

That afternoon, I stood behind the living room window
watching for a car to appear on the driveway. The gardener,
a tall, craggy, silent man whom my father had kept on part-
time after the war, kept pushing the mower back and forth
across my line of vision. Its motor made a whirring hum
that got inside my head. I couldn't stop thinking of the
time my father had run over a field mouse with the

machine; I'd found it sliced open and bloody in the grass.

A car rolled by the window. Two nurses brought my mother into the front hall, then left. Hearing her approach, I stepped into the hall. Her coat swung open; she was very thin inside it. Behind a mist of tangled hair her eyes looked like glass.

"Mother?"

I couldn't tell if she'd heard. Her face was turned away from me. She drifted past, dragging her fingertips along the wall. I watched her slowly climb the stairs. She vanished into the shadows at the top. Clenching my fists, I opened my mouth to call up to her again, but her bedroom door shut hard.

Her coat hung crooked over the banister where she must have dropped it. I yanked it off and kicked it down the stairs.

The next day when I got home from school, I immediately began practicing the piano, playing some of Robert's music by ear. But Miss Gilly came into the living room to tell me that I was to change into my good shoes: my mother wanted me to come to her room. As mad as I was at my mother, I'd been hoping she'd be well enough to see me. Now that she'd actually invited me upstairs, though, I hung back.

"It's spooky up there," I said.

"I know, dear," Miss Gilly said. "But I'll save your tea for you. I've got that almond coffee cake you like."

She watched me pace around the kitchen. Ever since I'd let my turtle go, she'd been watching me like this. When she'd found its empty bowl, she'd demanded to know what had happened to it. I said I'd set it free. Why? she demanded—when I'd loved it so. I told her that turtles couldn't survive in captivity. That's when she gave me the strange look. "Well, yes, I reckon the poor little thing's better off," she said, the outrage gone out of her voice. "Splashing around with his friends, feeding on minnows and whatnot."

I thought she'd stop watching me after that. "There's nothing _wrong_ with me!" I told her now, staring back.

"Of course there isn't, dear," she said. "But if you don't feel up to seeing your mother, I can have a word with her."

"I'll go," I said.

I climbed the stairs and walked gingerly into my mother's room. The door clicked shut behind me. I stood very still, my eyes adjusting to the dim light. Most of the curtains were drawn, giving the room the look of a cave with heavy cloth walls. At the far end, my mother lay back on a chaise lounge in a rumpled blue bathrobe. Her arm hung down, fingers touching the floor. There were cigarette burns in the carpet near her fingertips.

"Hello, darling," she said, sitting up. "I'm so glad to see you."

"Hello."

"Don't you want to come in?"

I went to the bureau and picked up a clock, a silver hair-brush clogged with hairs, a tiny crystal bottle with a rubber bulb attached to the top. I squeezed it. Mist sprayed out. The air suddenly smelled like flowers. The room was silent except for the hum of the lawn mower outside the window.

She cleared her throat. "How are you, Jerrett?"

"I'm all right," I said, and put down the bottle. "How are you?"

"I'm much better." She let out a breath. "Thank you." A wavy ribbon of smoke rose from a big china ashtray on a pillow beside her. She looked toward a gap in the curtains that let in a shaft of sunshine. "Everything's so bright in here," she said. "Would you close those curtains for me?"

I pulled them almost shut, smoothing the material with my fingers. I left only a sliver of light streaming through. Now the air glowed deep gold around her reading lamp. It cast one side of her face in deep shadow; the other cheek was a pale powdery white.

"You could move that chair by the dressing table over here," she said, smiling. "I've got a very nice story book to read to you."

I sat down in the chair, but didn't move it toward her. My feet hurt in the new shoes. After a while, I heard my mother reading aloud. As she turned the book's pages, some of them flaked off in her hands.

The story was about a girl who lived in an enchanted glade of pine trees on an island. She grew tiny and talked to mice and all the other little woodland creatures, including fairies that had wings like butterflies. My mother's voice got soft and high as she read. Sometimes it grew sleepy; her eyelids fluttered, but she roused herself.

31

"Oh look, a giant's coming!" she said.

I went to the chaise lounge to look over her shoulder. The girl in the book was in black and white, which surprised me, since I'd pictured her in the pastel colors my mother's voice took on. She was riding a miniature horse across a meadow beside a white castle. Some fairies ran alongside through the flowers. Only the giant's feet were shown: heavy black boots like our gardener wore. They were bigger than the girl and even the horse.

"The girl's called Miss Marian." My mother looked up at me. The ashtray full of cigarette butts wobbled on the pillow beside her. "She's got the same name as I do. My mother used to read to me from this book when I was a little girl. I haven't looked at it for—for more than forty years." She stared at the front of the book, her glasses crooked on her nose.

The girl on the cover was in color: smooth pink cheeks and pale hair that splashed over her shoulders. She wore an old-fashioned yellow calico dress whose outline was worn away. "I used to like to rub my fingers over the dress," my mother said.

I tried it. The cardboard was soft, like felt. I pulled my chair over to the chaise lounge. She started reading again.

At nine, I was too old for books like this, but I was intrigued by the idea of my mother being a little girl who could ride a horse and talk to tiny animals. The air in the room was warm and heavy with the scent of cigarette smoke. As I looked at the pictures, the meadow where Marian played became our back lawn on a hot summer day. My gaze wandered to the gap in the curtains where the faint roar of the mower streamed in. I pictured myself running through the grass ahead of Marian and the fairies to warn them out of its way.

My mother's voice faded. I waited. Her mouth pitched down at the corners, cracks appearing in her lipstick. She gripped the book with both hands. Between the last page she'd read and the back cover were nothing but some flakes of paper with broken lines of print on them.

"The story's just *vanished!*" she said. "All those pages!" Her eyes went damp. "I was sure the whole story was here—"

I watched her try to fit the bits of paper together. Her fingers were trembling; paper fluttered down to the carpet. The ashtray rocked.

"It's okay," I said. "You can just tell me the story." By now I badly wanted to hear how it would turn out.

She slumped back against the pillow. Strands of hair stuck to her temples like cobwebs. "I don't remember it," she said finally, and shivered. "I'm sorry, Jerrett. I—I just don't know what happened."

"Why don't you?" I asked, but she didn't seem to hear me. "It's such *hell* when you can't remember things! Good things—that you thought you could never forget!" She pushed her finger under her glasses. "Please, would you reach me a tissue?"

I took the box from her table beside the chaise lounge. Wadded up tissues lay scattered on the floor below it like dead moths.

"Perhaps we could—" My mother took a tissue from me and wiped her eyes. "Do you think we could make up the rest of the story?"

"All right." I waited again. But from the way she was biting her lip, I knew that I was the one who was supposed to make it up.

She gazed at me. I leaned over to look at the last picture in the book, trying to curl my toes inside my tight new shoes. I pictured Miss Marian sitting on the grass beside her horse with the fairies gathered around her. She looked over her shoulder—something beyond the picture's edge was approaching. The giant, probably. I stared at the crack in the curtain. Dust motes swarmed in the narrow shaft of light from the window. They seemed to be making a terrible noise. Now I saw Marian and the fairies running through the grass just ahead of a huge roaring lawn mower.

"Couldn't you *try*, at least?" she asked.

A story was coming to me—the way unplanned streams of notes did when I was playing the piano by ear—but I couldn't speak it out loud.

"Oh, hell—never *mind!*" Her head dropped back, sinking into a pillow. Her eyes had that same terrible glassy look in them that I'd seen as she'd drifted up the stairs the day before, ignoring me.

"No!" I clenched my fists. "I know what happens!" I pictured the mower chasing Miss Marian and the fairies over the grass. They panicked, fleeing every which way. The huge blades caught one fairy and sheered its wings off, leaving bloody stumps at the shoulders. The mower roared like thundering bass notes over a bump and bore down on Miss Marian. She sprawled on her face into the grass. ...

"Jerrett?" My mother turned her face back to me. Her lips were quivering as if about to fly open. I expected a scream, but instead heard a sigh. "I'm sorry. I gave up too soon," she said.

"What?"

"That was an awful thing to do, wasn't it?"

My throat constricted. I nodded. Then I stared at the open book again. "I think... the fairies fly away with Miss Marian—back to that magic place where the trees are." I pointed to the earlier pages that hadn't flaked off. My mother nodded, watching me.

"The horse gallops around in the air. And it—it gallops right in the giant's eyes," I said. "The giant's so scared of it he runs away forever...."

"Can the horse fly?"

"Sure," I said, though I hadn't seen any wings on the one in the book.

"That's lovely, Jerrett." My mother smiled. "When I was your age, I was very fond of a horse like that. He was in another story book. He was called Pegasus," she said. "Yes, now I remember—that's what I named our horse that pulled the hay wagon. Poor old thing, he was so dilapidated. I'm afraid people weren't always very nice to him. So I gave him that name—like the winged horse—to make him feel better."

"You really had a horse?" I asked.

"Oh, yes." She sat up, her bathrobe rustling. "It's so wonderful to be able to make up things the way you did," she said. "You mustn't ever let anyone take that away from you—" Her words came out jumbled like laughter. "Will you remember that, darling?"

"Yes," I said, and I did.

"Good!" My mother heaved a sigh and tilted backwards into her pillows. Her hand struck the ashtray. It toppled off the chaise lounge and hit the floor with a loud thud. "Oops!" she said.

I heard footsteps on the landing. The door opened. Miss Gilly stood in the doorway, her hands on her hips. The ashtray lay unbroken but upside down on the carpet. Lipstick-stained cigarette butts lay scattered around it among the tissues. The toe of one of my new shoes was dusted with ashes. Miss Gilly glared at my feet, then looked up at my mother.

"What's the matter here?" she demanded. Her face was dark red.

"Nothing's the matter," I said.

I stood up and took the book from my mother's lap. She watched me. Her hand fluttered into the air and rested on my arm for a moment.

Miss Gilly squatted down beside the ashtray. "What a bloody mess," she said. "You go downstairs, Jerry. This isn't your concern."

But I wanted to pick things up. When I'd put all the cigarettes I could find into the ashtray, I set it and the book on the bureau, pushing the crumbled pages between the covers as best I could. My mother watched me, smiling. Then she seemed to drift off to sleep, her glasses resting at an angle on her face. I tiptoed out of the room.

In the kitchen where I waited for Miss Gilly, the oven gave off an oppressive heat, and when she appeared, still red-faced, the room seemed to grow even hotter. I knew she was cross with me, but she was often that way, and her moods always blew over quickly.

"What were you doing in there all that time?" she asked. "Reading that story book, were you?"

"Uh huh."

"What on earth was it about?"

I pushed my finger along a scratch in the table. "Just a story."

"I never knew she even had any children's books." Miss Gilly slid the coffee cake out of the oven. "Oh look, Jerry, this is just the way you like it."

We took it and the tea things into my old room, where my play table was still set up by the window. The coffee cake was glowing hot, with almonds set in the hardened dribbles of white sugar. It gave off a sweet smell that I'd always loved.

Miss Gilly cut a large slice for me. I picked an almond off the top, then set it down on my plate.

"Are you all right?" she asked me.

"Sure."

She looked at me the way she had once after I'd been exposed to someone who had measles, as if she expected me to break out in them, too. Then she leaned over to lift the lid from the teapot. Steam rose into her face, making her scowl.

"I should have just left her mess on the floor for your father to find when he comes home."

I sat forward. "He's coming home?"

Miss Gilly rolled her eyes in the direction of my mother's room. "I dare say, that was the whole idea."

"What do you mean?"

"Nothing, dear." She pushed my plate closer to me. "Let's enjoy our peace and quiet here, while we've got it."

The house was silent. It did seem more peaceful than usual. The low hum of the lawn mower made the pane of the open window tremble slightly, but the sound stayed outside, fading gradually. I took deep breaths of the cool, grass-scented air.

- THREE -

I picture Robert and me, both teenagers, clumping along the wooden sidewalk in our boots. Sepia-tinted clouds hover above the roofs of the stores along the town's rutted street. A wagon rolls past us in the opposite direction, its horse's hooves blurred out of focus.

Robert stops in front of an open doorway. Over it hangs a hand-lettered sign: LANGLEY'S DRY GOODS. The letters look like drunken stick figures leaning against one another. A boy of about seventeen stands ramrod straight behind the counter. He watches Robert and me with a steady critical gaze that makes me wonder if my shirttails are out.

"I need something here." Robert squints to control his tic. The store flickers like a shadowy nickelodeon scene. "I won't stay long."

The shop is bigger inside than it looked; we have to walk far to reach the counter. A sooty smell leaks out of a pot-bellied stove in the corner. An old man stands behind a side counter, waving a cigar in his hand as he talks to someone. He wears a suit with a loud tie spilling from the vest. A shock of white hair falls over his eyes.

He is Bill Langley, famous in town for his carousing and womanizing. The boy is his son Dean, tall and hawk-nosed like his old man, but neat in a high-collared jacket and pressed trousers. He, too, is well known—class president, member of the high school football team, Sunday school teacher. Everyone says that if he weren't here to keep track of the inventory, the store would go under, as all Bill's other enterprises have over the years.

Dean leans over the counter and gives my hand an awkward, hard shake. "Hello," he says, a half-smile on his lips. The greeting is welcoming yet so impersonal that I sway in place, both drawn in and repelled. My fingers curl over my palm, recovering from the handshake.

Dean looks at Robert. "Well?" he asks.

We stare around. The shelves lean forward, about to dump their goods all over us.

37

"Tennis rackets," Dean says. "A complete line of self-improvement books."

"I don't know," Robert says, squinting hard. "I wish I knew."

"Sheet music?" I ask.

Just then the old man calls down the counter at us. His face is flushed; he grins out of the side of his mouth. I see whom he's been talking to—a woman whose red hair swirls high on her head. In the smoky light, her silhouette is rounded in front and behind like a Gibson Girl's. She goes around the counter to take the old man's arm and strikes a pose, her parasol open, as they face a big box camera on a tripod.

"Go on, boys, it's easy." Bill Langley points his cigar toward the camera.

Dean tilts his face away, frowning.

Robert steps behind the camera. I glance at Dean, clenching his fists behind his counter, and I try to shout at Robert, "Don't do it!" But my voice is dammed at the bottom of my throat. The floor tilts under me. I stumble into an explosion of flash powder. Everything turns a blazing white before my eyes.

When the room comes back into focus, I am, strangely enough, the one standing behind the camera, my hand clutching the rubber bulb that has caused the explosion. The red-haired woman is gone. Robert and the old man are leaning toward each other over the counter, looking at something.

"We're closing," Dean says to them in a low voice.

Bill Langley raises his hand from the counter to shield Robert from Dean's glare. He beckons to me. Grinning, I move closer. "J'ever see one of these, sonny?" he asks, holding up a rough wooden flute. He blows on it—tweet!—and cigar smoke streams out the end.

Robert and I laugh. Dean glares at the smoke, his nose twitching.

"Must be some kind of magic in this one." The old man peers into the tube. As he leans forward, his gravy-stained necktie swings out from his vest. "On the house," he says, tucking the flute into my shirt pocket. I point to Robert, and the old man hands him one, too.

We step away from the counter and begin to blow into the flutes, squeaking and squawking, our laughter turned to notes that swoop around the room.

Then above the noise floats a ribbon-like tune, a slow, moaning cowboy ballad. It must be the old man's tune, I figure. But when I turn to look, he's gone. The place where he stood has turned to blank smoky air.

It's Dean, my father, who's playing, his face as flushed as my grandfather's was, his eyes sad and lonely above his moving fingers.

⌒

The morning after my mother swallowed the pills, Miss Gilly had called Robert at prep school, where he'd gone several days after the cocktail party. He went straight to New York and, after dozens of phone calls, found my father and told him the news. Miss Gilly expected Robert to come home with my father. But when the taxi pulled up in front of the house, only my father was in the back seat.

"How was school today?" he asked, pausing outside my old room, where I still had meals and tea with Miss Gilly. In years past, when he'd come home from work, he sometimes walked into the room, put his briefcase down, and squatted beside me. A silver chain glittered on his vest. He pulled it, and a watch popped out of a little pocket. The watch was gold and shiny and cool against my ear where he held it so that I could hear the ticking. I always wanted to hear the ticking. As the glass lost its coolness and became warm, though, he took it away and slipped it out of sight into the pocket.

"School was okay," I said. I'd been drawing a map; I bore down with my pencil so hard that its point broke. His gaze passed from me to my map to some stubby crayons strewn around the table.

"If you're going to be a cartographer," he said, "you'll have to learn to be more careful with your tools." He picked up a crayon from the floor and set it down carefully beside my hand. "There."

I could tell that he wanted to be helpful, but I couldn't look up at him. The hairs at the back of my neck prickled. Suddenly I blurted out the one question Miss Gilly had told me not to ask: "Why did you go away?"

Miss Gilly made a faint groaning sound behind me.

"Mother was sick," I said. I knocked the crayon to the floor.

"She's—she's better now," my father said finally. He took an off-balance step backwards. "Things are going to change around here." I heard him go up the corridor, through the kitchen, into the hall, and up the stairs, where his footsteps faded.

"Did you see the way he glared at me after that question of yours?" Miss Gilly asked, letting out her breath. "Enough to turn a person to stone."

"I'm sorry." I started to rub a line on my paper with my eraser. "What's a cart-ographer?" I asked.

"Damned if I know, Jerry."

I'd learned how to find words in the dictionary. A "cartographer," I discovered, was a map-maker. I decided to use the word in my next letter to Robert. Miss Gilly said he'd probably gone back to prep school from New York—at least he'd told her he would.

I'd learned to draw maps because of Robert. Long before I'd moved to the attic, he had taken me there to show me the hidden passageways under the eaves behind the plywood walls. Entering through the back of a closet, we crawled into a long dark tunnel on our hands and knees. The beam from his flashlight ignited swirls of dust motes ahead of us. He kept his hand on the top of my head so I wouldn't bump it on the roofing nails whose points glittered like rows of teeth from the low slanting ceiling. By the time we reached his hiding place where he kept a big photo album, I'd stopped being scared.

That night, I'd dreamed of a maze of passageways and staircases concealed behind the walls of the house. I slipped into them through secret doorways in the backs of closets. I followed them down to the cellar and out beneath the lawn into the woods. I emerged through trap doors hidden under the leaves.

When I woke, I could picture the network of tunnels so clearly that I drew a map of them. Afterwards I made more and more elaborate maps until I didn't know if I was remembering the passageways from the dream or was making them up as I went along.

I showed a map to Robert. He studied it carefully. From the smile on his face, I could tell he knew about the tunnels, too. I told him he could have the map. "Thanks. But you hang onto it, pal," he said, handing it back. "You never know when you might need it."

The "new regime," as my mother called it, meant that my father would come home regularly every night on the 5:36 train "to spend more time with the family." In the evenings, he and I kicked a football around in the yard, while my mother watched us from the terrace, sipping ginger ale from her highball glass. (The crystal decanters on the dining room sideboard had been emptied down the sink.) Sometimes she smiled and clapped at us, and I felt that we were stage actors with an audience of one. I felt like a conspirator, the way I had the night of the cocktail party, but it was all right now. By performing with my father on the lawn, I was making something up to her.

The football had come in the mail in a box of my father's old things that my grandfather had sent from Nebraska. He was leaving his house to move into a hospital, my father said. I had only faint memories of my grandfather from one long-ago visit. He liked to tell jokes in a funny German accent; he smoked cigars—outdoors, only—and knew how to make flutes from willow branches. He'd made some for Robert and me, but after a while they didn't work. The football, too, didn't work: it wouldn't stay pumped up, and my father threw it out, as he had almost everything in the box. I was glad to see it go—I had no idea how to catch the thing.

Each Monday and Thursday afternoon, I saw my mother waiting by the driveway wearing white gloves, a pale blue suit, and a pillbox hat with a veil that hid her eyes. A taxi picked her up and an hour later brought her back; then she went to her room to rest. Doctor's appointments, Miss Gilly said, and tapped the side of her head with her forefinger.

When my mother could drive again she took me to the library, where she checked out a dozen or so murder mysteries each week. We chose children's books and lingered in the periodicals room. She showed me pictures of strange, beautiful tropical islands in *Holiday*, and quizzed me from the "It Pays to Increase Your Word Power" section in *The Readers Digest*. I was the only kid in the fourth grade who used words like "tyro" and "effulgent" in his reports.

She liked to read to me from her own books, especially from one by Sir Walter Scott with ladies and noblemen in it

41

who spoke in rhymes. Often she stuttered and repeated lines. Now that she'd stopped drinking, she said, it was hard for her to keep her place.

"When I was a little girl, I didn't have nice books like these." She gazed at the shelves by the piano. "I was ashamed to go into the town library because I smelled from the barn." She showed me her leather-bound books by Shakespeare, Tennyson, Flaubert, and a book of my father's by someone called Zola, a name whose sound I liked. She opened it carefully. I saw a picture of a man talking to a woman in a long nightgown; they were in a bedroom with red velvet walls. On some of the other pages, the women had hardly any clothes on. My mother flipped the pages quickly until she found a picture of a crowded dance floor hung with paper lanterns. "Your father and I danced in a ballroom like that once," she said. "It was on board a ship crossing the Atlantic, just before you were born." I tried to imagine my parents dancing. Another picture showed people in an enormous glittering theater. "All the time we lived in New York, we never went to the opera," she said, and sighed. "One of my best friends and her husband had a box. But your father would never go."

"Why not?"

My mother touched the picture with her fingers. "My friend used to sing small roles in the opera, before she was married. She hated giving it up, but she wanted children so badly. . . ." My mother closed the book and slipped it back on the shelf. "This is my favorite," she said, pointing to a slim book in the glass cabinet over the writing desk: *Harp Weaver*, by Edna St. Vincent Millay, the spine read.

I stood on the chair to open the cabinet, hoping for more pictures, but the cabinet was locked. My mother rifled through the desk's drawer, looking for the key, but didn't find it. I could see her eyes starting to get damp behind her glasses, so I distracted her by asking her if she wanted to hear me practice the piano.

She said she did. I played "Moonlight Sonata," "Country Gardens," and other pieces my piano teacher had given me. My mother was usually good for about ten minutes of music, after which she excused herself to go upstairs to lie down. I was sad to see her go, but also very glad to be alone so I could play Robert's jazz. I needed to play by ear every day to keep from losing the tunes that kept bubbling in my head.

One evening my mother walked into the kitchen, a part of the house that had never been her territory, and announced a new idea to Miss Gilly and me: she wanted me to join "the family" for dinner.

"I don't mind cooking for you and Mr. Langley—" Miss Gilly wiped her hands on a dishcloth "—since I have to cook for Jerry anyway, and I know I'll get to eat with him. But if I have to eat all by myself in the kitchen while he's with you—"

"But he's old enough to eat in the dining room—"

"If you'd started him out there, perhaps he wouldn't be so nervous about eating—"

"If you weren't always telling him dreadful *stories* about me—"

"I'm sure I don't know what you're talking about!"

"You do!"

They were still at it when my father arrived from the station. He stood in the door listening, then stepped into the kitchen.

"I won't have scenes like this when I come home!" The kitchen went silent. He pushed me out into the middle of the floor. "What do *you* want to do, young man?"

"I don't know." I stared at the linoleum. Again I was an actor in a play, but this time I had to think of lines to say. "Well, I could—I could eat in the dining room on Miss Gilly's days off. . . ." I glanced at my father. When he nodded at me, I went on, "and eat with Miss Gilly when she's here."

"Fine. That's settled." He gave my mother a look.

"I'd like to get on with the cooking, Mrs. Langley." Miss Gilly clamped a lid on a steaming pot. "If you've no objections."

"You—" My mother glared at my father, then at me. "Oh, never *mind!*" She rushed out of the room.

I looked up at my father, clenching my fists at my side. "You made me say it—"

"You can't please everyone," he said. "Sometimes you just have to please yourself."

I went up to the attic to think about that. For the first time, I was glad I had a room to go to that was far away from everyone. As I sat at my desk, a smile slowly broke out on my face. Nobody had ever asked me to decide something before. Once

I had, they'd all agreed to what I'd said! Maybe things really were changing around here.

As part of the new regime, I received a full set of the Junior Americana Encyclopedia and a closet full of educational games, many of which I left in their cellophane wrappers for years. Miss Gilly said my father was "trying to make up for what happened with Robert," by giving me "the best childhood money could buy." I worried that Robert wasn't getting his fair share, but she pointed out that his closets, too, were full of sports equipment and games, and he was going to one of the most expensive prep schools in the country. "Money," she said, "is not the problem in this house."

When Miss Gilly had been a child in England, she said, her father's wages from the mine had barely kept the family alive. In her village, no one—except for the blood-sucking squire who owned all the land—had an extra farthing to spend on children. She'd left school at fifteen to work cleaning out bedpans in a hospital just to pay for her keep. "The money your father spends on country club dues could've fed and clothed our family for a year," she said. I knew this wasn't fair, and tried to think of ways I could make it up to her one day. She said I wasn't to worry about that. I was just to make damn sure I didn't do anything to make my parents sack her and send her back to England, where all the buildings had been knocked down by the German bombs and no one had enough to eat.

When my father suggested that I help with some yard work on weekends, Miss Gilly didn't have to push me to join him. One of my earliest memories was of him working outdoors. I'd awakened from a nap to hear chopping noises that seemed to be whacking the clapboard side of the house itself. I ran outdoors. My father was a solitary figure on the edge of the wide lawn. As he swung the axe, cedar branches flew off like huge green feathers. The axe opened a raw wound in the trunk of a tree. Chips of wood scattered to the ground. They looked like chunks of turkey white meat. I crouched behind a bush, my toes curling in the chilly grass.

My mother's voice shot past me from the terrace. She walked across the lawn, arms out at her side to keep from toppling over on the uneven ground. Her glasses reflected the gray glow of the sky. "You'll absolutely ruin the view!" she shouted, sounding as if she was about to cry.

"There's no view anymore. The place is shut in with trees."

"I like to look at *them*!"

"If they're too close together, they choke each other's growth. I've told you that." My father's voice was deep, growly. He yanked the axe from the tree and began swinging again.

My parents kept talking about the trees and the view, but I had my eyes on a wedge-shaped piece of turkey white meat on the grass. I crept up on it.

"Where did you come from?" My father stared at me as if I'd just popped up out of the ground like a strange mushroom.

I pointed to the wood chip. "I want it!"

Smiling, he picked it up and squatted down in front of me. I reached out for the wood chip in his hand. I felt it slipping into my fingers. Immediately I pushed it into my mouth and clamped my teeth over it.

My father laughed, lines rippling into the hollows of his cheeks.

My mother said, "Take that out of your mouth!"

My father said, "You really think he's going to eat it, Marian?"

I tried to shout, "Yes, I am!" but all I could say was "Mmph, mm-mmph!" I leaked laughter, saliva, snot. But now nobody was noticing me.

They were arguing about the trees again. My mother staggered back as the axe blade whacked into the tree trunk, making the air shudder.

I ran toward the house with the slice of wood clamped between my teeth. Miss Gilly closed the door behind me, stopping the voices. My lips tingled with a piney taste.

Afterwards, I kept the chip on the table in the nursery. I liked to put it on my plate and pretend to cut off bites with my spoon. In time, it darkened, stained with gravy. But it kept the hard, rough texture I remembered from the day I first touched it in my father's hand.

Now my father and I chopped down cedar trees only while my mother was away from the house. At other times we cleared brush, raked leaves, trimmed the forsythia bushes. One Saturday morning, he said he had an idea for "a project" we could make together: an underground house. His own father, he said, had dug a deep pit in his back yard and put planks over it for a roof. There had been boards on the floor and packed earthen walls, like the sod houses our frontier ancestors built on the Western prairies.

We walked into the woods with our tools over our shoulders, his a big long shovel, mine a smaller garden spade. He picked a spot beneath an apple tree. Then he hung his old sports jacket over a branch and started digging. I dug, too. Grinning, I threw dirt into the underbrush, where it made rain-shower sounds among the leaves. Another shower of earth followed—my father's, falling beside mine.

I could tell that he'd slowed down so I could keep up with him. Soon I worked up a sweat. He glanced over at me, then leaned on the end of his shovel to rest. I leaned on mine, and we gazed through the trees at the yard. Gray-green under the dark clouds, the lawn looked as if it would stretch on forever like a prairie. A strong damp smell rose from the patch of naked earth at my feet, forcing my nostrils to widen as I breathed. I'd never known that dirt smelled.

The next Saturday, we went out to the same spot, which was now a rectangle of muddy earth a foot or two deep. My father's shovel started striking rocks as he dug. "I hadn't counted on this," he said, frowning. "It's a different soil from Nebraska."

I stood well out of the way as he attacked the ground, sweating and grunting. When the shovel struck a rock, it clanged and sparks flew up. "Nothing worth having," he said, panting, "is easy."

I nodded, and furrowed my brows as I dug. I fell further and further behind his pace. At the end of the morning, the rim of the hole was as high as my waist. "A good start," my father said.

The next week, the earth in the pit was full of soupy mud. It took a long time for my father to bail it out with his shovel. I had to stay in a corner of the pit, out of his way.

The following Saturday, he carried some boards from the toolshed. They were for the floor and the roof, he said. But when we reached the woods, a strange thing had happened to the pit—several inches of water covered its floor.

"If something's worth starting, it's worth finishing," my father said through his teeth, and started smashing away at the sides of the hole with a pickaxe he'd brought from the toolshed. I'd never seen his eyes so wild-looking; the look in them made me retreat to the apple tree. Even there I could feel the violent reverberations in the ground.

One big rock was blocking his progress. He attacked it with the pickaxe. Sparks and mud flew in all directions. Finally the rock rolled out of the dirt. It made a sloshing sound at his feet. He stared down. He was standing up to his ankles in dark, murky water.

Slowly, he raised the pickaxe, his hands sliding apart on the handle. The big anchor-shaped thing swayed high in the air, one of its steel points hovering above his upturned face, the other taking aim at the treetops. I scuttled behind the apple tree, my nails digging into its trunk.

He leaned forward. His fingers suddenly sprang open from the pickaxe handle, as if he didn't dare hold it an instant longer. It dropped with a loud clunk and flipped over, one point embedding itself in the mud wall of the pit.

"All this time...." His eyes narrowed until they shut completely. "I've been digging into a rock spring! Nothing but goddamn rock!"

I didn't move. The woods were quiet around us. Hot sunlight shone through the tree branches. My father's gray hair stuck to his forehead. His arms hung down, his shirt damp and muddy.

"Dad?...."

He looked around and spotted me. "It's what you call hitting rock bottom." He sounded as if he were making a kind of joke, but he wasn't laughing. "But sometimes all you can do is to cut your losses. Sometimes it's all you can do."

He climbed up out of the pit and stood beside me under the apple tree. I let go of the trunk. For a moment, he rested his hand on my shoulder. His hand got heavy, but I didn't move away. Then the weight was gone.

I felt released. I sprang into the pit to retrieve the pickaxe.

Squatting down, he took it from me and pulled me back up by the hand. He was smiling. "Well, we gave it our best shot, didn't we?"

I said we had.

Without tools on our shoulders, we trudged up the hill together toward the shed.

My mother rarely came up to my room; when she appeared there one evening, I knew something unusual had happened. My father would be away for a week, she said, because his father had died in Nebraska.

I tried to picture my grandfather, the pink-faced old man with white hair who had visited us only once. Robert had told me that as a young man he'd worked on a cattle ranch out West, and sometimes had ridden on freight trains looking for work. He'd been a travelling salesman, good at making friends with lonely small-town waitresses and secretaries. He'd tried farming. He'd run a general store that had gone under. Now he was dead.

I seemed to be sadder about it than my father was. The night he came back, I heard him saying to someone on the phone, "The old bird died in a loony bin." When I told this to Miss Gilly, she said she wasn't the least surprised to hear it.

Later, I woke to hear music coming from the living room and tiptoed downstairs. I could just make out the shape of my father sitting at the piano in the dark.

"You can come in," he whispered across the room.

"I never knew you could play," I said, standing near the bench.

He played something that sounded like honky-tonk music in Western movies. "My old man used to bang away on a plinky old upright in the parlor. Sang, too. Always offkey." My father's voice sounded choked.

"How come you never play the piano?"

"Haven't got the time." He sat up straight. "But it's good that you can take lessons, learn classical music. You'll have time. You'll never have to work like I did."

I sat down at the end of the bench. "Why not?"

"Because I'm seeing _to_ it you don't, that's why."

"I want to hear some more."

He leaned toward me. I felt his breath in my hair. "Okay," he whispered. "Cowboy song."

Eyes like the setting stars, cheeks like a rose
Laura, she's a pretty girl, God Almighty knows
Weep all you little rains—wail, winds, wail
All along, along, along... the Col-or-ado Trail

48

I'd never heard him sing before. I grinned, staring at the silhouette of his face. He sat very still, his hands pressing down the keys until the last chord had completely faded.

"One more?" I asked.

He lifted his head, as if I'd woken him. "Can't remember any more," he said, and wiped his eyes. "Just as well."

"Why is it?" I asked.

He stood up and shuffled slowly out of the room. I wondered if I would ever hear him play the piano or sing again.

- FOUR -

In this picture, Robert and I are gazing at a long white antique car parked at the curb. The fenders rise like two ocean waves on either side of the gleaming hood. I love the way the hood reflects the tall buildings, bending them, edging them with light. The car's uniformed chauffeur puffs on a cigar and grins at me. I wave at him. Robert and I enter a door beneath an awning. The chauffeur follows us upstairs and, tipping his black-billed cap, flings open a door for us.

We walk into a room whose walls seem to be covered in red velvet, with curtains to match. I smell sweet perfume. In the corners, lamp shades give off clouds of beige light. From the next room I hear a woman singing in a high rippling voice, "Sempre Libera," from *La Traviata*.

My father strides toward us wearing a bathrobe and pin-striped suit pants. The door shuts behind him, cutting off the aria in mid-note. He glares at Robert. "What are you doing here?"

"She swallowed pills—she tried to kill herself!" Robert screams. "I want to go home!"

My father rocks back on his heels. Then he squares his shoulders, towering over Robert. "That's the last thing we need, you coming home!" he shouts. "You blame me for what she did—but you don't know anything about it!"

Robert's eyes blink hard. The room flickers like an old movie.

"She said she'd be content when I got her a country house!" My father's arm shoots out at Robert. "She said she'd stop drinking! She'd stop shaming me, prodding me on, goading—"

Every time Robert tries to speak, blood dribbles from the corner of his mouth. There's blood on my father's knuckles as well. He wipes his fist on a handkerchief.

I yell at my father, but he doesn't hear me. He grabs Robert by the neck and flings him backwards. The curtains flap like huge red wings as Robert collapses into them. I hear a crash of broken glass. I run to the window. Outside, Robert is falling

50

slowly toward the street, his arms outstretched as if trying to embrace a current of air. He hits the sidewalk running. I crane my neck to watch him dash around a corner.

In the apartment, I search for the man in the uniform, as if he could tell me where my brother is going. The man's shadow slips along the wall. I hear him humming softly behind me. Yet when I turn to focus on him, he's gone; only the scent of his cigar lingers in the air.

After the first time Robert had gone away to school, Miss Gilly had said he might write to me. In case he did, I wanted to be able to read, though she said I was much too young. I watched carefully as her finger moved beneath the sentences when she read to me from story books. I began to recognize letters by their sounds. But the first whole word I learned to read was at the barber shop.

I was sitting in my favorite chair while the elderly barber snipped away at my hair. The other customers, like me, were reflected in the long mirror; we were a row of heads poking out of the tops of white tents. The place smelled of shaving soap and bay rum; a radio hummed advertising jingles. On the footrest below my dangling feet were letters in a silver scroll-work design. I slid along their slopes and whirled on their silver curlicues. Never had I seen such beautiful letters.

"What do they say?" I asked the barber.

"Read 'em," he said. His name was Al and Miss Gilly said he was "cheeky," which meant fresh, but I always asked for him, anyway. I liked his strange gap-toothed grin.

Now I narrowed my eyes, staring at the silver letters. Suddenly they linked together into a word. "KOKEN!" I shouted.

The customers all turned toward me in unison. Miss Gilly lumbered toward my chair. I sank down, pulling my sheet up so that only my eyes showed.

"What's the matter?" She scowled at Al. "Did you prick him? I told you to be careful with those scissors."

"No, ma'am." Al pointed to the footrest. "He was just reading."

Miss Gilly leaned over to squint at the word.

"KOKEN," I said under the sheet.

"What on earth does *that* mean?" Miss Gilly asked.

Al shrugged. "I guess it's the outfit that makes the chairs."

"You told him."

"Nope. He read it." Al poked my shoulder with his comb. "Right?"

"Right!" I sat up, pulling the sheet away from my face.

Miss Gilly's eyes opened wide. She told all the men in the shop that I knew how to read. I read the word aloud several times again. The men all grinned at me and some of them even applauded. Al said I was a real smart kid. Miss Gilly said of course I was, tossing him a scornful look, but with a faint smile pressed between her lips.

The next day, another miraculous thing happened. Along with the letters Miss Gilly pulled from the mailbox was a post-card addressed to me. I'd never had my own mail before. The card was from Robert. On one side was a red brick building even bigger than our house. Plants grew up the walls like long green fingers.

Miss Gilly started to read aloud to me, but I stopped her. I read the first whole sentences I'd ever read on my own.

> *Dear Jerry,*
> *This place is a prison but I'm going out for cross country so maybe it will get better. I miss you.*
> — *Love, Robert*

Miss Gilly said that "cross country" was long races through the woods—it was supposed to toughen boys up. I read the card over and over, feeling as if Robert were speaking into my ear.

I discovered a book in Robert's room that he'd had in kindergarten, which I would be starting soon. I read it many times. The little boy in the book was named "Dick," which amused me. I'd heard Robert give that name to what Miss Gilly called my "pee-pee." I was concerned that the boy named Dick was never pictured peeing in the book. (Neither was his sister Jane, nor the dog Spot.) I began to make references to my "Dick." This made Miss Gilly scold me in a way that made me both nervous and delighted. Chuckling, I whispered the word over and over to myself, just out of range of her hearing.

Years later, after my mother had recovered from the pills, I got another postcard from Robert in the mail. It showed a train with a white plume of smoke blowing back from the locomotive's smokestack. The card had the postmark of a place in Ohio. Its message worried me:

> Dear Jerry,
> *The flashlight is switched off here.*
> *The records are yours.*
> Love — Robert

What was he doing in Ohio, and not in Vermont where his prep school was? Miss Gilly and I didn't usually show his postcards to my parents, but this time she rushed off with the card to my father.

A week later, as I got down from the school bus, I saw Robert sitting on the stone wall at the bottom of the lawn. I ran to him.

"You want to play catch?" he asked. He had our baseball gloves with him. Throwing a ball back and forth was our way of having a conversation now—he had become very quiet. His silences drove my mother crazy, but I didn't mind them. I liked being quiet, too.

"How come you're home?" I asked him.

"They found me," Robert said, and handed me my mitt.

"Why aren't you at school?"

"I flunked out." Robert threw a hard strike. "It doesn't matter, I get to see Mother now," he said.

"Maybe you can go to high school in town, then you can live here." The idea got me so excited I threw the ball several feet over his head.

That night I hid outside the dining room overhearing scraps of what my parents were saying to Robert. My father made low rumbling sounds, my mother's voice rose and stopped as if a chord were being yanked around her neck. My brother never seemed to say anything.

"—leave him alone, Dean. No wonder he's got no—"

"—just bumming around like some kind of hobo—"

Miss Gilly set up the Pirates and Travellers board game in my old room and ordered me to play. Her radio drowned out the dining room voices. She let me stay up late in my pajamas reading in her chair.

I must have dozed off. I woke to hear footsteps in the corridor.

My mother cried out, *"Robert, don't! It's locked!"*

A car's engine roared. A crash shook the walls.

I ran barefoot into the garage. The back end of my father's Dodge was sunk into the overhead door. Long wooden splinters splayed out over the car's trunk like Halloween teeth. Bits of glass were splashed all over the floor. Robert leaned against the driver's side door; my mother stood behind him.

My heart was slamming in my chest, the loudest sound in the garage. "What happened?" I asked, starting toward them.

They both whirled around. "You'd better go inside," my mother said in a quavery voice. "Go on, now. Before your father comes!"

I heard the swish of a housecoat behind me. Miss Gilly pulled me back into the house. She took one look at the floor and rushed me to her medicine cabinet. The linoleum in the passageway was smeared with blood—mine. Sitting me on her lap, she dug tiny pieces of glass out of the soles of my feet with her fingernails. They were shiny red, like pomegranate seeds. One was in so deep that she had to press her teeth into the bottom of my heel to get it out. I was too old to be sitting on her lap like this; I felt as if she'd suddenly made me younger.

"You're a brave little boy," she said, and spat the glass into the waste basket. I went shivery all over. She bandaged my feet and tucked me into her bed beside her. Loud voices passed us in the corridor, then the room was quiet. I fell asleep with her arm around my waist.

The next morning, I awoke soaked with sweat. The bed was empty. A note from Miss Gilly said she was driving my mother to the doctor's office. My father was outside trying to free his car from the garage door so that he could go looking for Robert. My brother was gone.

I got dressed and put Miss Gilly's fluffy bedroom slippers on my feet. The soles hurt now. Everything was strange. The table and chair in my old room seemed to be have been slightly repositioned during the night. I shuffled out to the garage.

My father stood in a patch of glare tugging at strips of splintered wood. He had opened a big jagged hole in the door behind the car. Seeing me, he dropped his hands to his sides, panting.

"Why—are you—wearing—those silly slippers?" he demanded.

Too startled to speak, I hurried back to Miss Gilly's room.

The sound of boards cracking outside jabbed at the air around my face. My brother was gone and my feet hurt and I was left with no one here but a man who was tearing apart the garage. I almost started to cry, but then it occurred to me that I probably wasn't alone after all: I knew where Robert was.

Several winters before, I remembered, Miss Gilly and I had gone for a walk with Robert in the woods behind the house. Robert spent a lot of time there, so he knew where the paths were. Miss Gilly packed a canvas bag with cookies and a big thermos of sweet milk tea. Where the snow was deep, she and Robert held me up by the arms and swung me along, my galoshes crunching through the white crust in long strides. The sun turned the ice-filigreed branches to strings of "fairy lights," as Miss Gilly called them; the clear shells broke off, tinkling to the ground, and I could eat as many as I liked.

We sat on logs under the snow-laden branches of a tree beside the brook; Robert said it was his favorite spot in the woods. I thought of it as the Three Bears' house. Miss Gilly looked like a mama bear in her huge second-hand fur coat with the fuzzy hood covering her head so that only her bulbous red nose was visible. I pulled the hood of my snowsuit low over my forehead to look like a baby bear. Robert, though plump as a bear, wasn't furry; he wore cowboy boots, dungarees, and an old military-looking jacket.

As we sipped our tea from tin mugs, he asked Miss Gilly to tell him about the places where she'd been a nanny for members of the British embassy staff—Cairo, Egypt, and Paris, France. The Nile River was lovely, she said, but the rest of the city was filthy. In Paris, though, there were beautiful parks with fountains and statues. She'd floated above the rooftops in the basket of an enormous hot-air balloon and saw tiny people scurrying along the banks of the Seine River below. Listening to her, I drifted above the treetops of Paris in a bright blue balloon.

"Someday..." Robert said, and I could tell that he was picturing places far away, too. Then he had to leave our picnic early; he always had homework and tests to do over.

"It's a pity he didn't have a nanny to give him tea when he was a child," Miss Gilly said, watching him trudge away through the woods. "It might have made all the difference."

Later that afternoon I climbed the stairs to my brother's

room, though my mother had left instructions with Miss Gilly that I wasn't to bother him. When I opened his door, he was hunched over his desk.

"You can come in. I'll never get these problems done, anyway," he said, turning toward me. He had a plump face and a lopsided smile. His old flannel shirt, which my parents were always telling him to tuck in, was hanging over the bulge of his stomach. He didn't seem bothered by me, though he winced when he talked; the skin around his eyes flickered as if invisible insects were beating their wings close to his face. When he opened his fist on his desk, a pencil stuck to his palm for a second, then fell to the blotter in two pieces.

I liked the grown-up smell of his room. He was sixteen, but as he showed me around, he spoke to me as if I were his age and could understand everything, so I felt as if I did. On his bureau was a baseball signed by all the Brooklyn Dodgers. His shelves were full of record albums. He took some down and opened his suitcase-shaped Victrola on the floor. Then he sat next to it the way a kid would and patted the carpet. Sitting beside him, I watched him slowly pull a record out of the album's page. He held the black disk by the edges with both hands the way my mother held her priceless china plates.

"This is called boogie woogie," he said, showing me a record's label. "It's a kind of music they played when jazz was coming up the river from New Orleans."

I pictured musicians poling a barge through the water. Robert's nervous tic stopped as soon as the music played. He closed his eyes to listen; so did I. The baseline notes sounded like their names: boogie-woogies. They rampaged into the room, confidently thumping everything out of their way as they strode back and forth. The treble notes scampered all around them like white rabbits. When the record finished, I opened my eyes. Robert opened his at the same time. Magic. I grinned. "Play it again!"

"Shhh!" He glanced sideways at the door, as if my parents were listening from their rooms.

"Don't they like music?" I asked.

"Not this kind. They like the things you play." For the past months, a woman had been coming to give me piano lessons.

Keeping the volume down, Robert played record after record for me, showing me each label. I loved the names of the piano players—Pine Top Smith (I pictured a man with a cedar tree growing out of his head) and Cow Cow Davenport (I pictured the living room couch with horns and a tail).

My favorite record was called "Night Train Blues." I pictured a locomotive chuffing rhythmically toward the house at night, its blue headlight beam shining through the windows, filling Robert's room with an aquamarine glow. When the record was finished, he put it away and shut the top of the victrola, but the blue tint stayed in the air, and I kept hearing the train's rhythm in my head.

"Can I come back again?" I asked.

"We're brothers," he said. "You ought to be able to come any time you want."

I helped him pick up the records.

"Let's go upstairs," he said. "I'll show you something amazing." He took a flashlight into the attic with him, and shone it into a closet at the far end of the room.

"Want to go into a secret passageway?"

"Sure," I said.

We crawled through an opening in the back of the closet that led into a long tunnel under the eaves. "Where are we?" I asked. We had stopped at a brick wall where another tunnel started to our left.

"Miles from everywhere," he whispered, shining the flashlight beam along the dusty floor.

I held onto the cuff of his dungarees. My elbow bumped against a metal box. A big book that had been leaning against it flopped down onto the floor. "What's that?"

Robert pulled the book onto his lap and opened it. "Mother and Dad's album. They used to keep it in the living room."

I shifted closer to him. As he flipped the pages, they made a whispery sound. Dust-smelling breaths blew against my face. The pages were blank. Corner mounts framed black empty spaces like mute open mouths. Some ripped corners of photos remained: a patch of sky, the toe of a boot, a feather in a lady's hat—tantalizing scraps that made me want to scream with frustration. I realized I knew nothing about my parents' lives. I tried to imagine whole pictures in the blank spaces.

"Stop!" I said—a photo appeared. A middle-aged couple walked along the sloping deck of a ship—my parents, with smiling faces. The ocean's waves seemed about to capsize the ship, though that was probably just the camera's tilted angle. Among the waves, I saw what looked like a strange diamond-shaped fish, though it could have been just a patch of reflected cloud or the shadow of something outside the edge of the picture.

Then the flashlight beam illuminated a sepia-tinted photo: I saw a young girl sitting on the back of a hay wagon. Robert turned more pages: a teen-age girl in a middy blouse hugged books against her chest. A group of girls in white dresses—the one with glinting round spectacles was my mother, Robert said—sat on the steps of a house. The last photo was of an apartment building's door. In wavy, faded handwriting, a caption read, "Greenwich Vill 1922 E S-V M."

The flashlight suddenly switched off. Feeling suspended in pitch-black space, I squeezed closer to Robert. The floor sank beneath me like the deck of a ship. "Where are we?" I asked, my voice quavery.

"The vanishing point." Robert spoke softly in the darkness. "We could be anywhere in the solar system. Or nowhere at all." Silence. He seemed to have drifted off into the galactic night.

"Robert!" I gripped his ankle.

He switched on the light again. "It's okay, Jerry," he said.

I stared up at his face. The flashlight beam illuminated the whites of his eyes and the fuzzy fringe of hair above his forehead; the rest of his face was cast in deep shadow. Behind him the tunnel, with its sloping nail-studded roof, stretched out before us into deep darkness.

"Why'd you do that—turning off the light?"

"I have to know I can vanish when I want to." He glanced around into the tunnel. "There's always an escape route."

I remembered that.

My father was still chopping away at the garage door to free his car when I left Miss Gilly's room. I found a flashlight in the pantry cupboard and tiptoed upstairs to the attic. Sure enough, I heard a scraping noise from deep under the eaves. "Robert!" I whispered.

The noise stopped. I peered into the tunnel at the back of the closet. Another flashlight beam lit up. Robert was sitting cross-legged under the rows of nail points with a metal box in his lap.

"Hi!" I crawled in, immensely pleased with myself for finding him so quickly. "Can I stay with you?"

His tic made lines appear beside his eyes. "Okay, a few minutes. Hold this—" He handed me his light and knelt over the strongbox. Grunting, he wedged a long steel tire iron under its lid and twisted it until one of the hinges gave with an angry crack. Then I took a turn, grunting the way he had as I pried the steel bar in the place he'd set it. I felt something snap, leaving a buzz in the palm of my hand. The box's lid clattered under the slope of the ceiling. I grinned.

"What are you looking for?" I asked.

"Evidence," Robert whispered. He reached into the box and pulled out a handful of photographs.

"Are they the ones from the album?" I asked.

Robert shook his head. "Too big."

There was a photo of a general store on a street with uneven wooden sidewalks, and one of a high school football team. Another showed a man in a rumpled suit, standing on the porch with a wicker suitcase beside him. His face was a blurred grin.

"That's our grandfather," Robert said.

"I remember him," I said. "I heard Dad tell somebody he died in a loony bin."

"I was listening in on that phone call." Robert stared at the photo; the man seemed to have aged in the last few moments. "It was quite a story."

"What happened?"

Our grandfather, Robert said, was a pauper at the end and a lifelong atheist. But he spent the last months of his life building a church on the grounds of a state mental hospital, where he lived in the old folks' wing. All day he collected pebbles and pressed them down in long straight lines on a dirt area that the staff called the recreation yard. Sometimes he knelt down under one of the oak trees and called on the Lord to reveal exactly where He wanted the walls erected.

I remembered my grandfather as a huge man with a grin that collapsed his toothless mouth and made you think of a jack-o-lantern left outdoors too long after Halloween. It was a salesman's smile, Robert said: sometimes he could be heard discussing the price of stained glass to Jesus in the same hearty voice he'd used to pitch vegetable peelers, home wine-making kits, and all the other products that had so often landed him in bankruptcy courts.

59

His behavior was no stranger than that of many other patients, such as the lady who sang obscene nursery rhymes all day, or the man who collected his drool in a jar, or another man who carried a cardboard sword and called himself General Ulysses S. Grant. People got used to seeing my grandfather lurching about the grounds in his baggy raincoat and old uniform cap, searching for small stones. At first no one paid much attention to his church. But after a while, it gave him so much to talk about at meals that everyone began discussing it, as if they, too, could see walls rising outside the dining room window.

One Sunday morning, Robert said, the old man announced that the church was finished. He cleaned himself up for the first time since he'd arrived at the hospital. He brushed his white hair, shaved the stubble from his chin, put on his double breasted suit and a wide hand-painted tie. Then he walked out onto the yard and, standing at one end of his pebbly diagram, delivered a sermon. No one came to hear it, but several residents sat in canvas chairs under a nearby tree to watch him wave his arms and shout across the grounds. After the service, he made a sharp right-angle turn around an invisible altar and left by a gap in the pebbles. He rejoined the others under the tree, mopping his brow with a big checked handkerchief.

The next Sunday, five or six residents got dressed up and attended his service. The following week, there were a dozen or more. Ladies took dresses they hadn't worn in thirty years out of suitcases. Men brushed out suits and made special trips to the thrift shop in town to select colorful neckties. The staff helped them drag chairs out to the pew area, and some staff brought chairs for themselves as well.

Soon, nearly everyone was attending the Sunday services. A choir was formed, which the old man rehearsed and directed. Someone supplied a wooden cross. The staff made an altar out of orange crates and a tablecloth. Ulysses S. Grant left his sword outside, the drooling man put his jar on the altar as an offering, and the woman with the obscene nursery rhymes recited them only to herself during the services, her voice getting quieter each week until finally her lips stopped moving altogether.

As long as the weather stayed warm, it was pleasant to sit in the sunlight surrounded by lines of pebbles, listening to the old man's voice fading in and out of consciousness. When he pointed at the Bible scenes he said were depicted in the stained glass windows, everyone gazed up, seeing not merely expanses of blue summer air, but New Testament pictures in blazing red and gold. The preacher's sermons were quite lucid and full of good jokes. One Sunday, he married two of the residents. The staff began to bring their families for services. The local newspaper featured him on its church news page.

He died in the fall, just as the weather was growing chilly. On a gray Sunday morning, the residents and staff put on warm clothes and held a memorial service for him in his church. Then all the pebbles were raked up before the rains could wash them away. The residents selected bright-colored ones to keep in their rooms. There were enough left over to border a flower garden, which was named after him and dedicated with a bronze plaque.

"The church," Robert said, "was the only successful venture of our grandfather's life."

I watched Robert turn the album's pages. He came to photos of World War I biplanes with their pilots. In one, my father, looking very young, draped his arm along his plane's fuselage. The propeller rose like a tall flame behind him. He wore high shiny boots, breeches, an Army Air Corps tunic. Aviator's goggles were pushed up on his forehead; a scarf was draped rakishly around his neck. His eyes were bright as he stared up into the sky; I'd never seen that expression on his face before.

"He was in the first generation in history to fly. A few minutes after this was taken, he was probably up there—" Robert touched a cloud in the sky. "No one had ever been there before."

"But he crashed once," I said, remembering the war story that Robert had told me. As my father's plane swooped low, his bombardier released leaden cylinders that made the air rock with their faraway booming. Planes plummeted in smoking arcs through the air. His own plane was strafed. He crash-landed in a field. There, he pulled his wounded bombardier from the flaming wreckage and dragged him to safety.

Robert and I used to reenact the scene, spreading lead soldiers on the attic floor under the slanting sunbeams that swirled with dust motes—anti-aircraft flak—from the small attic window. Over and over we crash-landed my father's tiny lead

61

plane, scratching jagged lines on the floorboards. We choked and gasped as the flames roared around us. We took turns being the wounded bombardier, pitching forward in his seat, writhing in the smoke. Every time, the pilot's strong hands gripped our wrists and pulled us out of danger.

Robert took the last picture from the box.

"Did you find what you wanted?" I asked.

"Sort of." He stared down at the photo. A huge antique car was parked in front of a beach cottage. A uniformed chauffeur sat in the driver's seat; in back, behind curtains, a woman's face was silhouetted, her hair piled on top of her head. We both stared at the picture. I kept waiting for Robert to explain it, but he finally just pushed it back into the box with the others and rammed the ruined lid onto it. The scraping sound made me shiver.

He lay on his back. "They're going to start looking for you pretty soon," he said. "I don't want to get you in trouble, too."

"I don't care," I said, lying down beside him.

"It'd make everything worse, believe me."

"How long are you going to stay here?"

"I don't know."

"How *long*?" I hit him in the face with my flashlight beam.

"Hey, don't cry, Jerry. I'll be fine, really."

"Why did you break the garage door?"

Robert shielded his face from the beam of white light. "I don't know. I don't understand most of the dumb things I do."

I wiped my eyes. "You're not dumb."

"Thanks, pal. But if you stay here talking, my goose is going to be cooked." I heard my father walking around downstairs, and knew he was right. Robert tousled my hair.

"Okay," I whispered, "I'll come back and see you, though."

On my way downstairs, I thought of a cooked goose and wondered how he was going to stay there without food. I could make some peanut butter sandwiches to bring him. But how would he go to the bathroom? If he peed on the floor, would it drip through the ceiling and give him away? I wanted to ask Miss Gilly, but I realized I couldn't do that. It was strange, having secrets from her.

The police came the next morning at breakfast. The man who talked to me didn't wear a uniform, he wore a suit like the school principal. He asked me if I knew of any places my brother might be. I shook my head hard. I could feel Miss Gilly eyeing me all the while. When the man left, she folded her arms across her chest and headed toward her room.

"Where are you going?" I asked, my voice sounding squeaky.

She paused in the doorway. Her face, surrounded by matted gray curls, looked exhausted. "I've got to go pack my suitcase, ducks."

"It's not your day off. You can't go!"

She gave me a sad look. "I'm for the chop, Jerry."

"Why?" I started to tremble all over.

"Here's what I reckon's going to happen," she said. "That detective will come back and start asking you questions again—"

"He's a *detective*?" I knew what a detective was from the Sunday afternoon radio shows Miss Gilly and I listened to. Lamont Cranston—known as The Shadow—and Mr. Keene, Tracer of Lost Persons, could always make people spill the beans.

"Oh, yes. And when he finds out you know where Robert is, and he tells *them*—" *Them* was always my parents. "Well, they'll think I knew all along too. And this time they'll sack me, sure as fate." She lumbered off toward her room.

"Wait—"

"Never mind that I've cooked and scrubbed floors and put up with those people's abuse all these years, just so I could be with you...." Miss Gilly's voice grew faint on the other side of the wall. "I reckon you don't need me any more."

I ran into her bedroom and buried my face in her stomach. "He's in the attic!" I blurted.

She took care of everything. Before the detective could come back to grill me, she somehow snuck Robert outdoors. Then he came back in, telling my parents that he'd been at a friend's place. All afternoon, the house reverberated with shouts and thumping footsteps. Miss Gilly and I stayed in the back rooms keeping the radio on loud. Neither of us got blamed for anything. Except, of course, I knew I was to blame for betraying Robert. He was to be sent away to a military academy.

The day he left we went outside for a last game of catch. Robert had cut off most of his hair because he'd heard that was what happened to cadets at the academy and he wanted to do it himself. Pale patches of scalp showed through as if he'd hacked the hair off with a knife.

"I'm sorry I told on you," I said, staring down into my mitt.

"Don't worry about it, Jerry. I couldn't have stayed up there forever," he said. "Anyway, I'll lose a lot of weight." He sucked in his stomach and smacked it, a hollow sound that made me wince.

"Don't do that!" I said.

"Okay, play ball." Robert walked to the mound by the tool-shed and waited for me to squat down into my catcher's position. "The Dodgers are ahead by a run but the Giants have the bases loaded. Two outs, last of the ninth. The pitcher goes into the stretch—" He glanced at the runners, his tic making him blink hard. His arm snapped around.

The ball hit the ground several feet to my left and skidded past my glove. I plunged into the bush after it. All the Giants, their cleats raising clouds of black dust, rounded the bases and thundered toward the plate.

- FIVE -

I see a British diplomat walking with Miss Gilly in the Tuileries Gardens. He calls her Alma. His white suit and straw boater look jaunty, yet his brow is furrowed. Today is his last chance to propose to her—he's just been assigned a new posting—and he wonders if he'll ever find the right words.

Her plump face is young and radiant as she strolls beside him in a long skirt with a high-collared, ruffled blouse. Like him, she's a little nervous—never before has she accompanied him to the park without the ambassador's little boy, her charge, to chaperon her. When he pauses before a statue of a woman on a pedestal, she says, "Ridiculous—a person standing up there half-naked in public. I prefer statues like Lord Nelson in Trafalgar Square—that make you feel proud of your country."

"Quite," he says, but gives the statue a backwards glance as they head toward the Seine. Feeling warm, he undoes the top buttons of his waistcoat and takes deep breaths of the river-scented air. A lone frog croaks somewhere. He gazes at a man and wife fishing from their houseboat, and feels about to explode with longing. The husband is robust, red-faced; the diplomat feels thin and pale, despite having fortified himself, perhaps too liberally, with brandy.

"Oh, a fête!" Alma says, as children run squealing past them. Ahead are gaily striped tents; hurdy-gurdy music and the scent of candied almonds float through the air. "And just look at that—"

He sees it, too: an enormous blue balloon sways gently in the breeze. It seems to be gazing up at the clouds as it strains against the net that tethers it. He has never held her hand before, but now he grabs it and rushes toward the balloon.

"Wait!" she cries, staring up at the great circus-colored airship. "What if its ropes break?"

She hasn't shaken off his hand; she's squeezing it, in fact! He thrusts some franc notes at the man beside the basket and pulls Alma with him. The little wicker gate opens. They stumble through.

A man steps up to them with a big tripod camera. Alma

65

grips the diplomat's arm with both hands, smiling giddily at the lens.

The flash powder explodes, obliterating the children, the tents, the park. Incandescence echoes in the air. By the time they have rubbed it from their eyes, the treetops are slowly sinking beneath them. Watching her smile down at the view, her soft curls fluttering in the breeze, he stops noticing the churning of his stomach. The Eiffel Tower shimmers in the sunlight. Traffic sounds fade; he hears the faint harp song of the balloon's cords.

"The river's so blue—just like a silk ribbon," Alma says. "When I was small, I always fancied a ribbon like that for my hair."

He stares at her face, trying to untangle sentences in his mind. Rooftops spread out below. His necktie, loose from his waistcoat, flaps like a kite-tail in the warm breeze. Alma is still holding onto his arm as if he is what is keeping her buoyant. Now! he thinks—

"Alma—" he gasps, and embraces her. "Stay with me! Marry me!"

Suddenly the basket jerks. He staggers, the blood rushing from his face. The balloon sways, suspended in space as if its ropes have broken loose from the earth. Blindly he kisses her eyes, her cheeks. Never has he done anything like this before.

"*Please!*" He presses against her dizzily, a moan flying out of his throat.

She blinks hard. "What are you *doing*?"

He drops to his knees. His hat tumbles off and rolls between her shoes. Half rising, he wraps his arms around her waist, buries his face against her breast.

She stops straining backwards. "There, there," she murmurs, and cradles his head against her.

He cannot bear to let go of her. Finally he tilts his head back. At the same moment he feels a warm stickiness in his trousers, and shuts his eyes tight in horror.

Gently she tucks his necktie into his waistcoat. "I don't know. . . ." She touches the place on her cheek where he has kissed her. "How could I ever leave that poor child? He'd have no one to take proper care of him."

"I . . . undertand—"He staggers to his feet, frantically tugging his jacket down over the front of his trousers. His stomach is churning. He gropes for the rim of the basket but misses it, his fingers clutching a length of rope. The basket sways beneath his feet. He's inadvertently given the signal to the people below. The balloon starts to descend.

He hears the laughter of children in the park below. The rooftops rise toward him, the treetops expand, the earth tilts strangely. Sheepishly he retrieves his hat from the basket's floor. His heart is a frog kicking as it falls through space. Now he feels the ground thud beneath the basket's floor.

"I'm so sorry, Alma," he says. "I don't know what got into me—"

Biting her lip, she takes one more look over the side of the basket. Then she steps out onto the grass. A child runs by, chasing a ball. "Not to worry," she says.

They leave the park in silence. The tremor in his legs lasts all the way to her embassy residence.

At the iron gate, she turns her face up to him. "It was the loveliest view I ever saw."

"I'll write to you, Alma—" He watches her walk away from him and disappear through the heavy door. For a moment, she stands at the window. Then she is gone, and the world is a flat, sunless place. He drifts off into the rest of his life, into the silence of years. Already he is beginning to fill it with the words of the first of his letters to her.

When my parents went on their annual vacation, Miss Gilly and I waved good-bye to them from the front steps as their taxi rolled down the driveway. Then we turned to each other and let out our breath.

I moved back into my old room downstairs. I no longer had to keep my voice down or say my prayers at bedtime. We ate in the dining room, and made a fire in the living room fireplace every afternoon, just like in the English country houses where Miss Gilly had been treated so well. I sprawled on the rug with my parent-forbidden comic books spread out around me. She sat on the couch in her lumpy old sweater and woolen skirt, a cup of tea in her hand. Sighing happily, she stretched out her bare feet toward the fire. Her enormous toes wriggled in the heat. They smelled like cheese.

At night, I washed in her bath-room, a kind of long closet filled completely with a tub, three of whose sides were flush with the tiled walls. I remembered when there had been room for two of us in the tub. The walls had vanished behind clouds of steam. Her knees stuck out of the water like red hippo snouts; I lay between them laughing while she scrubbed my belly. Kicking and squirming, I made big waves that swamped her wobbly chest. "Don't you dare get my hair wet, you little heathen!" she sputtered, but I always did. Then she had to wash it, and mine, too. We were covered with white lather that slurped down the drain when she turned on the shower. Kneeling, eyes shut in the hot rainstorm, we squeegeed the soap out of each other's hair. When she finished toweling her scalp, her graying black curls sprang out in all directions from her head. "Wild Woman of Borneo!" she said, bulging her eyes out and making me shriek with laughter.

I remembered the eiderdown comforter that lay over her bed like a silky pale blue cloud. Her previous employers in London had given it to her, she said; it was the only truly nice thing she had in the world—except for me, of course. I loved to dive into its whooshing softness. I couldn't cajole her into letting me have the eiderdown on my own bed, but when I woke from bad dreams, she let me snuggle under it with her. She wore a fuzzy flannel nightgown that gave off fragrant damp heat.

"Mind your great bony knees!" she muttered, and I lay still, listening to the curtains fluttering quietly beside the half-open window. Her stomach rose and fell; air gurgled in her throat and whistled out her lips. In a while, she turned toward me, her fingers moving on the top buttons of her nightgown. I wriggled in closer, feeling her soft flesh squash against my face. Her nipple felt like a giant raspberry in my mouth.

I'd moved a cot into my old room, but it wasn't very comfortable. I often went to sleep in Miss Gilly's room, curled up in the armchair beside her bed in my pajamas. One night I woke very late, feeling strange, as if I wasn't sure how old I was or where in the house I belonged. On the bedside table, her old radio murmured low, its cloth dial glowing faint orange in the darkness. The soft music was interrupted by her gurgling snores. Standing up unsteadily, I crept under the eiderdown beside her and dozed off.

I dreamed that I was waiting for her hand to undo the top of her flannel nightgown. When I opened my eyes, I still seemed to be in the dream, yet I was awake. I waited. Her hand didn't move. So I unbuttoned her nightgown myself, carefully so as not to wake her. Her breast rolled out against my cheek. She pressed my head gently to her as she slept.

Something new happened. I felt a stirring in my pajama pants. My dick was growing!

She must have felt it against her thigh, because her hand started brushing it away from her as if she thought it would bite her. "You behave yourself," she mumbled.

"I can't help it," I whispered

She sat up, rubbing her eyes. The moonlight glowed in the lace curtains beside her. I saw her breast resting on the folds of her belly like an enormous white dewdrop. Then it was swallowed up by her night-gown. She lay down with a lot of oofs and grunts, her back to me.

I tried to get comfortable lying against the two big mounds of her rear end. My dick ached, as if the skin around it were being stretched too tight. I moved back to keep from touching her with it.

Now there didn't seem to be room in the bed for the three of us. My own rear end was hanging out over the edge, getting cold. When she shifted her position, I grabbed the covers with both hands to keep from being shoved onto the floor, but I wound up sitting on the carpet anyway, buried under the blanket.

"Here—you give that back!" Miss Gilly groaned, flopping on the sheet like a beached whale.

I quickly covered her up. She began gurgling again. My dick was poking out of the fly of my pajamas. It wouldn't get smaller, no matter how I pushed it. Finally I took it into the hall to see what was going on. In the harsh white light, it had a strange pale purplish tint. Would it ever return to normal size? Would I have to get special pants go to school in, made with a kind of cage in the front under the cloth? I'd have to wait until the bathroom was empty before I went in to pee.

Somehow, thinking about this made my dick shrink. I didn't trust it in Miss Gilly's bed again, though, and returned to the armchair.

Robert sent a postcard from the military academy. My parents came back from Europe, and I moved back upstairs to the attic.

I kept my mail tacked to the wall beside my bed there. In her room, Miss Gilly kept her letters in a big square biscuit tin with the royal family's portrait on the lid. Her favorite family member was the prince, who I thought had a face like a puppy. He reminded her of the British ambassador's little boy she'd taken care of years before in Paris.

When she received letters from her friends, other nannies on vacations, she always read them aloud. But just before Christmas, a letter arrived addressed to "Miss Alma Gilly" that she wouldn't read to me. She tried to interest me in its stamps with sailing ships on them.

"Who's it from?" I asked. "Who?"

Her cheeks flushed red. "It's from a man I once knew. He's coming to New York and he wants to see me—it's preposterous!"

A stack of similar envelopes lay on her bureau beside the open cookie tin. I counted twenty of them, each with a seal on the back which she said was from British embassies in various South American countries. I demanded an explanation.

Holding her lumpy old housecoat together at her chest, she sat down on the bed. "Once upon a time," she said, "I met a foreign service gentleman in Paris. He wanted to be my friend. We went for walks in the park." She squeezed her hands together in her lap. "He took me up for a balloon ride, and asked me to marry him."

I'd often been intrigued by her faded photograph of a hot-air balloon. The picture was in the bottom of the tin. I took it out and stared at the figures in the basket below the balloon. The woman, wearing a long old-fashioned skirt and blouse, had Miss Gilly's plump cheeks, but the curls that fringed her head were light instead of dark gray. I didn't recognize the giddy smile on her face. The man stood off balance beside her in a white suit and straw boater. Miss Gilly took a long look at the photo before pulling it from my hand.

"That was taken twenty years ago. Every year, he writes me that he wants to marry me." She rolled her eyes. "Now he's in New York. He's invited me to have dinner with him at the Waldorf Astoria hotel."

I sat down on the bed beside her. "Are you going to marry him?"

"Of course not—don't be silly!" She pursed her lips. "He must be an old man by now. Sixty-four years old. And I'm nearly fifty."

"Then why do you want to have dinner with him?"

Miss Gilly wiped her forehead. "I don't know."

I bounced on the bed, begging to hear about Paris, the balloon, her friend. She dropped the photograph and the letters back into the tin, and put it on the top shelf of her closet, out of my reach.

This was the plan: Miss Gilly was to take me to New York for a day's sightseeing and drop me off at my father's office, where a Christmas party would be in progress. My father would take me home on the train while she went to have dinner with the English man.

"I don't want to go to the office," I said, glaring at Miss Gilly in the elevator. I didn't like the idea of the place: my father's company manufactured ladies' lingerie, a source of embarrassment when this had somehow gotten out at school. And I didn't care at all for the way Miss Gilly inspected herself in the elevator's mirrored panel, either. She never worried about how she looked at home.

"Wild woman of Borneo!" she said, trying to push down her springy gray curls. "I can't walk into a grand hotel looking like this!"

"That's true," I said.

She turned sideways, pulling open her thrift-shop fur coat, which was speckled with snowflakes. "I just wish I wasn't so bloody fat!"

"Weren't you fat, before?"

She smoothed her suit jacket down over her bosom and straightened the silk scarf at her throat. "Oh, I was always plump. He never seemed to mind. I reckon if I was any sort of a beauty, he wouldn't have dared...." She sighed. "But in point of fact, Jerry, he's made something of himself. He's the first secretary in the British embassy in Brazil now."

"So?"

"So he can afford to give me a nice night out. I deserve to be treated like a lady once in a while."

"I know where Brazil is." It was a stop on the Pirates and Travellers board game we often played. If you landed on Brazil, you had to stay there for three rolls of the dice, which seemed forever to me. But not to Miss Gilly. She always said it seemed like a lovely place to be.

"It's where they have the vampire bats," I said, scowling. Miss Gilly knelt beside me, her brow furrowing. "You're worried about being left with your father in that office, aren't you? I suppose I shouldn't just leave you there."

"He always has to stay at work late," I said. This wasn't strictly true; he only occasionally missed his train lately.

"We'll see, dear. I'm sure you'll like the Christmas party." At the one at church last winter, I'd had to make papier maché sheep for a crèche. "I'm too old for Christmas parties," I told her.

When the elevator door slid open at the top floor, I was sure we had arrived at the wrong office. Before me in the foyer stood a nearly naked woman. It wasn't a real woman, of course, just a very life-like mannequin wearing a Christmas bow over her belly button, and a lacy purple bra and half-slip manufactured by the company. She was holding her hand out toward me. In her palm was a big glass marble, blue tinted, clear as a crystal ball. Dozens, perhaps hundreds of these gleaming marbles filled a pool around the pedestal she was standing on. They seemed to be staring up at me. I approached her, transfixed.

"You come away from there this instant!" Miss Gilly grabbed my arm, her face flushed.

"S'all right," someone said. A bald man in a dark suit ambled over to us, sloshing a paper cup. "He can have a marble."

Miss Gilly stepped back, her fur coat bristling. "Who do you think *you* are?"

"I think I am—" The man bowed. "Edgar Bernbaum, Assistant Vice President, Marketing. At your service, madame."

"Mr. Bird-bom, I'll thank you to show us to Mr. Langley's office. This boy is his son—"

"No kidding?" The man blinked at me. His small beaky nose did make him look like a bird—a bald, bespectacled parrot in a gray suit. "Well, then, he gets all the marbles he wants."

I took the marble from the woman's hand and dropped it into my overcoat pocket. Her glossy lips seemed to smile at me. I stared at her over my shoulder as Miss Gilly yanked me down a corridor after Mr. Bernbaum.

The office was a maze of passages whose frosted glass partitions were only as high as the top of my head. Through doorways I caught glimpses of cubicles where bowls of punch were laid out on desks. People were singing "God Rest Ye Merry Gentlemen" in off-key voices.

"Straighten your tie!" Miss Gilly whispered at me.

Mr. Bernbaum opened a door and then backed away as if awed by something inside the room. I walked in. The door shut; the music vanished.

"Well, hello there, Jerrett." My father stood up from behind an enormous desk and reached across it.

"Hello," I said, leaning forward to shake his hand. I could feel his eyes inspecting my tie, blazer, and slacks. His office was the size of our dining room at home, with oil paintings on the wall and a huge window behind his desk. I gazed out at the rooftops of tall buildings that rose like blocks of black granite through swirling snowflakes. "How do you like this place, young man?" My father's bushy brows formed sideways question marks.

"I don't know," I said, feeling sweaty.

Folding his hands on his desk, he asked me what sights I'd been seeing. I wanted to tell him about Mr. Bernbaum's offer, but he looked too important, in his dark suit and gray silk tie, to be interested in marbles. Miss Gilly said she wanted to go "do something with her hair." I gave her a panicky look, but she left anyway. An awkward silence followed. Someone knocked on the door.

A young woman rushed in on a gust of perfume. "Mrs. Laura Miller's on the line again, sir," she said to my father.

"Jerrett—" My father stood up, pointing with his chin toward the door. At home he sometimes excused me from the room in the same way after picking up the telephone. I stepped into the hall, letting out my breath. The door clicked shut.

I looked for Miss Gilly up one corridor and down the other, my fists clenched at my sides, but she was nowhere to be seen. Gradually my panic faded, and I forgot about her. I decided to look for the woman with the marbles. In the first office I came to, somebody had hung out a lady's stretched nylon stocking full of gaily wrapped presents. On a desk some bottles surrounded a bowl of purple punch; steam rose from a miniature iceberg floating in it. I ladled myself a big paper cup full. It tasted fizzy and left a glow in my stomach. When I walked away from the table, the floor tilted strangely beneath my feet. I was lost. Walls of glass kept rising up before me. Fluorescent lights overhead made the air vibrate. I reached into my pocket to grip the marble, as if it would orient me, but I'd left it in my overcoat in my father's office.

The maze of corridors led on and on. In one cubicle some men and women were dancing. As I walked in, smiles froze and laughter stopped. At first I enjoyed producing zones of silence wherever I looked, but soon I got tired of this and ducked into an empty office. I was helping myself to more punch when a man stepped inside.

"Ah, young Master Langley." He tipped an imaginary hat. His horn-rimmed glasses tilted on his nose. "Mr. Bird-balm, at your service. Have you found the nymph of the marbles yet?"

I shook my head, grinning.

"She's a dream, isn't she? And all those marbles—like finding a pirate's chest full of jewels." He squatted down beside me, his lips bending into a smile. "D'you still call them clearies?"

I nodded. "That's right."

"And do kids still walk around holding them in front of their eyes?" He squinted through a circle he made with his thumb and index finger. "And everything looks like it's underwater?"

"Yes," I said. "Do you know where she is?"

"Where indeed?" He sighed. "Through the enchanted forest. At the end of the rainbow."

I cocked my head. "What did you say?

"First right at the end of the hall, just past Accounting." He stood unsteadily. "*Bon voyage!*"

I got lost again; all I found were more corridors, more cubicles, but no pool of marbles with a woman standing in it. I stopped for a drink at each unattended punch bowl I came to until I began to feel queasy. When I found a darkened office that seemed empty, I ducked inside, looking for a place to sit down.

Someone moved. Bubbles rose in my throat. In a chair, a woman was sitting on a man's lap. Her white bra glowed in her open blouse. The man's hand rose toward it. I held my breath, staring. Suddenly the woman struggled to her feet. The man stood too, trying to embrace her. I heard loud footsteps behind me.

"Just *what* d'you think you're *doing*?" Miss Gilly's voice knocked the man off balance.

The woman fumbled with her blouse. I lurched forward, but Miss Gilly grabbed me by the collar, my shirt tightening against my throat. A loud burp jumped out of my mouth, echoing in the cubicle like a frog in a well. Then she let go and I had to grab the door frame to stay on my feet. The man and woman rushed out of the room.

"Where on earth have you been?" Miss Gilly asked.

"Was looking for you," I mumbled. My stomach was churning.

"The goings-on in this place!" she muttered. She caught a whiff of my breath as she tried to straighten my necktie. "Stay *still*, you little heathen! You're going to upset everything!"

I escaped to the bathroom across the hall. The tiles shimmered light blue. The whole place was blurry, as if underwater. I managed to wash my face and focus on the mirror. I was strangely glassy-eyed. In the corridor, Miss Gilly pushed a peppermint into my mouth. The sweet taste made something start to rise in my stomach like a big bubble through sludge. Open doorways flickered by in pale waves.

In his office, my father had his topcoat on. "Sorry I didn't have time to show you around, son," he said. "But I've got to leave now."

Miss Gilly stared at him. "Aren't you going to take him home? I thought that was the *plan*, Mr. Langley." There was a strange catch in her voice. "I was going to go on to dinner with my friend."

My father shook his head. "Something's come up. I'm going to have to take a later train home."

I only half-heard this—I was remembering the marble I'd left in my topcoat, and began moving blurrily around the desk toward it.

"But I can drop him off at the station," my father said.

"What—and have him ride that train all on his own?"

"He's old enough, I should think." My father glanced down at me.

Miss Gilly frowned. "I'm not so sure."

I needed badly to get hold of the marble. I yanked the coat toward me from the chair, but the chair yanked back. Then I was off balance and the marble was bouncing on the hardwood floor at my feet. I sank to my knees.

"Are you all right?" Miss Gilly asked.

I wanted to stand up, but I couldn't. My mouth formed the word "yes," but suddenly a different sound burst out of my throat, along with a long gushing spasm of purple liquid. More followed, churning up out of me. I pitched forward, sprawling face-first into a warm puddle.

"Oh, Jerry, what have you *done*?" Miss Gilly knelt beside me.

Sitting up, I could see clearly again. I noticed for the first time that she had on make-up. Her cheeks were round and smooth; her curls lay in a soft fringe around her forehead.

"What the hell's going on here?" My father's shoes moved away from the puddle.

"I'm afraid he's got into the punch, Mr. Langley." Miss Gilly's lower lip began to quiver.

"Why weren't you looking after him?"

"I—I don't know what I could have been thinking of."

I leaned forward, my necktie dripping. "The marble," I croaked.

"Well, never mind." My father moved toward his desk. "I'll put him on the train. He'll get over this."

The office was terribly quiet. I didn't dare look at Miss Gilly.

Her hand fell slowly, and she began to stroke the hair from my forehead. "It's all right, dear," she said, "I'll stay with you."

Riding in silence on the train back to Connecticut, I squeezed the marble I'd somehow managed to rescue from my father's office. A chilly wind blew through the car. My mouth tasted rancid and I knew I stank. I was sure Miss Gilly could smell me.

Pressing one hand against her cheek, she stared past me out the window. Her curls were flat and damp on her forehead.

I picture the marble lying like a crystal ball in my hand. When I look at it from one side, I see Miss Gilly facing the window, her soggy fur coat gathered around her. From another angle, I see a rounded reflection of the city she is staring at. It glides past the train, building after tall building falling into the night without a sound.

Far across the city she sees a man in a white suit sitting in a hotel dining room. On the table a candle flickers. Beside it a small package waits. It is tied with a blue silk ribbon and is wrapped in silvery paper that matches the man's hair.

He imagines her unwrapping the package. Inside is a velvet-lined box that he will open for her. He pictures her face when she sees the ring—the face of a young woman gazing down from the sky at a city sparkling before her on a bright, sunny morning. He takes her hand, feeling the softness, the plumpness, the warmth. His breath stops as he slides the ring onto her finger.

He waits and waits for her. His gaze moves many times from the package to the door. The dining room is empty now. The candle has burned down to a wax stump. He tucks his necktie tighter into his waistcoat and takes a long look at his watch. Now he can no longer imagine slipping the ring onto her finger. He hears the box click shut. The silvery paper wraps itself slowly around it. The ribbon loops over and under the package. Its ends twist into a bow. The box falls from his hand into his jacket pocket.

Slowly, he leaves the dining room and walks out into the last years of his life, through the vampire-infested jungles of Brazil, to the white marble embassy rising on a cliff above a sea where the ships of pirates and travellers float motionless, never docking.

"I'm sorry," I finally managed to say. I stared up at her.

She blinked. The train bumped along the elevated track. Snowflakes slanted down out of the darkness, dripped sideways across the window.

"It's probably all for the best," she said quietly.

I tried to give her the marble, but she wouldn't take it.

- SIX -

I see a framed photo on the wall: two rows of high school boys in mud-soaked football jerseys and pants. Dean Langley, his hair parted down the middle in two slick wings, is the only one in a clean jersey.

His room is immaculate. A dictionary is lined up with the edge of a sturdy desk. A college banner and a picture of a grim white-bearded Andrew Carnegie cover the worst cracks in the walls. The striped bedspread and curtains match; he has ordered them from the Sears Roebuck catalogue with money from an after-school job at the livery stable.

Sitting at his desk in creased slacks, white shirt, sleeveless sweater, he hands me a book. It's my novel by Emile Zola about a French courtesan. "If the preacher had seen you with this," he says, "I would've been in dutch." Dean teaches Sunday school at the church which may sponsor him for a college scholarship. He confiscated the book from me when he caught me reading it in his class.

"What did you think of it?" I ask.

I've got him. He can't hide his grin—a look I've never seen on his face before. "I liked the descriptions of those fancy balls," he says, his voice hushed.

We hear voices from outside the window. The town's one street is rutted with wagon tracks; the weather-stained storefronts lean over the sidewalk as if about to collapse into kindling under the weight of the rain clouds overhead. Dean's father, in a rumpled double-breasted suit, stands in the street at an angle, as if leaning on air. It's a familiar pose—he's often seen stopping women to chat. Everyone feels sorry for his wife. Now he's talking to the red-haired woman I saw before in his old store. She twirls a parasol as she laughs.

Dean glowers at him. If he were a porcupine, he'd have shot a hundred quills into that rumpled suit of his father's, drawing blood.

As the woman walks off down the sidewalk, Mr. Langley bows and tips his hat. The men spectators grin, the women turn their faces away. Dean watches his father pick up his wicker sample case. We hear him walk into the house, his footsteps stumbling along the hall toward Dean's room. I can smell his cigar smoke.

"You in there, boy? I could use a hand."

With a whip-like movement of his arm, Dean slams the door. The crash reverberates through the house. Dictionary pages flutter with the sound of a crowd whispering. The bedspread hysterically wraps itself around a bedpost. The picture of the bearded industrialist slides down the wall and explodes into laughter on the floor.

I stare at Dean. He is a graying sixty-year-old man. Purple-faced with rage, he raises his arms and presses his palms against the wall as if holding back a swelling dike.

Gradually the room settles. The spread sighs back onto the bed. Andrew Carnegie rises up the wall and resumes his grim expression. The curtains hang stiffly on either side of the window.

Dean is a teen-aged boy again. His forehead is flushed but his face is determinedly composed and absolutely blank.

"Keep the book under your jacket," he says, showing me out.

I walk slowly along the sepia-tinted street, looking back. The crash of the door echoes in my chest.

"When I was your age," my mother told me, "I dreamed of having a room as big as this."

"It's very nice," I said. She'd had the walls painted Easter chick yellow; the new curtains had a cheerful Scotch plaid design. On shelves at the far end were scale model cars, Tinkertoys and Lincoln logs, an elaborate electric train set still in its box. Somehow, though, I couldn't appreciate them as much as I should have. Something was the matter with me; I didn't really belong in this nice room—this house, this town, this childhood.

During the day the attic was quiet, but at night, when I read inside the bell-jar of light from my bedside lamp, I had to try hard not to hear the shouting downstairs. Then I felt as if I were living inside a little dome vibrating on top of a pressure cooker.

My father's voice was a low rumble, my mother's a shrill whine. My father always seemed on the verge of striding across the landing to smack my mother in the mouth; my mother often sounded as if he'd already done it. I lay on my back with my sheet clamped between my teeth, whispering, "Shut up! Shut up!"

"I think you're afraid of yourself—" That was my mother's voice. I sat up. "—of what you might do to Jerrett if you let him get close—"

"Marian, if that psychiatric mumbo jumbo helps you, fine. But don't try to inflict it on me—"

"Can't you forgive yourself for Robert? It was years ago. *I've* forgiven you, why can't you—"

"Thanks. But sometimes your mercy can be worse than—"

Needing to go to the bathroom, I stomped down the stairs and rushed along the landing with my hands over my ears. As I went by, my mother hid her glass in the folds of her bathrobe. She'd started drinking again, as Miss Gilly had said she would, but now, having "things under control," she waited until five o'clock to mix her first cocktail. She smiled at me as I returned to the attic. Even with makeup, her nose was covered with faint red veins, and dark pillows of skin puffed out beneath her eyes.

Maybe they were bruises, I thought, as I lay in bed later. The voices finally ceased; silence hovered around me like a giant black moth's wings about to swing shut. I could picture my father standing over my mother, his fists clenched; she lay on the floor with blood dribbling from her mouth. My own fists clenched beneath the sheet.

I stopped going downstairs at night, preferring to pee into my waste basket and empty it secretly in the mornings.

Miss Gilly gave me her old wooden radio to drown out the voices. I found a country music station from West Virginia with a disk jockey named Wayne the Night Owl who kept me company plunking his guitar and telling stories about his hoboing days. He played songs on his harmonica that ended in lonesome train-whistle wails. I supplied the boogie woogie beat of the night train's wheels rolling along the track; the locomotive's light shone through my window and tinted the darkness blue around my bed.

Sometimes I dreamed of trains. But sometimes I dreamed I was a bombardier—not the man who went down with my father in his burning plane, but a boy drifting in the basket of an untethered balloon dropping bombs all over town.

Ridge Haven was at the end of a suburban commuter line— "The Last Station Before Heaven," as the town newspaper proclaimed on its masthead. It was a beautifully preserved New England village, with narrow country roads, fields, ponds, and deep fragrant woods. Old stone farmhouses, redecorated by junior executives, stood in apple orchards and fields.

Protected from view by high hedges were the estates of corporation presidents: sprawling Victorian mansions with rolling lawns, out-buildings, four-car garages which had once been stables. Senior executives like my father lived in places nearly as big, white colonial-style houses surrounded by lawns and woods.

A few miles from our property the country club's golf course began, a winding carpet of green with soft beige sand traps scooped out of grassy knolls. The clubhouse, an old gabled mansion, was surrounded by terraces and gaily striped awnings. When we ate lunch there on weekends, I had to dress up in my slacks, blazer, and tight necktie. Every Saturday and Sunday during the summer, I had a tennis lesson with the pro. Afterwards, I watched my father finish matches with his friends, and then the two of us would play. He shouted at me across the net:

"*Pay attention! Keep your eye on the ball!*" The harder I tried to concentrate, the more awkward my strokes were. The net gave twinges of hopelessness as my ball hit it and dropped back onto my side of the court with little apologetic bounces. My father seemed as frustrated about this as I was.

He signed me up on the Junior Tennis Ladder, a chart posted outside the pro shop. Names were printed in black ink on stiff strips of paper that could be moved from slot to slot up and down a long column. I was supposed to challenge boys two or three rungs above me on the ladder. If I beat someone, I would move up to his rung and he would drop to mine. But if I didn't challenge anyone, other boys who were winning matches climbed up the ladder over me, and I dropped each time to make room for them.

"The tennis ladder's like life," my father told me. "There's no standing still. If you mope around in one place with your head in the clouds—like your brother—other people get ahead of you, and you get pushed backwards." I nodded, my tennis racquet dangling from my hand. The diabolical logic of the system lodged in my head like a migraine. Still, I rarely challenged anyone. All summer long I tumbled in slow motion down the ladder of life.

Boom!—one of my bombs obliterated the club's pro shop, turning racquets to kindling. *Boom!*—tennis players in white shorts exploded all over the brushed clay courts, their limbs littering the smoking craters. *Ka-Boom!*—fire storms swept across the terraces; ladies in straw hats sipping ice tea burst into flames, bald men clutching golf clubs flew through the ruptured awnings. *KA-BOOM!* The club was parched earth, nothing standing but the caddy shack where the kids from PS 8 staggered out to wave up at me and cheer as my balloon drifted away overhead.

The boys on the tennis ladder went to the Country Day School. I was on its waiting list, but I had it on good authority that the place was full of snobs and sissies, and was able to resist my parents' efforts to take me out of the public school.

The kids who went to PS 8 all lived in what my parents called "the village," where the houses were closer together and the yards smaller than in the outlying areas. Many of the people were first-and second-generation immigrant families, mostly Italians. Some fathers worked in factories in Bridgeport, some were members of the town police and fire departments, some ran small grocery stores. Mothers took in laundry to help out. In front yards, grandfathers in felt hats constructed rock gardens reminiscent of the mountains of Sicily. Here and there were elegant older houses where New England spinsters rocked in antique drawing rooms behind lace curtains. Somewhere a dozen or so black families lived—the men were mail carriers, the women caterers and maids—but I never knew where their houses were. I thought they must have had a special, secret place of their own somewhere.

The commercial district looked as uncommercial as possible. No vulgar storefront displays were permitted. The zoning board—advised by the Historical Society and controlled by the Protestant families who owned most of the land—had determined the maximum size allowable for signs. Colonial white clapboard shops lined either side of the main street. Even the gas station looked as if it had been erected before the American Revolution. Many shops resembled private residences, with tiny green lawns and flagstone walks. Entering one, you felt you were in the tidy home of some elderly lady who happened to have some cakes or cashmere sweaters she might sell you if you asked her nicely.

There were no bars and only one diner, which had individual tables, not booths, and was called a tea room. Matrons ate long lunches there: sliced chicken sandwiches on white bread, no crusts. High school students could buy milk shakes and hamburgers but were not allowed to smoke or sit more than four to a table. There was of course no jukebox.

Only one store appealed to kids—the Corner News Shop. On its main floor was a large selection of candy bars, comic books, and magazines which included, in the very back of the bottom row, *True Detective* and *Police Story*, with dagger-wielding women in black slips on the covers. Upstairs were the kinds of toys—squirt guns, balsa gliders—that kids could buy with their allowances, not the toys my parents got me for Christmas, which came from FAO Schwartz in New York.

I got to explore the store on Sundays after church while my father picked up the paper and chatted with other men in tweed topcoats and Tyrolean hats. Because it had the thickest business section, he usually bought the *New York Times*, though it made him rant about its Truman-Democrat bias. He hated Truman almost as much as he had Roosevelt, who had handed over the country to the labor unions. I suspected that he also preferred the *Times*, because it had no color comics section. The few times my mother got him to buy the *Herald Tribune*, which she said had a better gardening section, he threw out the funnies. That comics rotted kids' minds (I assumed no grown-ups ever read them) was one of the few things my parents agreed on. I didn't protest; Miss Gilly got her friends to save the Sunday funnies and brought them to me after her days off.

I could tell that the *Tribune* was a Republican paper from all the pictures of Thomas Dewey it ran. In a classroom secret ballot, I voted for Dewey along with everyone else—except one person. All the kids gazed around at each other wondering who could have voted for Truman. None of us had suspected that there were any Democrats in our town, much less lurking somewhere right here in our school.

At last the teacher herself, a woman named Miss McQuater, confessed. A clamor went up, but she didn't look the least bit ashamed. Folding her arms across her chest, she said she thought that Truman would be the best president for the country's working people, of which she was one, she was proud to say. In the confused silence that followed, she called on me to say why I had voted for Dewey. I gave it some thought. Because he had color comics in his Sunday paper, I said. Everyone laughed, and Miss McQuater smiled, too. "I suppose that's as good a reason as any for voting Republican," she said. I was grateful to her for backing me up.

Miss McQuater was amazingly young for a teacher: perhaps thirty-five. She had curly black hair and big dark eyes. She wore purple blouses, plaid skirts, wide belts made of colored leather. Her wrist clinked with a bracelet of gold charms which she actually let us touch.

Everyone, girls included, fell in love with her. She could often be talked into telling us funny stories about her mischievous nieces and nephews, who were our age. It astounded us that a teacher could have a personal life. We more or less assumed that when we left school after the last bell, the teachers curled up under their desks and waited for us to arrive again the next morning.

Miss McQuater was occasionally grouchy, but she gave us warning when she came in, explaining that she'd been up all the night before on a train from Dover, Delaware—a city which began to take on an aura of mystery for us. When her face burst into a smile, we felt that we'd done something good to deserve it. She even thanked us for cheering her up.

She read us stories about knights and ladies, tales of true love which the girls liked more than the boys. When the boys in the back rows—the older ones who were repeating the grade—began whispering and hitting each other, she didn't silence them with icy looks, the way the other teachers did. She walked up the center aisle, her bracelet clinking, to argue with the "tough guys," as she called them. She pursed her lips hard and brushed the curls off her forehead, but eventually we heard a hoarse, musical laugh bubble up out of her. It was obvious that the boys were making noise just so that she'd go to the back of the class and talk to them. No other teachers would do that. Then one day, she didn't come to school. We had an elderly substitute who organized us into study groups and quizzed us on state capitals. I signed a get-well hurry-back card to Miss McQuater, and waited for word of how she was. No word came. Approaching the classroom every morning, we listened for her in the halls; they seemed bleak without her. After several weeks, though, we got used to the substitute and even treated her with a grim civility.

Suddenly Miss McQuater was back. Just before the first bell rang, she jingled into class in a loose skirt and purple blouse and shiny high heels. Wild cheers and applause greeted her.

This made her break out crying. Everyone stared. Leaning back against the teacher's desk, she wiped her face with a lacy handkerchief. Her eyelashes looked like dark wounded butterflies; her cheeks went a spectacular shade of pink. She couldn't speak for long moments, but she beamed a smile up and down the rows that took our breath away.

Finally she told us how much she'd missed us. We all tried to talk to her at once. Everyone assumed she'd been sick—that was the only reason teachers ever missed school. One of the boys in the back row called out, "What was wrong with you?"

Slowly she raised her face. Her damp eyes shone. "Nothing," she said. "I'm pregnant."

Recovering from shock, one of the girls offered congratulations. She smiled and swallowed hard. "I'm very happy about it," she said. Then her face fell; lines appeared in her forehead that we hadn't seen before. "But the school board's not happy. They wouldn't even give me permission to come say good-bye to you."

Good-bye? A hush fell over the class.

"They don't think I'm fit to teach you anymore."

"Why not?" I asked, and several others joined in.

"Because the people who run your town hate people like me—" She pressed her knuckles against her lips. "You see, I don't have a husband. The man I loved decided he didn't want to marry me. So I'm just going to go ahead and have my baby anyway." She narrowed her eyes at the flag hanging on its pole in the back corner of the room. "Do you think this makes me a bad teacher?"

I'd never heard of an unmarried woman having a child before. I think I'd vaguely assumed that it was against the law. One girl said that she had a cousin who'd had a baby without a husband, and then another girl said that she did, too. We all agreed that this didn't make anyone an unfit teacher.

Miss McQuater thanked us over and over, and hugged as many kids as she could get her arms around. My face was pressed into her soft blouse; I inhaled a dizzy mixture of strong perfume and sweat. And then she was gone.

The principal, a scowling bald man in a suit, stood in the doorway to keep kids from running after her down the hallway. When he left, the class was pandemonium. Every girl was crying, even two girls who could fight as well as any boy. One kid wrote, "Fuck the Prinsaple" on the blackboard.

At dinner, I told my parents about what had happened, wondering if they would be outraged, too. They were, but not in the way I'd hoped. My mother thought it was dreadful that the woman had been allowed to upset a classroom full of children with a story like that. My father was furious—*this* was what public education was coming to! I kept asking them why Miss McQuater's being pregnant meant she couldn't be a good teacher, but the matter was much too complicated to discuss.

I was kept home the next day while my mother tried to enroll me in the Country Day School, but there wasn't an opening. For the time being, I went back to PS 8.

The new teacher was a gray-haired woman who wore bulky cardigans and shoes that squeegeed as she walked briskly up and down the aisles. The kids in the back row never disturbed the class by fooling around; her sharp glances kept them in a state of sullen defeat. I got used to stuffing my brain full of facts.

But every now and then as I sat at my desk I would hear the clink of what sounded like a charm bracelet rising from the sidewalk beneath the window, and I would look out, hoping to catch a glimpse of a purple blouse and bouncy black curls—Miss McQuater on her way back to us from Dover, Delaware, with a baby in her arms.

The school resembled a brick armory surrounded by a fenced dirt playground. All morning it gave off a murmur of high voices and an aroma of mashed potatoes. At 3:20, the last deafening bell of the day released swarms of kids onto the playground.

I moved out the door with cautious strides, hoping I could get to the bus without being teased about the way I talked: I had a slight British accent concealed behind an acquired West Virginia drawl. A boy named Vince Marino never teased me, for some reason. He had a way of flicking his black hair off his forehead that I used to practice in the mirror at home, though my own blond hair was short and bristly. Never allowed onto the bus without creased slacks and an ironed shirt, I envied Vince who, like the other village boys, showed up at school in jeans and T-shirt and scuffed sneakers. I admired the freedom with which he careened around the school drumming on fire extinguishers, yelling to his friends in the halls, punching bigger kids in the cafeteria food line. He'd always been one of Miss McQuater's favorites.

When Vince asked me one day if I wanted to come over to his house after school, I immediately said yes, though I hadn't the faintest idea how I'd get home afterwards. I'd never done anything so impulsive.

I phoned home from Vince's house. Miss Gilly had almost called the police when I hadn't gotten off the school bus. Finally she asked me for Vince's address, and said somebody would come fetch me later.

"Your mom don't want you here, huh?" Vince asked.

"It wasn't my mother," I said, then wished I hadn't. I didn't want him to know I had a nanny. "It was my aunt." I was about to make up a story about an aunt who was visiting from Nebraska, but Vince wasn't surprised to hear that I had an aunt at home. One lived with his family, along with her daughter, Vince's cousin, a pretty dark-haired girl named Tina who played the piano at assemblies with me and was trying to get a scholarship to the Country Day School to study music. Also in the house were Vince's mother and stepfather, a grandmother, and four little sisters. They all lived in small rooms on the second floor. I loved the way the house smelled of spaghetti sauce that bubbled in a huge pot on the stove. Kids ran through the kitchen continually; adults yelled at them and the kids yelled back. This made me nervous until I noticed that nobody ever seemed mad at anyone.

Vince's stepfather, a contractor, sat on the living room couch in green work pants and a T-shirt; his feet in white socks rested on a coffee table. He wiggled his toes at the little girls as they ran past, making them giggle. In my house, nobody was allowed to put their feet up on a table or take their shoes off in the living room. I liked it here.

I liked Vince's mother, too, a plump young woman who gave off a smell of laundry soap. She wore no makeup at all; her face was shiny with sweat as she came out of the room behind the kitchen. For some reason she seemed to know who I was when Vince said my name.

"Why didn't you tell me you were going to have a guest after school, Vincent?" she scolded as we sat down at the kitchen table. "I could have straightened things up a little."

Vince flicked the hair off his forehead. "He's not a guest, Mom. He's just a friend of mine."

I grinned and tugged down the bill of my baseball cap.

She poured us glasses of chocolate milk, then sat down with us. The cookies she gave us tasted of licorice, though they weren't black. "Italian cookies," Vince said. "My grandmother makes them."

"They're great," I said, taking another.

The grandmother was standing by the stove watching us, a tiny old lady with a caved-in smile. Vince got up and helped her sit down in a chair next to me.

"How do you do?" I said, as I had to the other adults.

She stared at me and gave off a cackley laugh.

"She's a little feeble." Vince tapped the side of his head.

"Vincent!" His mother scowled at him.

The grandmother reached out toward me. I thought she wanted to shake hands. She put her bony hand in mine and hung on to my fingers.

"Mama—" Vince's mother started toward her.

The old woman said something in Italian, and gripped me tighter.

"That's just one of her tricks." Vince grinned. "She likes you."

"It's embarrassing your friend," his mother said.

"I don't mind," I said. "I like it."

This seemed to be the right thing to say. Vince's mother stopped looking worried, and refilled my glass. The old lady's hand didn't feel so bony anymore, just small and warm. This was one of the strangest things I'd ever done—sit at a kitchen table holding an old woman's hand. After a while, though, nobody seemed to take any notice, so I relaxed. I was even disappointed when the grandmother shyly slipped her hand away to reach out for a cookie.

As Vince left the house, his mother wrapped her arm around his neck, her hair brushing his face as she kissed his cheek. This, too, seemed remarkable. Watching, I nearly stumbled down the front steps.

Vince borrowed a bicycle for me from a neighbor and we took off for the town park. I liked the old bandstand partially covered with vines, the gnarled trees, and the lake that gave off a glow of bug-buzzing heat. A couple lay near the shore with their arms around each other. High school girls in swinging pleated skirts walked beside a field, pink bubblegum bubbles expanding in front of their faces. An old man raked leaves into a fire; the smoke plumed up, turning the air hazy, smelling good.

Some of the kids from PS 8 were playing touch football by the lake. They were boys the teachers never spoke to in class except to tell them to keep quiet and stop acting like dummies. But here they seemed older and more important. Vince ran over to join them, beckoning me to follow. I knew a lot about baseball, but I wasn't sure about the rules of football. The boys eyed me warily.

Vince and I were put on different teams. The captain of my team, a stocky kid called Angelo who wore his cap backwards, told me to block for a pass. When the ball was hiked, I moved in front of a kid who was running toward Angelo. He threw me to the ground as he rushed past.

"Hey—" I yelled, but he just rushed forward to slap Angelo. I stood up, brushing my slacks off, and shuffled into the huddle again.

"He ain't going to stop if you just stand there smiling at him," Angelo said to me.

"I'm sorry. I'll kill him this time," I said.

"Just take him out of the play, okay?" Angelo ran into position. The boys standing on the line with me made growling sounds.

I understood something now: the only way to be good at

this game was to care a lot about it. My father had told me this about tennis, but I'd never been able to work up much interest in the importance of winning. Now, though, I frowned fiercely as I got down into position. As soon as the ball was hiked, I lunged forward and tackled the kid trying to rush past me. To my joy and amazement, he tumbled to the ground.

"Will you fuckin let *go!*" he said, squirming loose.

I stood up, grinning. I didn't brush myself off, since I noticed nobody else did.

"What are you—from Mars?" The kid glared at me.

"You're just mad because I blocked you," I said.

A crowd gathered. "Leave him alone," Vince said, and took me aside. He explained that I couldn't tackle anyone in this game, and showed me how to block with my arms folded across my chest. I walked into the huddle with my arms already crossed tightly. Several kids were arguing about which planet was farthest from the earth—Mars, Pluto or Uranus. On the next few plays, the kids called me "Uranus," or sometimes just "Anus," for short.

Then Vince kicked the ball into the lake. We stared at it floating far out in the greenish algae like a peanut set in lime jello.

"Nice kick, dummy," Angelo said to Vince.

I knew what I had to do for Vince. Pulling off my loafers, I dove in. Weeds clung to my ankles like slimy rags, but I was a good swimmer—I'd had lessons at the country club. I pushed the ball ahead of me to the shore. I couldn't tell if the kids were grateful or not as I climbed out, dripping and trailing weeds. They had looks on their faces as if they were trying to keep from coughing. I handed the ball to Vince.

"Good going," he mumbled, and rubbed it on the grass.

"I'll just get dry," I told him. "You go ahead and play."

The boys looked at one another and then back at me. "Don't catch cold," Angelo said, and they all ran off.

After I'd wrung out my sleeves and pants cuffs as best I could, I decided to ride the bicycle around for a while. It was a battered, comfortable old bike; its fat tires cushioned the ride over bumps. I pedaled beside the lake, caught up in the sensation of coasting along without destination or purpose. The shadows of kids' sailboats rippled on the water. The smell of burning leaves drifted past me.

Under a big tree, I saw a man rolling a blue beach ball across a patch of luminous green grass toward a little boy, who flailed at it with his hands; the father clapped and retrieved the ball each time. The peaceful aimless rhythm to their movements fascinated me. Watching the two of them made me feel lonely, but also lucky, in a way, for noticing things that other people didn't appear to think were remarkable. The park seemed more open, more interesting than any place I'd ever been.

I heard a train whistle from beyond a clump of trees, a long faint cry that seemed to echo the way I was feeling. As I looked in its direction, I was sure I could sense a warm blue haze filtering through the branches and spreading around me. The sound faded. I stopped my bike and listened hard. But now the air was clear again, and I had the feeling that the sound wasn't one you could listen for. You had to be in the right coasting mood and just let it come to you, by surprise, of its own accord. I hoped I'd hear it again one day.

The game was breaking up as I arrived at the football field. I rode beside Vince and waved good-bye to his friends at the park gate. His home was across the street from the park, one of a row of frame houses with wide front porches, walks cluttered with toys, old trees spreading branches over the sloping roofs. But something about the place was different.

I felt its presence in the pit of my stomach before I actually spotted it—my father's big gray Dodge parked at the curb.

Vince did a kind of baseball slide off his bike, letting it fall sideways as he jumped off. I wanted to try the maneuver, too, but feeling the car's headlights watching me, I lost my nerve.

The scene in the living room had changed. Vince's father was no longer resting his feet on the coffee table. He sat in an armchair with his shoes on, his big hands resting on his knees. Two little girls stood stiffly on either side of their mother in the doorway. I could see the grandmother sitting at the kitchen table, glaring past them.

My father had the whole couch to himself. His dark suit and gray silk tie made the slipcover's flower pattern look shabby. An empty wine glass rested on the low table in front of him. And on the rug lay a rectangular wicker laundry basket full of ironed white shirts and towels.

"Hello, Jerrett." He gave me a long look, his frown moving down my shirt and pants to my feet. Then he stood up quickly and smiled at Vince's mother. "This has worked out very nicely—I can collect my son and the laundry at the same time."

I stared at the basket on the floor. "Laundry?"

He reached into his inside jacket pocket and pulled out a thin black wallet. Its leather was as shiny as his shoes. The little girls craned their necks to look at it. My father started to hand Vince's mother a bill, but she gestured toward her husband. He took the money and stuffed it into his pocket.

My mind was working slowly. Suddenly I realized: Vince's mother was what my parents always called "the laundress." I pressed myself back against the door frame.

"I appreciate your hospitality," my father said to the stepfather, and then turned to Vince's mother. "That was excellent wine, madam."

Vince's mother nodded. I tugged down the bill of my cap, aware of my reflection in the mirror beside the door—a skinny kid with smudged face and shirt, rumpled soggy slacks, and muddy loafers. I caught a whiff of myself: pond scum.

"Have you thanked Mrs. Marino?" My father smiled at me. The smile said, "Hurry up!" Everyone in the room saw it.

"Thank you," I said. "I had a very good time."

Mrs. Marino's expression was new; it reminded me of the way the boys had watched me on their football field. "Vincent!" She shouted suddenly, though he was right next to her. "What're you standing there for? Put that laundry in Mr. Langley's car!"

"Yeah, yeah." Vince grunted as he leaned over the basket. It was almost too long for him to pick up, but he got his arms around it somehow. I wanted to help him carry it, but he pushed ahead of me and avoided looking at me all the way to my father's car. After he slid the basket onto the back seat, he ran his finger along the hood.

"Some paint job. This car new?"

"I guess so."

"You got a radio in it?"

I shook my head.

Vince pointed to a dented sedan in the driveway. "We got a radio in ours," he said. Then he ran back inside the house, leaving me on the sidewalk to wait for my father.

Riding home through the town, I imagined myself drifting high above the street in my balloon. Its basket jerked as I released bombs—*KA-BOOM!*—and far below, smoke clouds billowed up with a delicious black stench, obliterating my father's new car. The smoky air around me was only exhaust fumes, though: a line of commuters' cars waited at a stop light. The street filled with traffic sounds. They were louder than usual—horns honked impatiently, the noise battering the windows. My father hadn't moved forward when the light had turned green. He was too busy yelling at me.

"*Look at yourself!*" He knocked the rear-view mirror sideways so that I had to see my hair spiking out from beneath my cap. "How could you go to someone's house like that? You represent the family! You can't go around looking like the son of—of some tramp!"

I squeezed against the door. The cars behind us honked and honked.

"*ANSWER ME!*" He began to pound on the steering wheel with both fists. His face went dark red, his lips bloodless. I'd never seen his eyes like this: the pupils seemed to quiver at me.

Suddenly I stopped cringing. "*I was playing football!*" I screamed. I felt the seat reverberate beneath me the way the ground had as I'd tackled the boy on the field and lay there, bruised and proud. I'd never talked back to my father before. My voice just shot out of me. "*Everybody got dirty!*"

His foot squashed the accelerator. The car shot through a red light and pulled over, screeching to a halt with two wheels up on the curb. He sat forward, his shock of silver hair hanging over his eyes. I loosened my grip on the armrest. I could see that he was making sense of what I'd said. His mouth opened and closed several times before he spoke.

"Did you score a touchdown?" he asked in a strange hoarse voice.

"No."

"Never mind."

I cocked my head. "What?"

He sat back in his seat. "I wasn't very good at football, either." He spoke so softly I had to lean sideways to listen. "But

93

I knocked myself out to make it into the team photo. I needed it to send with my scholarship application. My father had no money to send me to college."

"Why not?" I asked.

He shook his head. "The old man rode the trains from town to town selling kitchen gadgets nobody wanted and sleeping in cheap boarding houses. He'd come staggering back home through town, everybody smelling the whiskey on his breath, seeing the gravy stains on his necktie. He stank up our house with his cigar smoke. . . ."

"I remember when he came to visit," I said. "He smoked outside."

"I wouldn't let him smoke cigars in my house. One day I came home and he was standing out in the rain in his old suit, puffing away." My father shut his eyes, going silent for a moment. "Christ, I never meant for him to stand out in the rain, though!"

"It was summer, wasn't it? I mean, he wasn't cold or anything."

My father nodded, opening his eyes. "That's true."

"He made flutes for me and Robert."

"I remember those flutes. I used to have a drawer full of them." My father sighed. "He could be good with small children sometimes. Children and women and stray dogs." He started the car's engine.

Suddenly it backfired, a booming sound that echoed in the quiet street and filled the clear air with fumes. He glanced sideways, and I caught the flicker of a smile on his face before he accelerated off the curb.

That night, lying in bed with the radio on, I again imagined the balloon drifting above the town. But what I breathed now, as I descended for a closer look, was a smell more startling than the odor of bomb smoke or a backfiring car's exhaust fumes. It was the sweet scent of towels and ironed white shirts, of soapflakes and starch—the smell of that wicker laundry basket in the car's back seat. I could imagine lying in the basket swaddled in fresh soft towels up to my chin—this was the exact same basket in which I'd been driven home from the hospital after I was born.

I was furious with my father because I thought that he'd spoiled my friendship with Vince. And he had, in a way. But I couldn't picture Vince's face as clearly now as I could that of my father, sitting beside me, with his shock of silver hair fallen over his clenched forehead, and the brief smile on his face as he drove off into traffic.

I see the car turning up the driveway. My father was not there on the day when I first arrived at the house in the laundry basket, but today we are linked together by it, literally: the basket is too long for him to carry inside by himself.

"Can you give me a hand with this?"

"Okay."

I take hold of one end, and he the other, and, with me shuffling backwards across the garage floor and him stooping awkwardly, we carry that basket—again and again and again—into the house where I live.

- SEVEN -

I picture Robert walking to the mound. The dark red sun behind him bleeds across the grass of the town park. I hear a crowd in the bleachers: restless clapping, booing, the gathering thunder of feet against heavy boards. I walk up to him, removing my catcher's mask.

"A perfect pitch will win it," I say to him.

"You're the one with perfect pitch," he says. Then he looks around, his smile fading.

The opposing team stands along both sidelines looming like giants, their uniforms blackening in the deep twilight, the features on their faces erased by shadows. I give Robert the ball and return to my position behind the plate.

The batter, a tall man with silver hair and a hawk nose, chops at the air as if with an axe.

Robert goes into the stretch, his leather jacket taut along his arm. I pound my fist into my mitt, making a target for him. The crowd goes silent. He'll have to aim at the sound in my mitt— the last of the sunlight has flickered out in the trees behind him.

His silhouette moves. His arm cocks back, snaps forward.

I feel a great wind approaching. A blue light expands in the darkness, explodes in my face. The roar of a locomotive passes over me, knocking me to the ground.

But the ball is in my mitt.

During the summer when I was eleven, Robert left school. For a while, nobody knew where he was. Then he sent me a postcard which my father found in the mailbox. My parents called the Kansas state police, who picked him up hitchhiking two weeks later.

The night he came home I heard a row going on in the dining room while I ate with Miss Gilly. Afterwards, I snuck up to Robert's room with my new baseball cards.

96

"What was it like where you were?" I asked, sitting on his bed.

"Wide open spaces." Robert sat back in his desk chair. The military school had made him a little thinner, but it had taken most of his hair away; his head was covered with a bristly shadow. "I was on my way to a job, clearing brush."

"Can't you stay here and go to high school?"

"I'm too old. Anyway, if I stayed, I'd go nuts."

"No you wouldn't." I squeezed my cards tight. "I wish I could go away, too," I said. I meant, with him. "But not to one of those prep schools you went to."

"No." Robert looked up. "There's other kinds of schools. You could find a music school. I heard of one in Colorado...."

He looked at the cards in my hand. "You got some new players?" he asked, smiling for the first time since he'd come home.

We spread the cards out on his rug in diamond patterns according to players' fielding positions. I badly wanted to collect a complete set of Brooklyn Dodgers—my team and his—but cards of the famous players were hard to find. I'd recently traded twenty cards for a Gil Hodges. "D'you think I got rooked?" I asked.

"No, it's a beauty." Robert lay the card down in the first baseman's position. "Did you get Jackie Robinson?"

"Not yet." I grinned. I knew that if I could get Robert talking about baseball, he'd feel better, so I chattered on about Jackie Robinson. He was my favorite Dodger. I liked to hear Red Barber, the radio announcer, talk about the way he teased pitchers as he led off base. Base stealing was the part of the game I liked best. You could do something all on your own that was normally not allowed, but if you got away with it, everyone cheered instead of getting mad at you. I got in fights at day camp about who was the better player, Jackie or the Yankees' Joe DiMaggio. The camp, which was mostly for stuck-up Country Day School boys, was lousy with Yankee fans. It puzzled me that Robert, though a devout Dodger fan, also thought there were things to be said for Joe DiMaggio or Ted Williams or Stan Musial. He always wanted to be fair to everyone.

"Jackie had to wait till he was twenty-nine to play in the majors, just because he was a Negro!" I explained.

"Does that make him a better player?" Then Robert answered his question. "Yes, in the long run, it probably does."

97

The next night, I ate in the dining room with my parents and Robert. No one said much—the echoes of the previous night's shouting still hung like shadows in the corners. After dessert, my father sat up straight in his chair, focusing on Robert. "Well, what are you going to do with your life now, if you don't mind me asking?"

Robert looked down at his plate. "I'm thinking," he said, his voice quiet and slow, "of joining the service."

"Wonderful," my father said. "The son of the head waiter at the club is going into the army. We'll have lots to talk about, won't we?"

Robert looked up slowly, focusing on the candle flame between him and my father. "I hate your sarcasm," he said in a low, quiet voice that seemed to make his back teeth vibrate. "I hate the way it makes me panic, so I can never do anything but hang my damn head."

My father's mouth fell open. I gripped the edge of the table, looking from face to face, feeling both terrified and exultant. My mother's ice cubes clinked in her glass as she raised it from the table.

"Anyway, this should make you happy. . . ." Robert broke the silence. "I'm thinking of joining the Air Force."

My father's Adam's apple rose in his throat. "Oh. I see. Well, that's. . . ." He swallowed. "We ought to talk about this, Robert."

After dinner they went up to my father's room. Passing the open door, I saw them sitting on the bed with one of my father's big World War I aviation books open on their knees.

I told Miss Gilly about this. Having heard on the radio that a war against the communists was starting in Korea, I worried that Robert might get shot down there. Miss Gilly stormed upstairs to my father's room. I wished I hadn't mentioned Robert's plans to her—after all the years of telling me how risky it was to argue with my parents, she seemed to have forgotten this herself.

"Well, that man put me in my place!" Miss Gilly said when she came downstairs, her face purple.

"Is he mad at you?" I asked.

"Don't you worry about it." Miss Gilly gave me such a long hug that I wondered whom she was trying to reassure, me or her. "Anyway, a sensitive boy like Robert's the kind the Air

Force will keep on the ground, if they keep him at all," she said. Robert enlisted. On the night before he was to leave, my mother cooked him a steak dinner. My father seemed a lot more cheerful about Robert's decision than Robert was. I watched him chewing grimly as if with exposed nerve-ends instead of teeth.

"How are you going to spend your last day as a civilian, son?" My father wiped his mouth; a smile remained when he removed the napkin. "I can reserve us a court at the club tomorrow."

"I want to see the Dodgers play one last time," Robert said, and turned to me. "Want to come?"

"Yes!" I said before my father could object.

The train looked new, the sides of its cars gleaming silver as if illuminated from within. The windows reflected light like a row of mirrors. As soon as we pulled out of the Ridge Haven station, Robert yanked off his necktie and let out a long breath. "Erskine's on the mound today," he said, opening his newspaper.

I'd been staring out the window at a shelf of fat dark rain clouds hovering above the telephone poles, but said nothing about them. "Is Erskine still your favorite pitcher?"

"Mmm." He studied the paper. "But he hasn't been having a great year."

I had several Carl Erskine cards; they weren't hard to get. He had a sad, open face, like the man who ran the Gulf station in town. "What's he—about four and five this season?" I asked. Robert nodded. I twisted in the seat until I could see behind the paper. "What's that?" I asked, pointing to the page.

"Just a box score."

I wished he would explain what the letters and numbers meant, but his gaze was sunk so deeply into the newsprint that I didn't want to disturb him. Once he said, "It's probably dumb, going into the city now when I have to go back in tonight." He meant to the recruiting station, where another train would take him to a camp down South.

"It's not dumb," I said.

I loved being on the train—the clicking of the wheels beneath me, the long plume of sound the locomotive gave off when we went around the curves—but Brooklyn was even better. The streets crowded with people of all different skin colors, the bluesy music blasting from record stores, the swarthy old men talking in barbershop doorways, the sudden strange spicy food smells we walked through—everything made me stare, take deep breaths, stop and listen with my head cocked. The more foreign it was, the better I liked it.

As I rounded a corner, Ebbets Field appeared before me like the prow of a huge old freighter washed up onto the asphalt. The place gave off a faint roar that vibrated just above my head. I sensed another universe behind those walls, where gods roamed hidden from view; I heard the crack of a bat echo deep inside the place, and shivered. The afternoon was unusually dark and damp; massive banks of lights over the stadium flashed on all at once; I stopped in my tracks as the glow floated like a cloud of silver steam above the walls.

At a souvenir stand, Robert bought a blue cap with a gothic white B above the bill. "This is the official Dodger cap." He handed it to me.

"Hey, thanks!" I ran my finger slowly over the felt crown. "Aren't you going to get one, too?" I asked.

"The government's going to give me a cap tonight," he said.

"Wait!" I handed the vendor a crumpled dollar from my back pocket and grabbed another blue cap. "Here!" I thrust it into Robert's hands.

"Well, okay." He put it on. I was glad to see his bristly hair disappear beneath it. "For good luck," he said. "I'll need it."

I'd only seen black and white pictures of the stadium, and was startled to see that the playing field was in color. Under hundreds of artificial suns, the grass glowed green as if it had just been washed. The bases were as white as big vanilla cakes. An old man dusted off our seats with a huge mitten and Robert gave him a quarter, though the seats hadn't needed cleaning. My brother obviously knew that this was part of going to a ball game. He bought hot dogs for us, a beer and a cigar for himself, a Coke and peanuts for me. The hot dog squirted salty juice into my mouth; the Coke—forbidden at home because of the dangerous drugs it contained—made a fizzy laughing sound in my paper cup.

The seats around us filled during batting practice. Men called out to the players by their first names as if they knew them personally. These weren't Dodgers, they were Giants, but they were baseball players, the first live ones I'd ever seen. The field became a blur of balls being thrown around and smacked into leather gloves. My eyes ached from trying to watch everything at once.

"This is almost the best part," Robert said as a batter hit one lofting fly ball after another. "Nobody has to win or lose. They're just doing what they love to do."

He pointed out various Giants by name. Most I'd only vaguely heard of, players whose cards I'd traded away to get Dodgers. One Giant's name was familiar: Elmer Vlacek. His card said he was the only major league player born in Europe—in Czechoslovakia, which I knew was behind the Iron Curtain. Watching him, I figured that it must have been hard to grow up in a communist country where kids probably weren't allowed to play baseball. Elmer had a round face with one cheek puffed out from chewing tobacco just like any American ballplayer. He didn't look like a communist to me. I couldn't see the point of going to war to shoot people like him.

Kids in dirty shirts and jeans were hanging over the rail of the box seats below us, reaching for stray baseballs. One kid leaned so far over he fell onto the grass. Retrieving a ball, he scrambled back into the stands. A guard came running and grabbed him by the collar.

"Booo!" Robert shouted. I'd never heard him raise his voice to anyone before. Several other fans booed the guard, too. The guard let the kid go, but snatched the ball out of his hand and tossed it back onto the field. I booed loudly.

Then an amazing thing happened. Elmer Vlacek walked over, picked up the ball, and tossed it to the boy. He caught it, letting out a whoop. Robert laughed. I hoped Elmer would get lots of hits today.

"I sort of don't want the game to start," Robert said. "Once it starts, it's partly over." He looked at the ash on his cigar. "There's no big leagues where I'm going."

"Miss Gilly said you won't have to fly planes in Korea," I said.

"I'm only going to Alabama tonight. Boot camp. It'll be full of crackers there. You know what they are?"

I shook my head.

"They're the kind of people who called Jackie Robinson 'nigger' when he first came up to the majors. They don't like

Northern boys much, either." Suddenly he turned toward the field. "Hey, there's our Dodgers."

Now the field was alive with players in baggy blue and white uniforms. Dust clouds rose from under their cleats as they ran. I didn't need to look at the scorecard to recognize them. Gil Hodges had big ears, like his picture on my baseball card. Pee Wee Reese really was smaller than the others. When Jackie Robinson ran out to second base, he didn't deign to notice the boos mixed with the cheers. I watched him field grounders, sweeping his glove along the ground as if he were scooping up stationary turnips instead of fast-moving baseballs. Nothing got by him. He threw so fast to first base that the ball disappeared in the air until it exploded into Hodges' mitt. Over the stadium I could see the heavy clouds squatting on the roof, but the banks of lights gave the place a radiance of its own.

"Ladies and gentlemen," the public address voice boomed, "Gladys Gooding will now play our national anthem." Organ music filled the stadium. I hummed along.

The first batter walked toward the plate. But now thin diagonal lines of rain were filling the space under the lights. The air smelled wet. Robert kept looking up at the sky. The drops of moisture against his face made him wince continually. It was first time I'd seen his tic since we'd gotten on the train.

No one got any hits during the first three innings. Jackie Robinson didn't get on, so he couldn't steal any bases. Elmer Vlacek wasn't playing; maybe he was being punished for giving the kid the ball.

"I like games where there's lots of hitting and scoring," Robert said. "I wouldn't care who won if they started doing *something*."

"It's a pitcher's duel," I said. That's what Red Barber called games like this on the radio. "Maybe it'll be a no-hitter."

Robert shook his head. "They only happen once or twice a season. The odds against them are millions to one."

"Still—"

"You ask for too much, you get nothing at all," he said, his voice startlingly sharp. When he saw my face, his eyes started blinking furiously. "Forget that, okay? I'm just wound up today. You want some more peanuts?"

"Okay," I said, and he waved the peanut vendor over. The first peanuts were hard to open; my fingers didn't work well.

Carl Furillo struck out. He had the highest average in the league; if he couldn't get a hit, what chance did the Dodgers have? I had to go to the bathroom. It wasn't easy to find in the echoing cement caverns under the stands; the urinals were over-flowing and stank of old beer foam. When I came back, the field didn't seem green anymore; it was a dark, soaked gray. The players standing in their positions looked bored, waiting for something to happen. It occurred to me that a lot of baseball consisted of waiting around. Gray boredom and rain got into the park whether people booed or cheered. Looking down from the ramp at my brother hunched in his seat under the drizzle, I could see that he was just hanging around, too. I suddenly saw my own life as a lot of time spent waiting for nothing very ter-rific to happen. Like Robert, I couldn't do much about this. Maybe nobody could, not even baseball players.

I sat down again. "You okay?" I asked Robert.

"Sure." He sat up straight. "We got a run—look."

The scoreboard read:

Giants	0	0	0	0	R 0	H 0
Dodgers	0	0	0	1	R 1	H 1

"A double, an error, and a fielder's choice. You didn't miss much." Robert was trying to sound cheerful. "Look who's coming up."

The big man with the deep black face strode toward the bat-ter's box. Then he stopped. I leaned forward. Two umpires were talking to each other near the pitcher's mound. Jackie Robinson walked away from the plate. The rain had begun to pelt down.

The fielders ran into their dugout. Grounds-keepers rolled a huge tarpaulin onto the infield, turning it into an instant lake with raindrops bouncing like B-B's on its shiny surface. Behind us, people were taking shelter under the overhanging roof, but Robert just sat where he was with his knees drawn up, staring out at the slanting lines of rain.

"You go ahead," he said, his shoulders drooping. "I just feel like sitting here."

"Me, too." I pulled the bill of my cap down.

Robert didn't speak for a long time. Now and then he chewed his nails, something my father always got after him

103

about. The rain hissed faintly like air slowly leaving a balloon. The faraway bleachers began to fade into a mist.

"The game doesn't count if it doesn't go five innings," he said. Rain was trickling down his cheeks.

"It does, too!" I said.

He looked at his cigar. It had gone out.

I decided that I wanted to be the last person to leave the stadium if they cancelled the game; I'd rather be here with Robert watching the raindrops splashing in Brooklyn than be anyplace else in the sunshine.

After half an hour, the rain finally let up, though the dark clouds continued to lie low over the roof. The tarpaulin was rolled away. As the players ran back into the outfield, their cleats made splashes on the grass. I was soaked but didn't mind; the air was warm. With all my might I pictured players hitting doubles, triples, home runs that would make Robert jump up and down and cheer.

Jackie Robinson, returning to the plate, grounded out. Batter after batter grounded out, struck out, flied out. A few Dodgers got hits but were left on base. The zeros kept appearing on the scoreboard like blank mocking cartoon eyes.

Giants	**0 0 0 0 0 0**	**R 0**	**H 0**
Dodgers	**0 0 0 1 0 0**	**R 1**	**H 3**

Suddenly I turned to Robert, who was staring at the field as if he were already watching out the window of a train heading south to Alabama. "Hey, the Giants still haven't got any hits," I said. "Isn't that a no-hitter?"

He sat up. "Listen," he said. "There's three innings left."

"Okay, okay," I said, but I could tell by the way Robert concentrated on Carl Erskine as he warmed up on the mound that he was thinking about a no-hitter, too. Carl still looked like the gas station manager. When he took off his cap to wipe his forehead—the drizzle had started again—I saw that he was partly bald. I never knew players could be bald under their caps. Beside wiry Pee Wee Reese and huge dark Jackie Robinson and Gil Hodges standing like a mountain over first base, Carl looked very ordinary. He didn't throw the ball too hard, and everyone hit it somewhere. But not for a base hit.

"Only two innings more," I said, as the seventh 0 went up on the scoreboard. "And it'll be a no-hitter, right?"

"Shhh!"

"Why?"

"You're not supposed to say it. It's sort of like magic. Saying the words out loud might keep it from happening." Robert squeezed his empty beer cup.

"So if we keep it a secret, we could help. . . ." I shut my mouth.

"Maybe," Robert said. "That's the idea, anyway."

I noticed that the people around us seemed keyed up, as if they were all sharing a powerful secret. An old guy who'd looked like a bum was grinning and waving his arm in the air with every pitch; he didn't look like a bum now. The kid who'd picked up the ball during batting practice leaned over the front of the box seats with all his friends; the guard saw them, but didn't chase them away. He was watching the field.

Carl Erskine came up to bat and struck out on three pitches. "He's saving his strength," I said. Robert agreed. The people around us must have understood this as well—they clapped for Erskine as he walked back to the dugout. When the first Giant in the eighth inning grounded out, I could feel in my seat the vibrations of thousands of feet stomping.

"Attaboy, Erskine!" the old man shouted. "Humbaby!" The kids at the box seats' rail jumped up and down. The stadium rocked with cheers, the huge freighter shifting on moving waters. Then, as the next Giant stood waiting at the plate, the crowd hushed, as if a wind had died down suddenly. The world stayed precariously level. Then: a pop-up. The stadium rocked and trembled again. Grown men were jumping to their feet and yelling at the top of their lungs like kids. I'd never seen men in Ridge Haven behave that way.

"Get outa there, ya jerk!" Someone shouted at the next batter. No one even glanced at him.

I jumped up. "Get out!" I screamed. "Beat it!"

I looked down at my brother to see if my noisiness bothered him. He was never rude to people. But he just grinned up at me.

The Giant hit a line drive over third base. I covered my eyes. The crowd made a loud "Ohhhh!" sound that moved like a wave along the stands.

"It's just a foul ball," Robert said, nudging me.

"Whew." I dropped my hands from my face and stood on my seat.

Another pitch: the batter swung and missed. "Strike two!" the umpire yelled. The storm exploded again.

All the people in front of us were standing now, blocking Robert's view. "Don't you want to see?" I shouted at him.

He slid down in his seat. "Your turn—you tell me what's happening."

"Okay." The batter took a third strike. "He's out!" I screamed to Robert over the roar of the crowd. "The inning's over!"

Robert gave me the high sign, his forefinger and thumb meeting to make an **O**.

Everyone sat down while Brooklyn batted. We were just waiting for Carl Erskine to take the mound again. It wasn't like waiting for rain to stop. I sensed a new feeling in the air: people thinking that all the magic they were trying to work—by not saying the words "no-hitter"— might actually make it happen. All around me, strangers were grinning at each other and talking in hushed voices. Robert relit his cigar and sat back, the smoke rising from it like a tiny banner unfurling.

I knew I shouldn't say anything, but I couldn't keep still, and leaned close to whisper to Robert."You think, maybe. . . ?"

His whole face seemed to be struggling to speak. Finally he rested his hand on my head for a moment. Under the circumstances, it didn't seem like an awkward gesture.

Now Carl Erskine's methodical warm-up pitches were the most fascinating thing going on anywhere. People cheered every time he threw, even though there was no batter yet. I kept rolling my eyes along all the zeros on the top line of the scoreboard.

Giants	0 0 0	0 0 0	0 0	R 0	H 0
Dodgers	0 0 0	1 0 0	0 1	R 2	H 6

The first batter of the ninth inning chopped his bat beside the plate, glaring at the pitcher, aiming invisible line drives past his head. Carl's shoulders drooped. He looked tired and vulnerable. The gray outfield seemed vast behind him and the high walls of the stadium loomed out of the drizzle. Was he scared? I was. If he messed up, and if something bad happened to Robert in Korea—I remembered crashing planes to the floor in the war games we'd played in the attic, years before—then I'd look back and think, it all started with that day we went to

Brooklyn. Robert hadn't asked for anything as risky as a might-be no-hitter, he'd just wanted to see a ball game. Why did this dumb pitcher have to try to bring off something so impossible?

Then Pee Wee and Gil and Jackie all leaned forward around the infield, poised to spring to Carl's defense. The clapping and stamping and cheering from the stands died down a little. Carl straightened up. Suddenly he didn't look so hesitant and ordinary anymore. He threw a ball, a strike, and then the batter hit a grounder to shortstop. Pee Wee threw to Gil, and everyone jumped up to scream. Robert got to his feet. I started to shout insults at the next batter stepping out from the Giants dugout. But then I shut my mouth, feeling queasy.

"What's the matter?" Robert asked.

"It's Elmer Vlacek. He's pinch-hitting." For an awful moment, I had the impulse to shoot him down in cold blood at the plate.

"Oh." Robert winced at the boos starting up around us. "Well, if he gets a hit, he'll be a hero. If he doesn't, Erskine will be. Either way, it's pretty good, huh?"

I stared at Robert. Could he really be so cheerful? Not judging by the look on his face. His mouth was stretched in a grimace, his eyes narrowed. I could tell he needed this no-hitter even more than I did.

"I don't want to watch," I said, sitting down hard.

"Okay. . . . Strike one," he called down to me. Then he pulled me by the arm. "Come on, I need you here with me!"

I leapt to my feet. Standing on the seat, I leaned against Robert's shoulder. He clamped his cigar between his teeth.

I saw Elmer's body jerk around. His bat made a cracking sound that hit me between the eyes. A groan went up all around me. The ball went screaming into the hole between shortstop and second.

Suddenly Jackie Robinson sprawled onto the grass, one arm trapped under him, the other stretched straight out. The stadium rocked with noise. He had the ball in his glove. He'd caught it for an out!

Pee Wee ran over to him. Jackie stood up slowly, holding his stomach. His head down, he walked in a circle, brushed off his uniform. Then he crouched behind second base again. The roar of the crowd surged out of the grandstands.

107

I knew that the next batter didn't stand a chance. Robert was leaning sideways against me now. He seemed to know it, too. Carl was throwing hard, his arm snapping forward as he zinged the ball toward the plate. Strike one—pop! into the catcher's glove. Then a ball. Then a hard pitch, a perfect one right down the middle. . .and tap! a soft one-hopper bounced back to the mound. Carl grabbed it as if snatching a gnat out of the air. He turned and tossed a sure, slow strike to first base.

He had his no-hitter!

Suddenly I was caught up in a huge screaming mob. I stood on my seat and yelled as the players rushed to Carl and hugged him and smacked him on the back. They all ran together toward the dugout, heads up, grinning. Fans swarmed onto the field. Even as the stadium emptied, I kept screaming until my voice gave out altogether. I hadn't realized it, but I was clutching Robert's arm, my fingers digging into his shirt. I tried to say something to him, but only a scratchy sound came out of my mouth. He looked dazed, his mouth half open, his eyes fixed on the dugout where all the Dodgers had disappeared. When I shook him, a wobbly smile appeared on his face.

I would have been crushed on the throbbing stairs under the stands if Robert hadn't kept his arm tight around my shoulder. People were pressed up against me on all sides; all I saw was sweat-soaked backs of shirts until we were suddenly squeezed out into the daylight. The rows of brick tenements, the overhead wires, the gray cheesecloth clouds overhead—everything vibrated before my eyes.

I wanted to watch until the very last of the fans poured out of the stadium, and all the vendors rolled away their pushcarts. I wanted to stay in Brooklyn forever. Robert was in no hurry to leave, either. He wandered around with me, gazing at the people as if they were old friends. Finally he bought two scorecards and two official Brooklyn Dodger pencils.

As the subway train roared through the tunnel, I stood tight against my brother's side in the mob, swaying with him into the turns, feeling the train rumble around me like an echo of Ebbets Field's pandemonium. I could picture the stadium somewhere above me, the huge freighter still rocking, sailing away into a gauzy sky on raucous waves of applause.

At Grand Central Station, my face ached from grinning all the way from Brooklyn. Men in suits were racing for commuter trains as if this were an ordinary afternoon. The evening papers weren't out yet, so no one here but us knew that Carl Erskine had just thrown a no-hitter. At the very moment this occurred to me, Robert turned to me and said, "They don't realize, do they?"

"I know!"

He gave my cap's bill a tug. Then he stared up at the big clock over the entrance to the tracks. It was time to catch the train home.

When we'd found a seat, I hoped the train would break down on the way to Ridge Haven. Robert took out the score-cards he'd bought and handed me one. "You've got to help me with the box score."

He showed me how to fill in the little squares with letters and numbers that recorded what each batter had done, inning by inning. I remembered plays for him and copied his notations with my Brooklyn Dodgers pencil. It seemed important to finish filling in the squares before we reached Ridge Haven. We had it all done except for Elmer Vlacek's at-bat in the ninth inning. Robert chewed on the pencil's eraser. How could he have forgotten Jackie Robinson's diving catch? I reminded him, and he wrote it in, nodding.

"Now, watch this," he said, moving the pencil point. He wrote nine 0's in a row after "Giants." Then he drew a final round 0 under the total of hits. "Look at all those perfect zeros." He grinned.

I filled in the 0's on my own scorecard and carefully rolled it up around my pencil. So as not to make the pencil shorter by sharpening it, I decided never to write anything else with it again.

Trees and buildings flicked by outside the glass. Robert sat beside the window, the scorecard resting on his knee. His eyes were shut, all twitching subsided. I sat in exactly the same position beside him, except my eyes were wide open. Rain streaked down outside the train now, splattering the window. But those banks of suns over Ebbets field—those banks of perfect incandescent zeros—gave us a glow, and I felt it radiating all around my face. Robert and I were the only ones who could see it.

The aura moved with us as we climbed down off the train and got into my mother's car. Its interior was lit up by our grins, and my mother, seeing them, began to smile a little.

Robert told her how Jackie Robinson saved the day with his diving catch, and I wanted to tell her about Robert's player, the spectacular Carl Erskine—but he gave me a glance and I knew I mustn't tell anyone, not yet. No-hitter magic was still on; saying the word might make us go out like a couple of light bulbs. We kept them lit.

I watched Robert and my mother standing at the counter in the pantry while he poured gin over some ice cubes. Usually he didn't say much to her unless she asked him questions, but tonight they were chatting quietly as they had a drink together. It occurred to me that Robert was very much a grown-up now and had been for some time. I liked watching the two of them leaning back against the counter with glasses in their hands. I couldn't hear what they were saying, but now and then Mother made a laughing sound; she was inside the bulb of light with us now.

Then she heard my father's car on the driveway and finished her drink in a gulp.

Robert and I and Mother stayed inside our incandescent aura all through dinner. We saw my father's remarks spattered on the glass but they didn't reach us. When he started to tell Robert about how tennis was a better sport than baseball because you could keep playing it all your life and it helped you to make friends and business contacts, Robert looked at me and we smiled, knowing better.

My father had a going-away present for Robert: a leather manicure kit with a red silk lining. Inside, tight leather loops held in place odd-shaped clippers and tweezers. They looked to me like strapped-down silver insects. Robert and I had seen these kits in the window of an expensive gift shop in Grand Central Station; my father must have bought the gift there while rushing to catch his train. I could see that Robert was disappointed with it, almost angry, and suddenly the glass bulb seemed about to crack. But he reached out and took the leather kit from my father. He said "Thank you" in a quiet voice, and glanced at me.

Mother said Robert would be the only one in boot camp with anything so fancy. My father shot her a look that sliced through the air like a back-hand swipe, but she half-shut her eyes and it was deflected by invisible glass.

Finally my father began talking about his World War I Air

110

Corps boot camp, where he learned to fly planes made of wood and canvas and wire. Robert and I glanced at each other; I pictured the combat game we'd played on the attic floor: the pilot rescuing the bombardier from the burning plane. Gradually Dad's voice penetrated our incandescence. It shone too: a web of crackling white wires reflecting in the glossy dark surface of the table. Even Mother appeared to like listening to Dad's old stories. A glow surrounded the table, with all of us sheltering together inside it, as talk of warfare brought a rare peace to the family.

Later that night, we drove through the rain to the train station. Robert stood awkwardly on the platform with his duffel bag. He wore his baseball cap. We all waited in silence.

The train pulled in, its brakes scraping beneath its belly. Robert kissed my mother and shook my father's hand. Then he hugged me good-bye. I dug my fingers into his leather jacket, my eyes stinging. He gave the bill of my Dodgers cap a tug.

"We were there," I whispered.

He made the sign with his thumb and forefinger shaped like an **0**. Then, swinging his duffel ahead of him, he climbed the steps into the train. The car's door swung open. He vanished through it.

The train looked grimy in the weak station light. Slowly, jerkily, it started to gather speed. I smelled acrid steam. Up ahead, the locomotive gave off a rhythmic chuffing sound.

Breaking free of my parents, I raced down the station platform, shouting and waving wildly at the windows. The train's whistle carried my voice off into the night.

- EIGHT -

Naked and holding hands, my parents wait for me beneath the sea.

Among the wedding guests are mermen in top hats and purple dinner jackets, mermaids with fish-tails swishing below their ruffled ball gowns. People with legs are dressed in rags, or flowing ribbons of luminous seaweed, or nothing at all. Their mahogany skin gleams in the blue-green water. Bubbles rise from the mouths of the women as they laugh. Their pubic hair swirls like living anemones.

I arrive riding on a sea horse, a four-footed one. Embracing its neck, my face pressed into its soft flowing mane, I feel its muscles heave as it gallops along the sandy ocean floor.

My mother and father reach out to help me dismount. Conga drums thunder around us. The water ripples with a *merengue* beat. Everyone is smiling.

The band-leader moves to the altar, his baton under his arm. Resting on his tail, he opens a book of poems.

My parents stand before him. I hold the ring.

The ceremony begins.

Travel brochures began arriving in the mailbox addressed to me. Miss Gilly said they were rubbish and cleared them angrily off her table at tea time. She and my father hadn't been getting along since the night she'd objected to Robert joining the service; I thought this was why she was so edgy.

She caught on before I did what the travel brochures meant: my mother, who had sent off for them, was trying to interest me in going on a vacation with her and my father. Miss Gilly reminded me of the good times we always had while my parents were away. I told my mother I didn't want to go anywhere.

Pamphlets continued to arrive: not castles and snowy mountains now, but beaches and palm trees and people dancing by the light of paper lanterns. I became intrigued by a photo of a diamond-shaped fish that glided flat and silent along the

112

ocean floor; the more I stared at it, the more restless I became. My father still wanted to go to Europe, but my mother found an island called Haiti where he could keep up his French and visit a fort built in the time of Napoleon. One evening, he announced that he'd bought three tickets to the island.

Miss Gilly was so upset she hardly came out of her room. When it was time for me to leave, she insisted on packing my bag. My mother had already packed it, but Miss Gilly lumbered all the way up to the attic to re-fold everything, tucking peppermint drops into the corners. Big tears fell from her eyes onto my shorts. I'd be fine, I promised her—what could happen in two weeks?

In Haiti, I seemed to have new parents. My mother, especially, was changed. A perpetually bemused look played over her face: her lips relaxed at the corners, and the lines beside her eyes faded. I'd never noticed the color of her eyes before: they were pale blue, like the ocean. She looked almost pretty in a peach-colored sun dress and gay straw hat. The view of the harbor below the hotel terrace made her smile, so did the gaudy pair of toucans in the dining room, the chatter of the maids, the incongruous rainfall sounds of the palm branches shifting in the hot sunny breezes. She especially liked the hotel garden, where she spent the afternoons lying on a wicker couch reading dog-eared books of poetry she found in the lounge.

"Things so seldom live up to one's expectations," she said, gazing over the book into a cluster of twined pink-flowering vines. "But here...."

My father liked the beach and the hotel; he talked French with the manager and trounced men half his age on the grass tennis courts. While I swam in the pool, he went for long walks with my mother. Once, when they came back, she was carrying an armload of flowers he'd bought for her at a roadside stand; their color matched her cheeks.

My parents said they were turning over new leaves. The manager took a photo of the three of us standing among the new leaves, big waxy ones on the branches of the flowering tree that embraced us as we posed, smiling. I stood in the middle, in shorts and a polo shirt, looking up at my parents as the camera clicked. My mother leaned against my father's arm. Her hair was platinum in the sun, and swept back, no longer fluffed out like confused feathers. My father was tanned and bare-chested, his arm resting on her shoulder.

We took a trip to the ocean. Running through the water, I nearly stepped on a small diamond-shaped manta ray. It brushed past my ankle, a breath against my skin. Leaning over, I saw it through my goggles for one clear instant. Its side flaps waved slowly like wings. As it shot away, its tail left a trail along the sandy bottom. Its soaring movement through the water was so beautiful that I forgot to be scared. I swam after it. If the ocean's floor had dipped down, I would have plunged after the magical creature, succumbing happily to narcosis of the deep just to keep it in sight.

My father said that Port-au-Prince, the city at the bottom of the hill, was one big slum. I was never to go by myself; anything could happen to a white boy there. I'd never known that whole countries of black people existed, but I got used to it more quickly than my parents did, maybe because I'd gotten to know some black kids at school, where the teachers were careful to treat them just like everybody else. I felt bad that the Haitians were so poor, but my mother said that the natives of countries like this were never really unhappy because they didn't know about any other way to live.

I had the run of the hotel grounds; I could swim in the pool, play shuffleboard and badminton, and order fruit drinks just by summoning a waiter. The part of the hotel that interested me the most, though, was the gift shop, a dimly lit room fragrant with sweet, dark wood smells and populated by mahogany figures that the clerk said were Dahomeyan spirits. "*Attendez*," he said, smiling and wiggling his fingers in the air. "They cast a spell on you for all your lifetime."

I liked the paintings of undersea deities: fish-tailed gods in top hats and mermaid goddesses with pointed breasts. My favorite figure was a wooden horse. It was heavy and smooth in my hand; its nostrils flared, its eyes bulged wildly, its mane splashed back in carved wavy lines as if it were galloping through surf.

The horse's restless energy got inside me. I hadn't planned to disobey my parents, but one afternoon while they were taking a nap I rode one of the hotel bicycles down the winding road to the city. Without my parents, I felt as if a faint grayish screen were lifting from before my eyes. The colors, the sounds, the smells—all were extraordinarily vivid. Gliding along the streets, I wanted to gulp down the contents of whole bakeries, rum shops, grocery stores. Women cut the pink guts out of fish with long knives. Carpenters' saws rasped through boards. Fishermen caulked their boats with handfuls of sticky black pitch. Spiced cooking scents floated past my face. I could smell the damp coats of donkeys as they brushed softly against me in alley-ways. And I smelled people themselves—glistening shirtless men, women whose bright dresses stuck to their bodies in dark stripes of sweat.

For hours I walked my bicycle through the market, moving with the flow of people. My restlessness was calmed: I was where I'd longed to go even before I'd known such places existed. In the market stalls, mangoes and papayas glowed with heat. A woman fruit-peddler with fat arms shouted in my direction. I grinned back, working up the courage to approach her; I felt as if I'd been starving for ages and hadn't realized it. Pointing at some bananas, I gave her a big Haitian coin. She weighed the fruit on a tin scale that hung from chains, handed me a bunch of yellow bananas, and counted out some small coins as change. The touch of her fingers startled me, as if an electrical current had jumped from them into me.

The sun glared down onto my bare head. I'd forgotten the canvas hat my parents had told me always to wear in the sun. The bananas were hot, which made them sweeter. I tossed the skins into a gutter where other people had dropped their fruit rinds. Dizzying odors rose in waves as the rinds broiled in the incredible heat.

Some boys were kicking around a ball made of rags and twine. How could they have so much fun playing with a ball like that on a crowded, littered street? But they were—running at full speed, yelling and laughing. I'd never seen soccer before. When the ball flopped toward me, I dashed into the game. The ball ricocheted against everyone's feet; I got off one good kick. After several minutes running in the sun, I felt the cobblestones slipping under me and stumbled back toward my bicycle. Trickles of sweat filled my eyes, and my head was spinning.

Several boys from the game followed me. Now I noticed that their undershirts had big holes in them, showing patches of dark skin; their shorts were ragged and dirty. I wanted to jump on my bicycle and ride away fast. When the boys held out their hands, I gave them the rest of my bananas. We all peeled bananas and silently ate.

A small boy held something out toward me. A cigarette. I took it. The paper was yellow with dried sweat. He handed bent cigarettes around. Producing a wooden match, he walked up to me with the flame cupped in his hands. I sucked in the heat and managed to blow smoke out without coughing. The boys grinned. Then they swaggered away. I carried the cigarette around until it burned my fingers.

But now I was seeing people differently. Those boys weren't the only people who were poor—everybody was, at least compared with me. What my mother had said couldn't have been true. Not all the people looked unhappy; plenty of them were smiling as they worked or talked. But when they weren't smiling, a lot of them looked hungry or sick or exhausted. Hungry, sick, exhausted was what you were if you didn't have enough money. The people pushed heavy hand-carts over the uneven pavement. They had to carry burlap sacks on their backs heavier than anything I'd ever carried in my life. The muscles in their legs and arms bulged like cables about to snap. Didn't that hurt? Didn't these people hate me?

An old man approached dragging a foot wrapped in a filthy bandage. When he spotted me he limped right over, as if he'd been expecting to find me here. My stomach tensed. He reached out his hand. It had practically no fingers; sticky dirt was congealed on the stumps. I'd read about lepers in a social studies book but had never expected to meet one. It hurt to look into his eyes, they were so sad and rheumy.

He said something in _Creole_. Did he think I understood it? But strangely enough, I did, in a way. I pulled all the paper money from my pocket. How could I give it to him without catching leprosy? Suddenly he stuck out his other hand. It had all its fingers. I gave him the bills.

"Thanks," I mumbled—for the clean hand. The old man's face wrinkled into a crazy smile. Yet wasn't I the crazy one for thanking him? He limped away.

Feeling disoriented, I sat down on a piece of broken cement beside the harbor. The heat baked my scalp through my hair. Sunlight bobbed like scraps of silver foil on the blue water. Sailboats glided by. Gulls soared back and forth. Everything was so beautiful here, and yet people were so poor. I was glad all my money was gone.

I pushed my bicycle up a side street. My sense of direction was lost in the sun's glare. The air made hot currents against my skin, swirling slowly in front of my eyes like tinted water. I began to flow with the human traffic again. The bananas in my belly seemed to have fermented, their fumes rising into my brain.

I was drawn into a maze of narrow alleys where the houses were painted bright green, blue, pink. I'd never seen such a place. It was like entering a dream. Sunlight ricocheted off yellow window shutters. Chickens scuttled away from my bicycle wheel. Second story French doors opened onto wrought-iron balconies. Bed-sheets billowed out from them, casting bluish shadows onto the cobblestones below. I'd never known that shadows could have colors.

Hearing drum music above me, I glanced up. Three women on a balcony waved to me crazily. Their dangling hoop earrings and kerchiefs made them look like lady pirates. I waved back. The women laughed. Their lips stretched wide; their cheeks shone pale brown in the sunlight. Bouncing their breasts, they danced in time to thudding *merengue* music from a radio in the doorway behind them.

Two of them had on long print dresses that hid their feet; their swaying movements reminded me of the mermaids in the paintings. The other woman, the one in the middle, wore only a short skirt and a purple bra. Her mouth was so shiny and red she looked as if she'd just been eating raspberry sherbet. Her lower legs were a creamy beige, and she was barefoot.

She held out a rum bottle toward me. But of course I couldn't reach it. I shook my head, smiling. She thrust out her lower lip as if disappointed. One of the other women hit her on the back of the head, and this made them all whoop and laugh again.

The woman in the bra stepped close to the railing and fixed me with a hot dark gaze. I stared back, gripping the bike handles to keep my balance. With a flourish, she reached up under her skirt. Shutting her eyes, she slowly spread her legs. I held my breath. She gave a little shudder, and pulled her hand out. Her bracelet clinked like tiny bells. Her hand rose, thumb and forefinger pressed together in

117

front of her face. The music seemed to grow louder.

Like a magician, she smoothed something invisible with dancing flicks of her fingers. Smiling into my face, she passed her hand beneath her nose. Her nostrils twitched. Her eyes rolled back. It must have been a hair she was showing me—or pretending to. She leaned toward me and opened her fingers, releasing it.

Her naked arm swayed back and forth as she pointed into the air. I turned my head, following the magic hair's flight. For a second, I was sure I saw it in the sun's glare. Down, down it floated like a transparent butterfly. She motioned me to catch it. I didn't plan to move, but suddenly I felt a strong force tipping me off-balance like a hot wind blowing against my back. I stumbled toward the balcony, cupping my hands before me.

Suddenly loud applause was splashing around me in waves. I blinked hard. A crowd had gathered. People were laughing and clapping. A man and a woman pointed at my pants—I had an erection. I couldn't stop laughing, myself. People seemed to be applauding it as much as they were the woman. She was still leaning over the balcony, her hand outstretched toward me. I smiled up into her gaze. She made a kissing sound with her lips. Then, flouncing her skirt, she vanished through the doorway.

I might have wandered around in a daze all afternoon if a man hadn't seen the hotel's name on my bicycle and walked me part-way up the hillside. I stumbled along with the sun perched on my head like a blazing chicken with red-hot talons. I kept picturing the woman on the balcony. Had I actually seen her? Just when I was beginning to doubt it, I saw a single curly hair glowing on the ground at my feet. It moved with me, it wriggled and writhed along the surface of the road. When I leaned over to pick it up, it melted into the broiling red clay. I wiped my eyes hard; incandescent ghost-hairs spiralled across the insides of my eyelids.

Under the palm trees near the hotel gate, I felt an amazing ache pulsing beneath my scalp. Puddles of shimmering water hovered just above the lawn, then disappeared as I stepped toward them. My bicycle dropped silently away from me.

I shuffled toward the room I shared with my parents. I had to squint through the ache. A printed cardboard sign hung from the door knob: Please Do Not Disturb. I knocked on the door.

"Just a minute!"

I opened the door. An exhalation of heat nearly knocked me over. The sweet scent of fruit was everywhere. My scalp felt like the skin of a pounding drum. I saw two beds and a cot, a sliced-open papaya on a table. The shade was drawn over the window, but a stripe of blue-green light trickled in along the floor like a tiny, shimmering river.

I saw the feet of a man with bare legs. A man wearing my father's bathrobe. Looking like my father. Sitting on a bed. Beside him, a woman with a bare back. A woman lying with a sheet wrapped around her waist. Turning over. Looking like my mother. I swayed in place in the doorway.

"Hi," the man said, as if nothing were out of the ordinary. He was actually smiling.

So was the woman. She sat up, holding the sheet to her pale chest. Her hair blew in the breeze from the fan. My mother hated fans because they ruined her hair, but this woman didn't seem to mind.

"Did you have a nice time?" she asked.

I nodded slowly. To speak would make my head crack open. The window curtain blew. The bright stripe on the floor was no wider than a hair. It swam with a watery motion before my eyes. I tumbled headlong into it.

I was in bed for three days, feverish with sunstroke. Every time I woke up, my mother was sitting beside me. It was strange to find her there. As a small child, when I'd been scrofulous with skin allergies, Miss Gilly had always been the one to fuss over me. My mother didn't fuss; she just stayed by my bed. I woke, dozed, woke. She read poetry aloud: Scottish lakes and islands and misty glens. She rubbed cool lotion into my burning forehead. I didn't remember eating, but I must have, because sometimes I saw her holding a spoon above my face.

Out of bed, I'd sit in the shade of the hotel garden with her. She watched me with the same pleased, curious expression with which she gazed at the bizarre tropical flowers or the chameleons that puffed their pink throats in and out on the flagstones. She fetched glasses of cool limeade for me, watching me drink as if this was some sort of miracle: bright green liquid flowing out of the glass into my body. Then she asked me if I wanted more, hoping, it seemed, that I'd say yes. At home, I was constantly told not to trouble my mother; here she actually seemed to enjoy taking care of me. My father, too, appeared to like being around me and my mother. The trip to the fort was cancelled, but he didn't seem to mind. The three of us played cards, swam, went for short drives in a taxi into the mountains, and there was never an argument. Stranger still, neither of them scolded me about going into the city alone. I dozed in the front seat, woke to hear them laughing and chatting together behind me.

Every evening before dinner, we drank planter's punches (no rum for me) in the bar, an open-sided thatched roofed hut on the terrace beside the dance floor. I'd never seen gaudy pink drinks like these at home—only light brown or clear liquors were allowed there. A cruiseship had docked down in the harbor, and its guests came to the hotel to crowd the dance floor. The band played American music from the 1920s; middle-aged men and women glided through the lights that sprayed out into the darkness from a revolving mirrored globe. I liked watching my parents dance. They whirled with amazing ease among the other couples, and when they returned to the table, out of breath, my mother was singing to herself.

Often the band played *merengue* music. In the light of flaming torches, Haitian women in skirts and bathing suit tops performed a "native dance" on the terrace. Swaying their hips, they flashed raucous red smiles at the tourists. I could see that all the smiling was fake—the dancers seemed to be doing cute imitations of the women on the balcony. Men from the cruise ship joined the women on the dance floor, forming a loud white and brown conga-line around the pool.

"Being in the tropics makes some people forget how to behave," my father said.

My mother smiled over her pink glass.

I went for a walk through the hotel garden, touching the huge waxy petals of night-blooming bushes, thinking again about the woman who'd gazed down at me from the balcony. I remembered her smile, her outstretched hand, the way her curls sprouted from beneath her pirate head-cloth like beautiful black lace. I missed her badly. Had she really thrown me a hair? I found myself looking for it among the flowers' tendrils. The high-pitched static of cicadas receded before me as I wandered along. I pictured the woman dancing there in the dark garden like one of the Dahomeyan-spirit mermaids. Undersea plants in the shapes of feathers and butterflies swayed around me in the liquid darkness. I glided among them, my arms outstretched like the wings of a manta ray.

The next morning, my temperature still wasn't normal; I had to stay close to the hotel another day. Restless, I went for a walk behind it. There, I was surrounded by coconuts lying on the ground under some palm trees. I picked one up, cradling it in my arms. It felt like a big green egg out of which some strange marine creature might hatch. I took it back to my room and stuffed it into my suitcase.

The bag smelled of peppermint. Miss Gilly's candies had melted inside. A rush of worry passed through me—I'd forgotten to send her a postcard.

I bought some with my last coins, and mailed off a card to Robert, too, remembering the one I'd received from him just before I'd left. He said he was in the stockade for talking back to an officer, but it was worth it. I knew that a stockade was a kind of jail like the parts of Western forts where the U.S. Cavalry used to lock up renegades and Indians. I pictured the house at home surrounded by high walls and wooden turrets. I didn't want to think about going home.

In the gift shop, I searched among the carvings for my wooden horse. I wanted badly to hold it in my hands again, though there was no question of buying it now. My father wanted me to learn to handle money wisely; I knew that he'd be firm about not lending me any. I couldn't find the horse anywhere in the shop. The clerk told me he was very sorry, someone had bought it. He showed me others, but they were lifeless imitations.

Sitting with my parents on the terrace on our last night in Haiti, I watched another torch-lit dance show. Afterwards, the women swished among the tables in gauzy skirts that soaked up the pastel colors of the bar's paper lanterns. Some of the men from the cruise ship invited them into the bar, draping arms around their waists.

My parents and I found a table behind some palmettos near the badminton court. Soon my father went to the room. My mother said she'd join him in a minute. I could tell that the waiter had forgotten to leave the rum out of my drink. I gulped it down, feeling dizzy. Figures flickered past the spiky bushes; notes of laughter flew by me like shuttlecocks.

"Are those women courtesans?" I asked my mother suddenly.

She shifted her position so that her face was partially hidden behind the brim of her straw hat. "Of course not, dear. They're just dancers. Wherever did you get such ideas?"

"A book I read." The one by Emile Zola in the living room, I remembered, but didn't mention it.

My mother gazed off through the palmettos. "Well... I suppose the women are what you said, really." She shrugged. "I certainly never expected to see anything like that at a hotel like this."

"Do they like the men? Or are they just acting?"

"What strange questions you ask!" She laughed, her cheeks flushed.

I knew that if I weren't in this place and full of rum, I'd never dream of asking her such questions. Nor would she have allowed me to. "Everything's strange, here," I said.

"I know—isn't it marvelous!" She stretched out her legs, her bare toes wriggling in her sandals. "Anyway, let's hope some of the women are having some fun and aren't just acting."

"Okay."

Reflections of purple lanterns shone on her glasses. She sat back, lifting her straw handbag onto her lap. "You've spent all your allowance, haven't you?" she asked.

"Yes." I cocked my head. "Why?"

She set something on the table before me. "I thought you might like this...."

It was the horse from the gift shop. The polished wood glowed in the light, its mane splashing over its neck.

"*You* bought this?" I asked.

"Your father and I saw you with it in the shop. You didn't see us. We watched the way you held it in your hands."

"Thank you!" I reached out slowly toward it. "But I thought—are you sure it's all right with Dad?"

"I'm sure. It was his idea to buy it for you." She smiled. "Do you like it, darling?"

"Yeah!" I ran my hand along the horse's mane.

She smiled. "You know, sometimes there have to be exceptions to rules." She stood up unsteadily and drained her glass.

"Could you tell me how long—" She touched her fingers to her lips, and her cheeks flushed. "I mean, I know you probably aren't very tired, since you slept this afternoon. How long do you think you'll be staying up?"

I was used to being told when to go to bed, not asked when I wanted to. "An hour," I said, ready to negotiate.

But all she said was, "An hour, fine," and kissed me on the ear.

I watched her walk away down the path toward the room, her skirt swaying against her ankles. She even walked differently here.

I went into the bar and sat down at a table, where I turned the horse this way and that, gazing at its wild mahogany eyes. Now all the stools and tables were empty. Where had the women gone? I ordered a planter's punch and slurped it down, tasting the rum. My fingers stroked the horse's carved wooden mane. From below the terrace, music was drifting up from the city on the warm breeze with the cries of nocturnal roosters. I could make out the shape of the cruise ship in the harbor; outlined with carnival lights, it glowed like a constellation of stars on the pitch-black water.

I had another sweet drink, then another. I was sure I heard a woman's laughter rippling through the garden beside me. Out of the corner of my eye, I saw the woman dancing there. But when I faced her, she swam into the shadows that flickered among the plants, leaving the reverberations of her fish-tail in the air.

The waiter helped me to my feet. The gaze of night-blooming flowers followed me to the room. The air was dark inside, but the curtains glowed faintly. Two beds and a cot were incandescent white. The room tilted as I staggered through it.

The people I'd found after my return from Port-au-Prince were back again. Now I knew who they were, and what they'd been doing. My mother's face was partially hidden in the pillow, her hair fluttering in the breeze. Beside her on the same bed was my father. Their bodies, side by side, formed S shapes under the white sheet. Over them, invisible fan blades whirred rhythmically, a sound like the echo of whispers.

I dropped onto my cot. The room began to revolve. I

groped for something to steady me. The horse's head dug into my chest. Holding onto it tight, I rode back over the undulating cobblestones of the city.

-NINE-

Alma stands weeping before the dark stone embassy. The diplomat rushes up to her.

"Oh Jerry, it wasn't your fault." She says, wiping her eyes. He—I pick up her suitcase and grab her hand. We rush across the park where the children usually sail their toy boats in the fountains. Today the fountains are dry. All the walks and benches are empty. Even the pedestals stand vacant of statues beneath the leafless trees.

Two people block my way in the icy fog. I barrel into them. The man sprawls to the pavement, a deep gash opening in his forehead. My foot comes down on the woman's hand as I step over her; I leave her scream behind.

In the deserted fairgrounds, the striped tents have turned to metal skeletons. The hurdy-gurdy stands rusty and silent, its spindly legs sunk in gray snow. The river's current has stopped; the barges are set in hardened black glue.

But on the other bank I see flowering bushes ablaze in the yellow sunlight. "Hear the music, Alma!" I point to the people dancing the *merengue* on the shore. "Come on!"

I tug her toward the balloon. We scramble into its wicker basket. I begin throwing things out to lighten the load—so many boxes of toys, games, construction kits. Slowly, the balloon rises.

It floats above the ground, but won't rise into the clear air above the cedars and elms that line the park, no matter how many things I fling over the side. I try to lift Alma's suitcase but it is made of lead. Jagged tree branches scrape against my face. I hear a terrible rip overhead. The basket drops with a groan through liquid fog. It bursts against the ground. I sprawl half out of the basket onto the pavement.

"*Alma?*"

She's gone. I peer into the fog, searching for her. The collapsed balloon settles over me like a heavy rubber blanket.

⌐

I rode in the front seat of the taxi from the airport to Ridge Haven. The air inside the car, clogged with gray silence and cigarette smoke, faded the pink straw of our souvenir bags to a dreary off-white. My parents, wedged into opposite corners of the back seat, kept glancing at each other. Why? When I turned to look at them, my heart thumping uneasily, they glanced out the windows.

The car turned into the driveway. The yard was still covered with grayish snow, and the tree branches looked like tangles of wire. The house's white clapboard had faded; the windows were dead.

Inside, the house felt like a place I hadn't lived in for years. No lights were on. A strange musty scent hung in the hall. I dropped my bag and headed through the kitchen toward Miss Gilly's room.

"Jerrett, come in here." My father's voice stopped me cold.

"In a minute," I said over my shoulder.

"Now!" he said in a tone I couldn't ignore.

In the living room, the heavy drapes were drawn over the windows the way they usually were at night, though it was afternoon, or had been a moment ago. My parents sat in the armchairs on either side of the fireplace. There was no fire.

I sat on the couch, shivering. "What's the matter?" I asked.

My mother winced as she cleared her throat. Her skin was powdery pale; the taut lines around her mouth had returned. "Jerrett, you've been too old for a nanny for years," she began. "We tried to let Miss Gilly stay on as a kind of housekeeper, but she was never happy—"

"Is she on vacation?" I asked. My heart was beating so hard I had to cross my arms over my chest.

My mother leaned forward in her chair, a determined smile bending her lips. "We took you on our trip because we wanted you to see how nice things could be, just the three of us." Her eyes behind the little veil of her hat were damp, full of an awful pity. "And we thought it'd be easier on you if you weren't here when Miss Gilly moved out—"

"She's *gone*?"

Both my parents were talking; their lips moved in unison.

"*You sacked her!*" I screamed.

"*Don't* you raise your voice like that!" My father's fist hit the armrest of his chair.

"Dean, he's upset!" My mother turned back to me. "Your father and I agree on this—"

"How can you agree? You never agree on anything! It's not fair!" I staggered to my feet. My shin banged the coffee table; an ashtray wobbled noisily on it. "Where *is* she?"

"She's at one of her friend's houses," my mother said. "You can call her, and you can even see her once in a while—"

"*If* you behave yourself," my father said.

"*I behaved* myself! It didn't do any good!"

"Jerrett! You get back in here—"

But I was gone, stumbling headlong out into the hall and through the kitchen. The door of Miss Gilly's room was shut tight. I shoved it open. Her bureau top was bare. The open mouth of her closet gaped at me: empty, hushed, holding its breath. I yanked out the three drawers of her bureau—empty, empty, empty.

My parents' voices approached. I slammed the door and twisted the bolt just as the doorknob turned. I tugged the bedspread back. The mattress was naked with ugly brown stripes. Miss Gilly's eiderdown was gone! Where was the eiderdown? I fell onto the bed.

From time to time, my mother tried to talk to me through the locked door. My voice, high-pitched and jagged, drowned her out: "EXPECTS ME TO TAKE CARE OF THIS GREAT BLOODY HOUSE—COOK THE DINNER, DO THE LAUNDRY—WHILE SHE LIES UP THERE IN HER BED HUNG OVER—" My mother's footsteps retreated. My father sounded thundery. I shut my eyes and yelled: "HIM—ALWAYS AWAY ON THOSE SO-CALLED BUSINESS TRIPS— EXPECTING EVERYONE TO STAND ATTENTION WHEN HE COMES WALTZING HOME—" His footsteps faded, too.

My mother returned. "Jerrett, *please!* Speak in your own voice!"

"*No!*" But that was my voice. "Why did you sack Miss Gilly?"

"Because... you're our son. We wanted you back, before it was too late."

"Go away!" I covered my head with the heavy bedspread.

After a long time, I half-dozed. My parents stuffed Miss Gilly into a sack and pushed her into the country club pool. I sank to the bottom with her, the sack tightening around my neck....

I ran my fingers along the seams of Miss Gilly's down comforter, searching for the spiny tips of feathers. *If you pull all the feathers out, dear, what am I going to have to sleep with?* Miss Gilly wrapped the light, soft eiderdown around me. *We'll never run out!* I promised. She pushed it toward me—*Go ahead, then, Jerry—take all you want.* I pulled one slowly with my thumb and forefinger. We both watched. A long black feather slipped out of the seam. She smiled—*Oooh, isn't that a lovely one, dear?* I brushed it against my cheek—*It feels good.* She shut her eyes—*Try it against my eyelids.* I brushed it slowly against her lashes, then along her lips. They moved—*Oh, it's all silky! Such lovely things, feathers....*

I sat up. Something at the top of the closet caught my eye. Miss Gilly's biscuit tin. I climbed on a chair to take it down. Buckingham Palace was stony dark in the corner of the lid. The king and queen smiled phony smiles at me. The prince looked younger than before, shrivelled and waxy, a little painted corpse. I yanked off the lid, stared at the silver bottom. Empty.

In the morning, I was awakened by sunlight blazing in the curtains. My father's car hummed past the window, then the air in the room was heavy with silence. I smelled something just outside the door. I opened it a crack. A plate of buttered toast and a glass of milk lay on the carpet. I kicked over the milk glass and stomped on the toast.

Footsteps approached. I ducked back into the room.

"Aren't you feeling any better?" My mother's voice was soft in the corridor.

"No!"

Around noon, I smelled food outside the door. I opened it a crack. Asparagus soup, my favorite, and a piece of chocolate cake. I took the tray inside. I was so hungry I ate everything and licked the plate.

Nothing appeared at tea-time. There would be no more tea-times, I realized; an important part of each day was cruelly empty, cancelled. I sat on the floor in the closet and drew an X in the plaster wall with the hook of a coat hanger. I gouged it deeper and deeper, enlarging it until it was the same height as I was. Cancelled.

In the evening, my father arrived home early. "I wish you'd come out, son," he said from behind the door. "We could play catch...."

Playing catch was what I did with Robert. I remembered the time the detective had come to question me after Robert had smashed into the garage door with the car.

"Are you going to tell the police?" I yelled finally.

But my father had left. I found myself waiting for dinner, and getting furious when no one came to the door. Eventually I heard footsteps, and a plate being put down. In a few moments, I looked out into the corridor. Faint voices came from the dining room. Silverware clinked.

"You'd better leave me alone," I said into the darkness, and snatched up my supper.

I curled up on the closet floor and went to sleep lying against the wall under the X, my head resting on the biscuit tin. In the morning, I ached all over. I had plaster dust in my mouth. The room was beginning to smell—I'd been peeing in the sink.

I tiptoed out the door. My father's car was gone from the garage. So was my mother's. I was alone in the house. "Good!" I said in a loud voice. The voice faded into the walls. I'd never been so lonely in my life.

A bowl of cereal had been left on the kitchen table for me, but I ignored it and, taking a flashlight, went up to the attic. I crawled under the eaves and kicked the photo album, strong box, and photos as far into the darkness as I could. But now there was nothing to mark Robert's spot. I sat down on it. The flashlight beam gradually grew weak. Darkness gathered around me, feeling heavier and heavier. Finally I crawled out into my room.

Sunbeams streamed through the attic window. My suitcase was lying open on the bed. Someone had unpacked it. On the bureau top, among the china animals that Miss Gilly had given me over the years and much bigger than them all, was the mahogany horse.

I snatched it off the bureau. It gave off a terrible restless heat; the skin of my hand felt scorched. I ran with it downstairs, through the house and into the garage. My arm cocked back. I flung the horse against the garage door.

It didn't break. I glanced around for something to hit it with. My tennis racquet leaned against the wall. I used it to whack the horse against the walls. After several smashes, the racquet's strings snapped and the frame looked as if had cradled an exploding grenade.

The horse lay at my feet, its body slashed with scratches, its legs broken off. Trembling, I backed away. The horse's wooden eyes watched me from the floor.

I spent the day in the woods sitting beside the brook. After a while I began to see something darting just below the surface. I remembered the turtle that I'd set free. But this creature moved too fast for a turtle; it was as quick and elusive as the patches of sunlight glinting on the water.

The manta ray.

"I remember you," I whispered.

I slipped beneath the water, growing small and flat. I burrowed under the surface of the ocean floor, shot out in a silent puff of sand, turning sand-colored. I darted in and out of flowering anemones. I was gone in half a blink—too fast to be seen clearly, never showing my whole self. From then on, people who tried to touch me would feel only a shiver of water against their skin. They would look down to see a diamond shape sliding along the ground, a fleeting shadow, a passing cloud's reflection.

When I returned to the house that evening, the garage had been swept. The tennis racquet, wrapped in newspapers, was hidden in a garbage can. There was no trace of the horse.

My mother stood at the kitchen sink staring out the window. "Jerrett! Where have you been all day?" she asked, hearing me in the pantry.

"Nowhere." I stood near the doorway, my gaze fixed on the wall. Flattening myself, I slithered beneath its white paint.

"I found the—the remains, in the garage." Her voice was quavery. "That was a dreadful thing you did."

"I don't care," I said.

"Somewhere, deep inside, you do care about that horse."

My eyes filled with tears.

"I know this is very hard on you. But you'll get used to us."

I slipped deeper under the paint, turning paint-colored.

She leaned sideways to peer out the window again, lines appearing in her forehead; she'd heard my father's car in the driveway. "We don't have to say a word about what you did."

"It can't make any difference any more what I say." I glided along beneath the surface of the wall and out the door.

Miss Gilly sobbed on the other end of the telephone line when she heard my voice. "For years, I knew it was coming!" she gasped. "But it tore the heart out of me! You know the way your mother yanks those bloody great weeds out of the garden—and all the dirt flies—and a big hairy clump of roots comes ripping out of the ground? That's what it felt like, Jerry!" I pictured Miss Gilly pressing her hand against a ragged hole in her chest, and my own chest ached. "I'd never have abandoned you—never!" she said.

"I know, Miss Gilly."

"They told me a few days before you left—that I had to get out. They said if I told you, it'd spoil your trip."

"I'm sorry!" Tears flooded my eyes.

"It was nothing you did," Miss Gilly said. "You must never, never blame yourself for this!"

"I can't help it, sometimes. If I hadn't gotten you worried about Robert enlisting—"

"That was just the straw that broke... it was just an excuse!"

"I can't stand it in this house!" I said. "When can I see you?"

"I'll come pick you up at school. We'll have tea at the bakery."

"When?"

"If I do it without your mother's say-so, she'll give me a bad recommendation. I'll never get another position." I heard her choke back a sob. "I'm not even a citizen—and I'm fifty-two years old!"

"I've got some money in the bank. You can have it."

"No, no, no. I'll find something, dear." She blew her nose, an explosion in my ear. "And as soon as I'm working, I'll come see you."

I waited, marking time. My whole life in that house felt like marking time.

I woke up each morning with grief clamped over my head and squeezing my chest like tight rubber. The world looked gray, sucked dry of all but muted colors, as if I were looking out at everything through smudged glass. Few smells penetrated the glass; all sounds were muffled. I walked slowly, my shoulders hunched over, my mouth partly open to get enough air. People had trouble hearing me. My mother asked me if I was sick. I shook my head.

"Then do try to be pleasant once in a while, won't you—at least at dinner," my mother said.

I knew what she wanted—for me to be part of a cheerful welcoming committee that would make my father want to come home on early trains. I made a deal with her: I'd act cheerful if I could see Miss Gilly once a week. She agreed.

I finished the school year, and turned twelve. Miss Gilly found a new job and went to Maine for the summer with her new family. She sent three postcards a week.

A few cards came from Robert, too. One said that he'd run away from the Air Force. It gave a secret address that he said I should write to from now on. I said nothing about this to my parents.

On the night before school was to start in the fall, my mother cooked a steak dinner like the one she'd made Robert the night before he'd gone into the service. I was too tense to eat much, wondering what it meant. I found out during dessert.

"A place finally came open at the Country Day School," she said. The candlelight flickered in her face; she blinked hard.

"We enrolled you in the seventh grade," my father said.

My parents watched me in unison. Something inside me scuttled away as if a hard blow to the stomach had dislodged it. Shadows shifted in the corner under the window; part of me, shadow-colored, hid there.

"The fact is, Jerrett, you can't get into a good prep school unless you have a good private school behind you," my mother explained. "The junior high in town is for boys who are just going on to the high school. Its standards simply aren't good enough."

I put down a forkful of cake. The melting ice cream on it had turned to diarrhea. "I don't want to go to a good prep school," I said. "I want to go to music school. Robert said there's one—"

"We'll have *plenty* of time to discuss it." My mother's eyes pleaded with me not to make a scene.

My father watched me over a forkful of dripping brown cake. "The Country Day's a fine place. You'll be with boys more like you."

"You just decide things for me!" I said, but in the voice of a lost cause, breathy and faraway, as if I had slipped outdoors already and was listening from the other side of the window. Yes, there was my face reflected in the night-black glass, watching me. Had my parents heard me? Not really. I jumped to my feet, knocking my chair over.

Deaf to their protests, my reflection and I darted across the window into the shadows and out of the room.

The Country Day School covered a green hillside like a toy village. It had once been the estate of a gentleman farmer, whose brick mansion now housed most of the classrooms. Outbuildings—a crafts shop, a theater, a chapel—surrounded the main hall. Playing fields, once meadows, were mowed to the texture of soft baize. From the outside, the buildings looked weathered and antique, but everything inside was new: walls smiled glossy white, the dark wood floorboards beamed as if regularly buffed with virgin chamois. Some classroom windows offered a view of dwarf deer grazing among birches on the neighboring estate.

When I'd seen kids wearing Country Day uniforms in town, they'd looked to me like members of a visiting croquet team. Here the uniforms perfectly matched the environment of grass (green blazers for both boys and girls) and geometric flower beds (plaid skirts with knee socks for girls). I had to wear a blazer, but it didn't make me feel as if I blended in. I felt like a foreign exchange student.

The girls hugged their books to their chests as they stood talking in high, breathless voices. The boys spoke in mocking tones and moved in packs. They charged along the gravel paths as if they owned them, which of course they did; they'd been at the school for six years and had their cliques and friendships well established. I knew none of the rules of the road, and left a trail of skid marks in the gravel.

One afternoon, a tall boy who was on the football team took a seat next to me on the bus. His blazer was a worn, languorous shade of green. Resting his arm on the top of my seat, he squinted at me as if the brightness of my new blazer hurt his eyes.

"The problem is, kid, you haven't been initiated yet." His wide-open blue eyes made me almost believe he was trying to

133

help me out. "All new kids have to be initiated. Once it's over, you'll be able to make friends."

"I don't want to be initiated into this school," I said.

He looked at me as if he were talking to a turkey the day before Thanksgiving.

At recess that morning, I was told to run with a football to the edge of the field. Boys clustered around me, bouncing the ball off my chest. I refused to catch it. They gripped each of my arms and walked me toward a copse of trees. Their laughter echoed across the grass toward the old brick walls of the main hall. From a window we must have looked like an illustration from the school brochure: chums in their uniforms enjoying a lovely autumn afternoon together. Sunlight streamed down through the tree branches, dappling the soft green grass. A spicy scent rose from the fallen leaves. A crow cawed and flapped away.

I was surrounded by grinning faces: freckles and bristly blond crew cuts and eager bright eyes. Someone tackled me from behind. I was rolled onto my stomach, but I refused to cry out or struggle. This made stuffing leaves down my back a boring task. I was buried beneath a writhing, pummeling mass of bodies. Someone thumped my head against the ground.

Now I strained to fight back. Too late—my arms and my legs were pinned down. Elbows dug into my stomach; buttocks squashed my face. I breathed damp flannel, crotch sweat, farts. My face was slithery with snot, my own or others', I couldn't tell. My zipper was yanked down. Handfuls of leaves were thrust into my pants. My crotch was alive with wriggling worm-like fingers. They yanked my dick, they squeezed my testicles. A sickening ache roared through my groin. I cried out.

Fingers squirmed into my mouth—someone was stuffing leaves into it. My jaw was the only part of me that could move. I clamped it shut.

A scream—not mine—rose from somewhere in the mass of bodies. I bit down harder. The fingers jerked frantically. Salty blood trickled down my throat. I felt bones crack between my teeth. Boys scrambled away. The screaming was louder. The fingers slid out my mouth. Someone rolled on the ground beside me—the injured boy, his hand clutched against his chest. I sat up, spitting blood and leaves. I laughed until

134

I coughed, choked, and threw up onto the grass.

An ambulance rushed the boy to the hospital. When he returned at the end of the day, his entire hand was in a plaster cast. The headmaster, a tennis crony of my father's, talked to me in his office about the seriousness of my offense. Tiny white hairs curled out of his ears. I focused on them until he was through talking. He wanted me to promise I'd make a better effort to adjust. I said nothing.

"How was school today?" my mother asked when I got home.

"Fine," I said, giving her a theatrically cheerful look. When she tried to touch my torn blazer pocket, I darted away.

"Were you playing football in your good clothes?"

"Something like that."

"Well, I'm glad you're joining in games, anyway. I suppose boys your age just like to roughhouse." She gave me a worried glance. "The headmaster called about this roughhousing, though. He said he had a nice talk with you about it." she said.

"He said that we had a *nice talk?*" I cocked my head.

"Yes. You see, when you're in a really good school, the headmaster takes a personal interest in each boy."

"What did he say?"

"He said you promised to make a strong effort to adjust." My mother smiled. "Isn't that true?"

"No," I said. I wouldn't lie, but I wouldn't explain, either.

Eventually I did "adjust"—I had to. I acted as if I wanted to belong. I pretended to look up to athletes and to look down on clumsy "weenies," to make fun of the "retards"—the men who raked the grounds and the women who served in the cafeteria. The kids seemed relieved that I'd stopped trying to be different. They were sure that the gift of their acceptance would make me so grateful that I'd forget my grievances against them. I camouflaged my real self—the manta ray that scuttled deep into a private tropical sea when no one was looking.

Piano was the only subject I liked. Every lunch period I stayed in the practice room with Vince's cousin, Tina, who had gotten the music scholarship she'd wanted. She was further along than I was, at least in classical music. I ate my sandwiches while she played, watching the reflections of sunlight flicker on the bare white walls as if ignited by flying musical notes. Tina rarely spoke, but sometimes she smiled at me over the keyboard and I smiled back. In a way, I wanted to talk to her, to ask to carry her books to the bus, but I understood why she liked to be quiet.

She, too, had an act at school, I'd noticed. When she laughed along with the other kids, her nose wrinkled and her face took on an almost desperate expression. While she played the piano, though, her features relaxed; she was her real self. I started practicing every moment my parents were out of the house.

In public school, I'd been among the top one or two students; at Country Day, I had the lowest grades in my class. I liked reading the books, but my mind slipped away from class discussions. In tests, I filled in blank spaces as quickly as possible in order to escape the classroom ahead of everyone else. The teachers acted as if they weren't exasperated with me and told me I was making progress. They sent concerned notes home, but I took them from the mailbox before my parents could see them.

On Tuesday afternoons Miss Gilly picked me up at school in the six-year-old Hudson she'd bought with the severance pay my father had given her. She always parked it away from the parents' sleeker models. I liked its long bulbous body and small windows; it reminded me of a car out of a children's book. The air inside was always rich with her peppermint scent and the damp heat given off by her old fur coat. She wrapped her arms around my neck as I slid across the seat. I gripped the fur at her waist, my face nuzzling into her shoulder. When I sat up straight, she beamed at me, her plump cheeks glowing, and stroked my hair.

"I always get here early," she said. "I like to look at the school building, knowing that you're somewhere inside."

"I always look for your car from the window," I said.

At the Swiss bakery, we sat at a table in the back, far from the counter where matrons cooed and twittered while waiting for their pastries. The handwritten menu listed cream puffs, Napoleons, jam-tarts, but we always decided on the almond cake to have with our tea.

"D'you remember these coffee rings we had while your parents were in Europe?" Miss Gilly dipped a piece into her teacup and popped it, dripping, into her mouth. Then she took out her handkerchief and wiped her eyes. A lot of subjects made us feel choked up. I didn't want her to worry about how badly I was doing at the new school, and she didn't want to depress me with the details of her dreary new position with a couple who lived in a nearby town. She was much too old to start over again with a tiny baby, she said. Fortunately the people were away at horse shows most of the time. When they were at home, they constantly interfered in the nursery. But at least the woman didn't drink.

"Speaking of which, how's your mother getting along in that house without any help?" Miss Gilly asked. "Staggering around in the filth, I should imagine."

"She's hired a cleaning woman two days a week," I said. "She doesn't have time to do housework, with her meetings and everything."

"She's started all that again—Historical Society and Library Board and whatnot?" Miss Gilly pushed air out from between her lips. "She must be too busy to cook. You're looking thin."

"Everything comes out of the freezer. Frozen minute steaks, frozen chicken pies. Even frozen TV dinners," I said. "My father says there ought to be a law against selling them to people who don't own a TV."

"It's a wonder he comes home for supper at all." Miss Gilly shook her head. "Does he still miss his trains?"

"Not so much."

"Well, I reckon he's getting on for that sort of thing, isn't he? He must be nearly sixty, now."

"They're trying to have a family life," I said. "That's what they say, anyway."

"Hmph." Miss Gilly brushed cake crumbs from her lap. Her beige suit, the one she'd always worn to present me at cocktail parties, had faded and was tighter around her stomach. A paisley scarf covered most of the red wattles under her chins. She sat back and sighed.

It was a relief not having to be constantly cheerful. Silences between us weren't uneasy. We sipped our warm tea, smiling at each other from time to time and picking away at the almond ring. The waitress, a skinny woman with a gray braid, rushed back and forth muttering in German. Cups clinked at nearby tables; puffs of sugary scents floated out of the kitchen.

Miss Gilly took out a box of English Oval cigarettes and lit one. "I started these things when I took the new job," she explained. "There's nothing else to do around that great empty house."

"I smoke sometimes, too," I said. "Same reason, I guess."

She slid a cigarette and matchbox to me. "Keep it under the table," she said, glancing toward the counter. "Your mother's friends must be thick as thieves in this place. If one of them sees us..."

I lit the cigarette. "I have to hide everything at home. At school, too. I'm pretending to be somebody I don't even want to be. But what if I turn into him, really?"

"I hope you never change inside," Miss Gilly said.

"I don't feel like I have an inside anymore." I took a hard drag on the cigarette. "I act like my parents' son, they act like my parents—like everything's fine."

"They're wonderful at pretending. Especially your father. Your mother could fall down dead at his feet and he'd say she just decided to take a nap on the carpet." Miss Gilly dipped another piece of coffee cake into her tea and chewed it thoughtfully, her jowls jiggling.

"I always have to be careful what I say. If they gave me the sack, where would I go?"

"Don't be silly. They couldn't do that to you."

I shrugged. "They did it to Robert, didn't they?"

She looked up from her teacup. "What do you hear from him, Jerry?"

I told her about the last postcard he'd sent. Strangely enough, she said I should show it to my parents. "He'll need their money for a lawyer if he gets caught," she said. "You can't just walk away from the military."

"He's gone somewhere they'll never find him."

"I hope so...." Miss Gilly shook her head slowly. "D'you remember the cocktail party when that Mrs. Miller came? I should never have said anything to Robert. That started it."

I leaned forward. "Started what?"

"Robert never told you? About the row with your father, after he'd spoken to your mother that night? Heavens, I thought you knew."

"No. What—?"

Miss Gilly put her finger to her lips. The waitress was standing over the table. The bakery was about to close, she told us. Miss Gilly sighed and paid the bill. What little tea was left was cold and black. We stirred in sugar, and sipped it as slowly as possible.

In the car outside, Miss Gilly wouldn't talk about the night of the cocktail party. I was curious, but after a while, I didn't push her to talk. Like her, I didn't want anything about my parents to interfere with our afternoons together.

She never wanted to drive any closer to the house than the bottom of the driveway. I said good-bye, hugging her tight, and walked up the hill, my cheek still glowing from being pressed into her fur coat. My mouth was sticky with the taste of glazed almonds. The sounds of cars on the road faded; silence rushed toward me from the house.

At the bottom of the front lawn, I put my green blazer back on. I became lawn-colored, camouflaged. The sky grew murky. The house was enclosed in a foggy liquid like a fake castle in an aquarium whose water has gone stale.

I climbed over the wall. I was inside the glass box. Weighed down, I became flat, the only possible shape for survival here. I skimmed gray-green above the grass. I turned gravel-colored as I swam along the driveway. I darkened as I vanished into the castle's back door.

- TEN -

I picture a Sunday evening in winter, with snow piling up silently in the darkness outside the windows. The room is dark and hushed, too. Flames are chuckling in the fireplace and the console radio's dial glows expectantly. I'm sprawled on the carpet gazing far into the fire; my parents are sitting together on the couch behind me. Armchairs shaped like hibernating bears cast furry shadows onto the floor. We're all waiting for seven o'clock, when from sunny California Jack Benny and his family will troop out of the radio into our living room.

As soon as they arrive, my mother sits back with a relaxed smile on her face. The show's theme music is my father's cue to loosen the knit tie he wears every night for dinner; his jawline loosens, too, and he waits for Jack's first line. I'm already grinning.

All Jack's friends seem to live at his house, like a family. They like to tease each other, but tempers never flare. Mary, Jack's wife, laughs off her husband's stinginess; when she says "Oh, Jack!" I picture her eyes rolling at him, and him beaming back in response. Dennis Day—who I assume is their grown son—annoys Jack with goofy kid-like remarks, but even so, Jack always tells him how beautifully he sings in his sweet Irish tenor. Other family members drop in. Don Wilson, a huge uncle, interrupts the banter to tell us about Lucky Strike cigarettes, which (like Don himself, Jack always says) are round and firm and fully packed. Phil Harris, a kind of black-sheep cousin who my mother says is "cheap," though she laughs loudest at his wisecracks, comes by to tell crazy stories about how drunk his band-members got last night. And finally, Mr. Kitzel, the grandfather, reports his doings to Jack in a nasal voice which reminds me of the German accent my own grandfather put on to make me laugh.

I hear my father laughing and turn to stare up at him from the floor; he glances down. We exchange grins. It's the only time we ever intentionally look each other in the eye. My mother's head rests against the cushion near my father's shoulder. She looks as if she's having a pleasant dream, but her eyes are open, watching us both.

In the flickery glow of the fireplace, I see my parents' faces grow round and mischievous. They begin to banter with each other. My mother chides my father, her eyes rolling tolerantly. My father, beaming, shrugs and raises his hand at his side, palm up. My grandfather laughs through his nose.

I play the piano with the band, and Robert sings "Danny Boy" in his lilting tenor voice. The crackling logs echo my parents' clapping; the applause piles up in the soft darkness around us, never melting away.

༄

Over the next year, Robert sent me postcards from Idaho, Montana, Wyoming. I liked to picture him riding in boxcars across the plains and mountains of the West. Then the following fall, when I'd turned thirteen, Robert sent me a pictureless card from Alabama.

Dear Jerry —
Back in the Air Force stockade. Dad's lawyers have fixed things so I can try again. But keep that address I gave you, just in case.   Love —   Robert

I paced around the attic kicking the wall, my bed, my desk. My father must have intercepted one of Robert's postcards in the mailbox again. My room, the house, the yard, the town— they all seemed like a series of stockades, walls within walls.

My parents tried to avoid talking about Robert. When his name did come up, they turned away from each other as if a meeting of their glances might produce sparks that could set off an explosion. The house's combustible atmosphere also seemed to be endangered by notes flying up from the piano. I practiced obsessively until my mother screamed into the living room that it was time to do my homework, and my father yelled downstairs that I could at least play something a little more harmonious.

My parents were again determined to create "a harmonious family life." This meant keeping busy and staying away from each other as much as possible. My father changed into his work clothes as soon as he arrived home from the office and attacked the yard with lawn tractor, rake, sickle, and axe. My mother sometimes walked partway across the lawn to shout at him: please, please don't cut down any more trees! And he shouted back: they're blocking the view! Then my mother came inside again and made herself a drink, but now she filled her glass only with plain soda water.

She filled her days with PTA and library board meetings. She headed a fund-raising drive for the Historical Society. Gray cigarette smoke puffed out her nostrils as she talked on the phone, jabbing her pencil in the air to give society members point by point instructions. She had to use her "nice" voice constantly—notes of self-deprecating laughter and carefully modulated light tones—to keep from sounding "pushy."

At school, my piano teacher found me a brochure for a music school in Colorado; it must have been the one Robert had told me about. But when I showed my parents the brochure, they refused to look at it.

"It's all very well, playing the piano for fun," my mother said.

"But you can't make a *career* out of it," my father said.

Agreement: harmony: a conspiracy against me. I ground my teeth, smiled, nodded. And slipped silently away: the manta ray. I forged my father's signature on the music school's application form. When my advisor gave me applications to New England prep schools where Robert had been incarcerated, I threw them out.

I wrote to Robert:

I feel like some kind of secret monster in human disguise in this school. But the more I pretend to like the place, the more the parents pretend to like me and each other, and we keep it up—because if we didn't, the house would explode, we would all kill each other like at the end of Hamlet, all the characters lying around the stage with bloody swords sticking up from their stomachs, except here it would be tennis rackets or maybe yard tools.

Things are real confused around here, maybe it's because Mother's stopped drinking again, even after five o'clock. I think it makes her lonely.

She starts talking about something that she's been thinking about as if I've been listening to her thoughts all along, I leave the room while she's talking and when I come back an hour later, she starts right up again as if I'd never left. How there's never any parking places near the library, the way the gas station man never cleans her windshield without leaving a smudge, how the doctor can never find anything for her headaches, stuff. It's always boring and I feel bad because it's a very big deal to her that I listen to her, but pretty soon I think of some excuse to leave, and then I feel worse but I still don't go back to listen.

School is shit, except Music. The teacher took us to New York to the Metropolitan Opera. Mother went crazy to hear that—all the time she'd lived in New York, she never got to go there, for some reason, she wouldn't say what. Anyways, I thought it was going to be a lot of screeching but I liked it. The way the lights came on, all the red velvet boxes glowing like a sunrise in a canyon. It was called La Traviata, and it was the same story as a book I read by Alexandre Dumas Fils called La Dame aux Camellias, so I understood what all the singing was about. The end was sad but I loved it. They play operas on the radios on Saturday afternoons, I listen to them now. I still like jazz better, but you can't find it on the radio. Doesn't anybody play it anymore?

There is one song on the radio, Heartbreak Hotel, have you heard it, by this singer called Elvis Presley, it has boogie woogie in it you'd like. Without you or Miss Gilly here, a big fancy heartbroke hotel is what the house is these days. Elvis Presley is great, though, his voice sounds like he is melting girls' clothes off them with it, and he has long hair and sideburns like I am going to grow when I get the hell out of here. I'll have a sickle (motorcycle) like Marlon Brando in The Wild Ones, did you see that movie, it is really cool.

You remember old Mr. Touhy? You must have had him for math, the little tubby guy with the no-rim glasses and blue suit, he was at the school for thirty-seven years, he said. Anyways, he left. Here's why—he told us he'd heard from this old girlfriend he used to have in high school in Minnesota, he wanted to marry her back then but her mother didn't like him, so they neither of them married anybody else and they wrote each other letters all these years and she stayed home and took care of her parents. Finally they died and she wrote Mr. Touhy, hey come on back, we can get married now. So he did, he just quit in the middle of the week, and took off for Minnesota. All the kids think the whole thing is weird, since he is sixty-four years old, but to me it is really great. I picture him riding a big sickle along this highway in the moonlight with this nice little old lady on the back and they're both wearing those Marlon Brando

143

caps and leather jackets, vrroom vrooooom they go, so long Mr. Touhy, good luck.
I wonder if I'll ever find out why you had to leave. Are you ever coming back?
Love — Jerry

When television first came to Ridge Haven, the first to buy sets were the Italian families in town. Vince's family had one, though I rarely saw him anymore—he was at the public junior high school. Riding in the car past his house at night, I gazed at the flickering windows hoping to catch glimpses of the programs I'd heard about the year before at PS 8. Gradually the invention spread to the outlying houses and estates, but my parents still refused to buy a set. A TV aerial sticking up from the roof like a metal clothes tree would ruin the appearance of the house.

Then one evening, I went with my parents to visit a couple whose maid had a television. We all squeezed into a tiny room in the back of the mansion—the maid, my parents, their friends, and me—to watch a quiz show starring Groucho Marx. My father's ordinarily stony face broke into a wide grin. What made him chuckle most was the way Groucho tormented the announcer whose job it was to pitch DeSoto cars between contestants. My father had it in for salesmen.

He ordered us a television, but it was installed in our basement; even the best console models wouldn't go with the antique furniture in the living room. Several evenings a week, my parents and I sat on an old sofa in the dark, watching Groucho and other resurrected film stars and vaudevillians. The screen's flicker reminded me of the Sunday night fires we'd sat around with Jack Benny's family.

I liked the televised Dodger baseball games. On September afternoons I retreated to the basement to watch the familiar figures in baggy uniforms play ball. I mentally discussed the plays with Robert as if he were sitting beside me in the dark. How'd you like Robinson's steal? Do you think Erskine's going to win twenty this year?

Once my mother came downstairs to watch. "Who are you talking to?" she asked in the dark.

I jumped. "No one." I'd been smoking a cigarette, but she didn't say anything about it. Rules seemed different in the basement.

She sat down slowly on the other end of the couch. "I talk to him sometimes, too," she said.

"What do you say to him?"

"I promise him things will be different if he comes back."

"Do you really think so?"

The crowd booed a player who bobbled an easy fly ball.

"Isn't that terribly bad sportsmanship?" my mother asked.

"It's okay to get mad and yell in Brooklyn," I said.

"I see." A match flared in the darkness. She sat back, drawing on a cigarette. "Can I share your ashtray?" she asked.

"Okay." I pushed it toward her along the cushion.

She dropped her match in its direction, missing the edge in the dark. I picked it up.

"Robert used to tell me about baseball sometimes, but I couldn't follow all the rules," she said. "He must have thought I wasn't interested."

The next batter grounded out and jogged, head down, off the field.

"Why did he stop running?" she asked. "I don't understand why he gave up like that." She shook her head. "What happened, Jerrett?"

I had no answer for her.

A day before Halloween, some PTA ladies appeared at the weekly chapel service at school. Among them, dressed in a gray suit and pillbox hat, was my mother. When everyone was settled, she stood up and walked hesitantly to the podium. All the Ridge Haven schools were participating in a "Trick or Treat For UNICEF drive," she explained; she hoped we would all "pitch in" to collect money for underprivileged children around the world. The teachers led the applause. I glanced around nervously. The boys were grinning at one another.

"I guess this means you're going to chicken out on the raid," one of them whispered to me as we filed out of chapel. "You wouldn't want to upset Mommy."

"Fuck you," I snarled.

All week they'd been planning Halloween pranks, but I hadn't committed myself to going along. Now I decided not only to join them but to organize a neighborhood raid myself. My parents had been urging me to "cultivate" the school leaders; when four of them showed up for the raid, there was no question that I'd succeeded.

One boy was class president; his father, who rode the club car with my father, was the CEO of a Wall Street brokerage house. Another school leader, whose father was on the church vestry with my father, had the highest grades in school and owned a real German Luger with which he'd once shot his neighbor's cats. Another boy was the track team captain; his mother was being treated at a famous drug rehabilitation clinic in California. The fourth boy had lost his virginity in a whorehouse in Caracas, Venezuela, where his father had been a top oil company executive before moving to Ridge Haven and committing suicide a year ago.

"Hey, Langley, where we going?" the track captain called out to me as I walked along the roadside. They all looked at me.

I thought: This is dumb—I don't even like these guys. But the cool night air was making me unbearably restless. My pockets bulged with firecrackers. Overhead, a crazed moon cut a swath though the silver clouds as it careened across the sky. The clouds turned to incandescent fish skimming the ocean's surface. I was the manta ray again, swimming toward them through the night: huge, shadowy, deadly.

"This way!" I yelled, with a new authority in my voice, and streaked off down the dark open road.

Roaming the quiet neighborhood, we shoved porch furniture into pools, slashed tires, toppled cement statues, blew up mailboxes with cherry bombs. The smell of gunpowder flared in my nostrils, goading me on. The dark picture window of an empty house got in my way. I heaved a construction brick through it. The loud rain of glass made me break out in a laughing jag. I couldn't believe I was doing something like this, but there was no question of stopping now. Inside the house, I attacked armchairs and floor pillows with my jackknife. A snowstorm of stuffing swirled around me. The other boys had to hold me back from the other rooms.

I broke free and raced out onto the driveway, my mind deliriously empty. I was galloping now, not slithering or slyly darting; I pawed the gravel and snorted with laughter. As I staggered across a lawn, a patio wall rose up before me out of the darkness. The boys were lobbing little bottles of model airplane paint at it. I grabbed one on the run. My arm cocked back, snapped forward. It felt like the most spontaneous, most natural movement I'd ever made: a perfect strike flying out of the darkness and exploding against the flood-lit white wall. A huge purple flower burst into life; jagged petals throbbed on the brilliant stucco.

Then I was galloping full tilt up the moonlit road. I was still gasping and laughing when a police car pulled up beside me.

The police booked us all. Shining flashlights into my eyes, they thought I must be drunk, and made me breathe into a machine at the station. Two boys sobbed as they gave their addresses. Still trembling too hard with excitement to be scared, I confessed to splattering the wall—the police said they'd seen us running from it—but I denied doing any other damage they'd had complaints about.

The policemen were uneasy and polite with us. They let us get cups of water from the water cooler and wash up in the bathroom. While they phoned our parents, I waited on a bench beside a steel door. Through its scratched window, I saw a row of empty jail cells; a radio was playing country music somewhere inside. I wished the police would lock me up in there: it would be better than facing my father.

But when he did finally arrive to take me home, something strange happened: I felt a glow against my face—the after-flash of the glorious tropical flower. It formed a buffer zone between me and everyone outside it. I couldn't feel scared.

In the kitchen, he and my mother stared at me from the other side of my aura. They seemed to be "the parents" in some family drama in which I was a participant but also a spectator standing very far from the stage. The kid I saw on stage looked uncomfortable, yet as a spectator, I often had to turn my face away for fear I might suddenly choke with crazy laughter. The sounds the parents made were variations of the same voice, one low and scratchy with rage, one high and teetering on the brink of hysteria. They'd never been further away.

How could you A good home Every conceivable advantage Everything we've worked for all our lives Bring disgrace to your family Like some kind of hood How could you How Why How Why?

I couldn't think of any answers to the questions, and so said nothing. Wiping her eyes, the play's mother went out to the pantry. I heard ice clink in a glass. The father looked strange in his gray suit so late at night. He must have put it on

147

to remind the police of his position in the town.

He slammed his fist down on the counter. "Have you any idea what this can do to us if people find out what you've done?"

I shrugged. Who was "us"? All this man could do to me was shout.

"Plus, there was hundreds of dollars worth of damage!"

"I'll pay for it," I said. "I can work it off."

"You damn well will! There's a lot of trees that need cutting—"

"What?" The mother stood in the pantry door, a glass in her hand. "What did you say about cutting down trees?"

The father frowned. "This is between Jerrett and me. About him paying for his vandalism."

The mother drained her glass fast. She took a wobbly step backward. "Please—no more trees!" she moaned.

Leaning sideways, she bumped slowly against the wall. The glass slipped from her hand. It clunked onto the linoleum. I smelled gin. She sank to her knees.

I reached out for her. "Mother!"

Too late. She flopped soundlessly to the floor.

The father—my own father—lifted her in his arms. I ran after him up the stairs. He tried to shoo me away with insistent shakes of his head. In my mother's room, I managed to get the tangled sheets smoothed out before he lay her face-down on the bed.

"You see what you've done!" He glared at me, catching his breath.

"You didn't have to just dump her!" I yelled, wiping my eyes.

He stopped in his tracks. Returning to the bed, he tucked a pillow beneath her cheek. "It's not the first time—" He wiped his forehead, backing away. "She'll be okay, Jerrett, let her sleep it off."

I thought: at least try to remove her shoes. I rarely touched my mother at all; now I had to wrap my fingers around her swollen ankles to tug at the shoes. Her skin felt clammy. The air in the bedroom was musty with the smell of insomnia. From the doorway, a strip of light shone along the carpet to her bedside table. There, casting a little shadow, was an open medicine bottle. She must have taken some sleeping pills just before the police had called, and with the medicine in her system, the sudden gulps of gin had knocked her out.

She looked like a murder victim sprawled across the cover of one of her library mystery novels. Hearing my father's voice on the phone from the hall downstairs, I felt like an accomplice. I sat very still on the side of the bed and listened for the sound of her breathing.

My mother was befuddled but alive the next morning. My father did all the talking at breakfast. Arrangements had been made with the families of the other vandals, the police, the town newspaper. The charges were to be dropped, no story would appear in the paper, and the five parents would pay the cost of resurfacing the stucco wall. I was to say absolutely nothing at school about anything that had happened.

The other four boys had the same instructions from their parents. We crept through the day, glancing silently at each other in the corridors. The secrecy made me sick. Once I had to rush into a bathroom to throw up. Red-rimmed, haunted, rat-like eyes stared back at me in the mirror. I tried to picture the splash of flowering light, but here at school it had turned to a hazy penumbra that hung around me like a leaden cloak as I went through the motions of attending classes. No one else saw it—teachers and students spoke to me as if I were still the same person I'd been the day before.

In chapel at the end of the day, Tina from the music room— I'd been trying to get a movie date with her for months, without luck—played some incongruously cheerful Dvorak folk dances. Then the headmaster walked slowly in wearing ecclesiastical robes and a grim pink face. He gripped the sides of the pulpit with both hands and addressed the school. Beams of sunlight slanted down from windows like God's gaze and glowed in his white ear-hairs.

"I am very, *very* proud," he said, "of the students who have collected so much money for UNICEF." Then he paused, his brows lowering. "There are five boys here, however—five boys who brought disgrace to their school. . . ."

A hush fell over the assembly. The headmaster spoke in a slow sonorous voice: "These five were arrested for doing wanton, vicious damage on Halloween night." I stared into space, my teeth clenched. He told the school about the police's surprise that boys from such good families had behaved like delinquents. He described the ruined wall and the shame that these thoughtless boys had caused both their parents and the school. Then he slowly read out the boys' names. Mine was last. "*Jerrett Langley,*" he intoned. He let the silence hang.

As he glared at the vandals, their heads dropped one by one like scorched daisies. But when he got to me, something inside me stiffened. I'd been through this before—I'd been initiated into this school. I knew what it was like to be buried in shame. And I knew that no one could ever make me feel that bad again.

I lifted my head and glared back at the headmaster.

The dewlaps beneath his eyes quivered with rage. All around me, kids were turning in their chairs to stare at me. I bent the corners of my lips up and held a smile. The headmaster's gaze dropped from my face.

"Dismissed," he said finally, and walked away from the pulpit.

My feet moved strangely along the gravel path outside as if they were treading several inches above it. I took big gulps of fresh air. I just wanted to collect my books and get the hell out of this place.

But Tina was walking beside me. I slowed down.

"You must really feel awful," she said in a hushed voice.

I stopped. She paused with me. I scraped the ground with my toe. "Actually, I've felt a whole lot worse," I said. I seemed to have slipped out of my leaden cloak, and felt lightheaded without it.

"Weren't you scared, when the cops picked you up?" she whispered.

I shrugged, and turned toward her. Her eyes seemed brighter than I'd ever seen them. She brushed a strand of hair from her forehead, her gaze staying on my face.

"Did they put you in *jail*, Jerry?" she asked.

I noticed that a small crowd had gathered. Some young kids were pushing each other to get better views of me. Several girls in my class were leaning forward, waiting to hear me speak.

"Not actually in the cells," I said. "But I could see them right down this dark corridor. The prisoners were all clanking their tin cups against the bars. ..." I grinned at Tina, and let the silence hang.

The next Saturday night, I took her to the movies. She let me slip my hand into her sweater even before the newsreel was finished.

- ELEVEN -

A young woman arrives at the door of the poet's apartment with a book in her hand. She stands on the landing, her cheeks flushed. Her hair is light brown; she wears round rimless glasses. Hearing her knock, I open the door. She smiles, then her lips retreat to press against her teeth. "I hope I'm not disturbing Miss Millay," she says. "I've seen her coming and going on the street. You see, I live just three doors down. . . ." Her voice trails off as she looks at me.

I don't fit into the elegant scene she must have imagined, pale and unshaven as I am, and barefoot at ten in the morning, as if I might have just gotten out of bed, perhaps with the poet herself. In fact, I've been up all night at the piano working on my jazz opera.

"Do you want to leave some of your work for her to read?" I ask. Sometimes people do that.

"Oh, no. I'd just like her to sign my book. Her book, I mean." A nervous laugh escapes; she pushes it back into her mouth with a white-gloved hand as if she'd just sneezed. Has a husband with no time for poetry pressed those lines into her forehead? She's got on her best clothes, a gray two-piece out-fit with a loop of artificial pearls and flat shoes; it's what she thinks sophisticated Eastern college graduates wear. She has no idea that Edna fled Vassar to escape young women who looked like this.

"You can come in," I tell her, stepping back inside the door-way.

She enters and stands before the window. Despite her city clothes, she moves as if she's used to tramping across frozen fields in a storm. She knows how to wrestle a calf out of a snowdrift: good training, in a way, for presenting herself unan-nounced at the court of the Snow Princess to ask for an auto-graph. Slowly turning her face, she bathes in the dusty beige light that slants through the window, turning the brick wall to the texture of velvet. She gazes at the watercolor landscapes, the writing desk, the silver candlesticks—for candles burnt at both ends, perhaps she's thinking.

Suddenly I hear Edna stirring in the next room, and hope

that she won't be haughty or hung over when she comes in. Then, dispelling worries, she wafts through her doorway, all soft wools and white delicate skin. A silk scarf flows round her neck and down her shoulder. Her hair is a lovely red blur. She picks up a pile of papers from the desk, pursing her lips to whistle a tune to herself.

"Hello?" she says, suddenly noticing the visitor. Her eyelashes flick up, and she splashes a look at the woman: Are you interesting? Will you amuse me? Will you have lovely small white breasts? Will your story give my heart an ache and a poem? All these questions in a vibrating instant; then the lashes drop with an answer audible to me but fortunately not to the visitor: No? Oh well, never mind.

The visitor's cheeks flush. A beautiful young woman has never looked at her this way before; probably no one has. "I am Marian Langley," she says, reassembling her rehearsed greeting. "My husband and I live just down the block. I have often seen you, I've read all your poems, I've admired...."

Edna smiles without glancing in her direction. She reaches out to take the book the woman has been hugging to her chest. "It's very sweet of you to come...." She takes up a pen and scribbles on the flyleaf. "Now I'm afraid I have to rush—" Edna holds the book out in the air. Marian takes it. The poet puts on her cloche hat with both hands, throws me a kiss. Then she is out the door, stuffing papers into her purse as she drops out of sight down the stairwell.

Marian Langley gazes out onto the landing, her face lifted as if she is listening to a trail of musical notes the poet has left behind her. I hear them, too, and forget for a moment that it's just a pianist practicing downstairs. A trace of Edna's perfume floats in the air, a pale purple tint among the beige sunbeams.

"Things so seldom live up to one's expectations...." Marian pauses as an arpeggio flutters past. "But *this* is what I came to New York for...." Her eyes sweep around the room again. "It's like standing in the middle of a poem!" She holds the book in both hands, one wrist cradling it from beneath. I have a feeling that for her, things never will be like this again. I think, too, that she has no one to show her treasure to.

"Let's see it." I lean forward.

She opens the book and holds it out to me. Her hair falls over her cheek; she brushes it back, watching my face to see my reaction.

"*To Mary — Best Wishes — Edna St. V. Millay,*" I read aloud.

I can tell Marian didn't see this before. Now the corners of her lips turn down, try to rise again. "She must be thinking of more important things," she says.

I invent. "There's a woman called Mary in the poem she's working on. I expect you reminded her of the woman."

"Oh." Marian's eyes light up. The mistake in the flyleaf has new meaning, a special value now. She closes the book carefully and smiles at me. "Are you, uh... her husband?"

"Not me." I grin. "I'm sort of temporary."

"Oh." She's trying not to stare at my bare feet, which are dirty on the sides. "Well, you've been very kind."

"I'm glad you came," I say, and stand up to see her to the door. Edna's scent is faint on the landing. The piano music has stopped. We shake hands good-bye. Marian's string of pearls clicks against itself as she turns away. I wave to her from the doorway.

I wish that composers signed scores—I'd have liked to have had something of mine to give her.

◡⁊

At first, my father was furious that I'd been identified as a vandal at school. What the hell had he gone to all the trouble to hush up the whole incident for? My mother insisted that my public humiliation was enough punishment for one impulsive, thoughtless act.

"It wasn't an *act!*" I muttered.

Neither of them seemed to hear me. I wanted to shout it.

"And what kind of recommendation do you think Mr. Clifford will give you now?" My father demanded.

"The only recommendation I want is my music teacher's," I said.

They both stared at me. This time they'd heard me. I had their attention as never before.

"Well, it's the only one you're likely to get." My father spoke, then swallowed hard, as if realizing what he'd said.

I couldn't help it—I grinned.

After my crime spree, I felt closer to Robert, though he was far away; I didn't have to pretent to be different from him. And I didn't have to be terrified of upsetting my parents any longer. I'd done it, and the sky hadn't fallen. They'd shouted and wept, and though I still felt awful about my mother's collapse, she and my father had pulled themselves more or less together again. I felt light, with a new freedom to move around.

My detachment about the vandalism wasn't faked, yet I was more remorseful about it than I realized. Sometimes I remembered Halloween the way a drunk recalls revels from the night before with a blurry, disbelieving horror. I would wake in the night shuddering at what I'd done, picturing the owner of the house I'd ransacked catching me in the act. He rammed a cherry bomb down my throat; he sliced my dick off with the jackknife I'd used to disembowel his couch. Somehow I always managed to drag myself away to the moonlit road, keeping myself alive long enough to see the luminous purple flower burst into view against the stucco wall, and to take one last breath of the its tropical scent.

Working to pay back the money calmed me. Every day after school, I went into the shed to select the tools with which I would chop, trim, rake, and clear the yard until dark. I especially like chopping down cedar trees—attacking them with a cold, clear concentration, hacking deep gashes with my axe until they toppled to the grass with a sigh of branches. Then I dragged them off into the woods. With each tree removed, the lawn grew longer; I could picture it stretching green and open all the way to the horizon.

On Saturdays, my father and I worked outdoors. He seemed glad for some company, and didn't bring up my criminal past. The sounds of our axes ricochetted together against the house. To pry a stump out of the ground, we gripped it on either side and lunged back and forth until we heard the root crack from deep in the earth. I noticed that I was pushing harder than he was. He wasn't as strong as he'd been when he'd dug the pit for me in the woods, and had to rest more often. We dug the stump out, filled in the hole with dirt, and stamped it smooth with our boots. We rarely talked, but when we rested to wipe our foreheads, our hard breathing seemed like part of a conversation that we'd been having all day.

"When I first got here in 1932," my father said one afternoon, "the place reminded me of Nebraska. Of the time we had a farm." He rested his axe. "In winter the wind howled like mad. We lost hay bales, tools, even animals. My father and I had to plant a lot of trees fast—for a windbreak. He figured they'd keep the farm from blowing away. We planted cedars every day, week after week, digging holes, dropping in the seedlings." My father looked down into the hole we'd just made in the ground. "I suppose that's why I overdid it here, planting so many trees," he said. "When they grow too close together, they choke each other's growth. Your mother refuses to understand that."

I leaned on my axe. "What happened to your father's farm?"

"Oh, it went under eventually."

I stared up the hill at the house, and at that moment, the little bushes along the terrace seemed to sweep the air as if a powerful windstorm were stirring in them.

One weekday evening after working, I rested on the seat of the lawn tractor in the toolshed with my axe across my lap. I liked the way the gathering darkness melted the tractor's front end into the shape of the old black jalopy Robert used to have. I sketched in the hood and windshield, remembering the time Robert had taken me for rides through the lower fields behind the house. He'd told me once that he'd let me drive as soon as I was big enough to see over the dashboard.

When he hadn't come home for a long time from prep school, though, the car had disappeared. I wondered if my parents had sold it, or if he had garaged it in some secret place where it was still waiting for us to come drive it away. In the dark, I pictured myself driving it out of the shed and across the lawn toward the woods—

The light flashed. I blinked. My mother stood in the doorway, her hand on the switch. She'd changed into a fresh blouse and skirt for dinner, and her hair was brushed.

"What are you doing in here?" she asked.

I glanced up. "Just thinking."

"You must be exhausted. Don't you want to come in?"

I gave the tractor's steering wheel half a turn. "No."

She took a sip from her glass. "Are you mad at me, too?"

"What? No."

"I guess it was just your voice." She sat down on a bag of peat moss. "I'm worn out. I don't know how much more of this I can take."

"More of what?"

She didn't answer. Her glass had no gin smell; she carried plain soda water with her everywhere nowadays, as if she were in imminent danger of drying out.

"I'm sorry I've caused you so much trouble, Mother," I said.

"Well, thank you," she said. "But really, it's not you. Your father blames me, Jerrett."

"That's crazy. What for?"

"I keep trying to figure it out. It must be for things I did years ago." She lifted her face. "I think maybe I pushed him too hard, when we were living in New York."

I sat very still, not wanting her to stop. Until recently, I'd heard practically nothing about my parents' earlier life; now that they seemed to want to tell me about it, I was curious.

"I kept insisting there were other firms where he could make more money," she said. "I didn't understand that he'd have to do things he'd hate—that he'd have to get ahead or go under in the new job. I just wanted him to earn enough for us to get out of New York."

"Didn't you like it there?" I asked.

"In lots of ways, I loved it. The big libraries, the theater, the music. Manhattan felt like an enchanted island." She leaned back against the wall, gazing into the rafters beneath the roof. "I had very cultured friends in New York. Edna St. Vincent Millay lived near our apartment in Greenwich Village. She once autographed a poetry book for me...." My mother stared down into her glass, swirling the soda water slowly. "But after a while, New York wasn't any good," she said. "Your father... well, I thought that if we had a nice place in the country with a beautiful view—another sort of island, I guess...I thought that everything would be fine. That he'd take an interest in—in his home...." She took out a cigarette and fumbled with her matches.

I watched her strike one match, then another. Then I took the matchbook from her hand and lit her cigarette. "What happened then?"

The question seemed to jolt her. She stared around the cluttered shed: the tools hanging from nails on the rough wooden

157

walls, the grass-stained tires of the lawn tractor, the cracked flower pots. "My parents' house was so bleak," she said finally. "Nothing to see from my window but miles of flat stubbly plains, and pieces of old farm equipment rusting in the rain like dead animals. Living with so much dreariness, it can make you sick at heart!" She pressed her fist against her chest. "All my life I'd wanted a place where I could look out and be surrounded by tall, elegant trees. Can you understand how important that was for me, Jerrett?"

My hands fell from the tractor's steering wheel. "I think so."

"I'm very glad to hear that. Just when I'm sure you've written me off entirely, I discover you're quite willing to pay attention if I get up my nerve to actually talk to you."

All I could do was nod at her. It occurred to me that the same might be true for her—that she might listen to me, too, if I'd take the trouble to focus her attention instead of always slipping away from it.

Her smile faded. "Now why was I telling you all this?"

I shifted my position on the tractor seat. Her brow was furrowed, one eyebrow raised, and I remembered the way she'd looked at me years ago when she'd discovered that the end pages of her story book were missing. Then she must have felt the sound's vibrations in the floor: my father's car rolling up the driveway. "I've made us a roast for dinner," she said, standing up. "Aren't you coming?"

"In a minute," I said, and gripped the steering wheel again. But when I was alone again, the tractor refused to turn into a car.

Every evening, while my father put on his flannel slacks and sports jacket for dinner, my mother shouted questions up at him from the hall downstairs. What were his plans for the evening? the weekend? the vacation next spring? Behind the railing of the second floor landing, he returned brief, fast answers. Listening from the attic, where I was changing into the required clean shirt, I pictured my father at net on the tennis court, smashing lobs as they came flying at him—pok, pok, pok—one put-away slam after another.

There was a routine he followed at the table. He'd take a drink of ice water and then refill it to the top from the silver pitcher. After that he'd unfold his white linen napkin, lay it in his lap, and tuck a corner of it above the button of his sports jacket.

"Well, how has everyone's day been?" he'd ask.

My mother would start talking. My father pushed the food—some of it barely defrosted—around on his plate, giving no indication that he heard a word she said. Undaunted, she spilled out her day's frustrations: the terrible problems she had finding a parking space at the library, the dilemmas about which cocktail party invitations to accept, the interminably boring Historical Society meetings—

"They give me such a headache. Those women just tolerate me because of your father's position in the community," she said, turning to me. Tonight her voice was more urgent than usual. She smoked as she ate; her burnt matches soaked up gravy on the rim of her plate. "They think including me in the society will be good for their husbands' careers."

"Why do you go to the meetings, then?" I asked.

She sighed. "One has to take companionship where one finds it."

My father turned toward me. "And how was your day?" he asked.

I kept to an old script at dinner: my father's question was my cue to fill the air with words, lest dreaded silences open up that my mother would try to fill. I recited lines about cell division and the life of Mozart and the Battle of Gettysburg. I invented high test scores, tennis victories, social triumphs. A carefully staged peace settled over the room. The candles flickered like footlights. My father's fork clicked against his plate; my mother's soda water swished round in her glass until the bubbles fizzed out. The Toby mugs on the shelf behind her grinned at me, prompting me.

"And then after school," I said, "I cut down the two cedars."

My mother suddenly focused on me as if startled by a sound no one else heard. "Tonight," she said, "you asked what happened—"

"What?" My fork paused in midair.

"In the toolshed, you asked me...." She cleared her throat. "Well, we left New York, and we got this place, this lovely, elegant place. It was everything I'd always thought I'd wanted." Her mouth turned down at the corners. "And now your father's destroying it. He's been doing it for *years!*"

My father finally looked at her. "Oh, for Christ's sake!"

"Tree by tree. Tree by beautiful *tree!*" Her eyes blurred behind her glasses. "All that's left of them are the dirty bare spots in the grass. Your father's doing it to get back at me."

"Damn it, Marian, what's the matter with you tonight?"

"What hurts me so"— she stared at me— "is that he's using *you* to do it to me!"

I jerked back in my chair. "What do you mean?"

"What...do I *mean?* Nothing. I mean nothing at all around here!" Her voice rose higher. "Go ahead, Dean, make him cut down more trees—"

"Marian—" My father gripped his water glass. "If you're going to make a scene—"

"You couldn't *bear* the scandal about Jerrett's vandalism-" She leaned forward, her fingertips digging into her placemat. "But can't you *see?*" she screamed. "Can't you see how *you're* vandalizing this place!"

My father's arm shot out, a quick forehand slam. My mother rocked back, her face jerking sideways. For a moment I thought he'd hit her with his fist. Then I saw the empty water glass in his hand. Water was dripping down her chin. Her cheeks shone wet in the candlelight.

She staggered out of her chair. Pressing her hand to her mouth, she ran from the room. Her footsteps reverberated on the stairs. The crack of her door shuddered down the walls.

My father shook his head slowly, staring at her white napkin lying on the dark carpet. Slowly he picked it up and laid it on the table. He started patting my mother's wet chair with his own napkin. I turned my face away.

"Jerrett, help me clean this mess up, will you?"

He was dabbing at the carpet. For a moment, my father and I knelt together over the wet spot. I picked up an ice cube, making a tight fist around it. Then I dropped it and scrambled to my feet.

"No," I said.

"Where are you going?" His voice was scratchy in his throat.

I didn't answer. I wasn't sure, myself.

I stood in my mother's doorway, the toes of my sneakers not quite resting on the rug. The amber glow of a lamp dimly illuminated her; only when she raised her face to look at me did her features come into focus. She was sitting on the chaise lounge; a ribbon of cigarette smoke fluttered up into the darkness from an ashtray beside her. Her gray hair was snarled as if she had been tugging her fingers through it. The damp spot on her blouse made a dark stain.

"Are you okay, Mother?" I asked.

She gazed at me and swallowed. "Thank you. . .yes," she said, her voice almost a whisper. "It was only water."

I sat in the chair where I used to sit while she read from her *Little Miss Marian* book years ago. I didn't know what to say.

She walked to the door, shut it, and turned to me. "Jerrett, I have something to ask you...."

Suddenly I knew what she wanted, and spoke quickly before she forgot. "Stop chopping down trees—right?"

She let out all her breath. "Yes!" she said. "Would you mind terribly?"

"No—it's okay," I said.

"That's what I was trying to explain, in the shed." She let out her breath. "Maybe we can keep this place from turning into a prairie for a while longer."

"There's plenty of other work I can do," I said.

"Good." She returned to the chaise lounge and sat down. A smile moved one side of her mouth up. "Listen, I have something for you. It came this week." She lifted a brown parcel from the floor. "I'm a little afraid, Jerrett. I went to a special antique shop in New York where they say they can restore anything. But I don't know what kind of a job they did on this."

She began tearing away the paper. Inside was a lot of straw. I watched her spread it with her fingers until a patch of brown appeared like something hatching in a nest. A head appeared— it was the wooden horse from Haiti.

I grinned. "Hey, they fixed it!" The horse's mane gleamed in the lamp light. The scratches on its flanks were covered with shiny varnish.

"Are you glad to see it?"

"Yeah. . . ." I started to reach out for it, then dropped my hand.

"Don't you want it back?"

"I don't know."

"Oh, dear." She wrapped her arms around the horse.

"I might get mad again," I said.

"Were you mad tonight?"

The imprint of the ice cube burned in my palm. "At him. He shouldn't have splashed you."

"That's true. And I'm sure he knows it. It's been years since he's done anything like that...." She touched the stain on her blouse. "But it was only water. I'll bet he was cleaning it up in the dining room when you left, wasn't he?"

I nodded. "He wanted me to help him. But I wouldn't."

"No? Well, well...." She smiled. Bits of straw fell from her lap to the floor. "What am I going to do with this horse now?"

I could see the cracks where the legs had been glued. If the horse walked slowly, it would limp; if it tried to gallop, its legs would buckle under it. I knew that a real horse got shot when just one of its legs was broken; this one had four broken legs but somehow it had survived, just barely.

"I could put it in my room," I said. I'd packed away all the animals Miss Gilly had given me over the years. I was too old for lambs, bunnies, little china dogs. "The bureau top's free now."

"I see." She raised her face. "Do you think the horse will be all right there?"

"I hope so," I said.

She held it out toward me. As I took it, her fingers stayed gently pressed against the wood for a second. Then the horse seemed to rise into the air in my hands, its mane splashing back from its neck.

- TWELVE -

The diplomat lugs Alma's huge suitcase along the bank of the Seine, searching for her in the crowds. My necktie is gone; dark stubble outlines my jaw. Out of breath, I set down the heavy suitcase. An enormous ache drains from my body.

The Seine is a winding road. On it is an antigue car that's rolling toward me. I swing myself up on the running board beside the front seat, where an old man in a chauffeur's cap grips the steering wheel with both hands, grinning. I pull open the door, about to lunge onto his seat.

That's when I realize I've left Alma's suitcase behind. And where's Alma? I peer into the crowd, shielding my eyes from the clouds of swirling dust.

A little boy is lugging the suitcase along, frantically waving to me. I wave back. I'm not beckoning him to catch up. I'm just waving good-bye.

～

During the fall when I was fourteen, my mother got uneasy about Miss Gilly taking me to the Swiss bakery after school every Tuesday. To minimize household tension, I acted as if I'd outgrown my need to see her. Then, without my realizing it, I wasn't quite acting any longer. Miss Gilly's visits left me feeling disoriented. She talked to me as if I were at various past ages when she had sudden, fond memories of me, and as she spoke I felt as if I'd become those ages again. With her, I seemed to be walking through a landscape of little pools that I was always being tempted to fall into. The familiar warm water was wonderfully relaxing. The trouble was, climbing out was painful; I wasn't sure at first who I was when I stood up, dripping memories and shivering in the cold, harsh air of my new maturity.

One week, she spoke to me on the phone in a voice so faint I could hardly hear her. She was leaving Ridge Haven, she said. Soon. For good.

"*Why?*" I choked on my breath.

163

"They're moving to Florida," she said, meaning the people she worked for now. "I can't stay here with no job! I've got no home here—or anywhere—" A blast of grief exploded in my ear: she'd blown her nose. "D'you reckon your mother'd make a row if I came to the house this Tuesday?" she asked. "I just want to—to get something I left."

"It's okay, sure." An echo of the explosion was making a terrible commotion in my chest; I felt something there like an electric fan that's been dropped, its blades whirring frantically against its wire cage. "We can have tea here," I said. "Mother'll be away."

"It'll be like old times, won't it, Jerry?"

I swallowed hard. "Uh huh."

I'd gotten back my composure, or so I thought, when I walked across the school campus to meet Miss Gilly the following Tuesday. Her brown Hudson was parked under a tree as always; I felt her watching me through the windshield. As soon as I slid onto the seat, she wrapped her arms around me, pulling me face-first into the bosom of her old fur coat. The fur against my skin reminded me of the eiderdown I'd snuggled under in her bed. Now my nose was pressed into the soft warm cave beneath her chin where her skin was pink and wattled. Gasping for breath, I tried to sit up straight.

She held my shoulders to look at me, giving off her old familiar scent of peppermint. "You look wonderful!"

"You, too, Miss Gilly." I managed an unsteady smile. Clouds of gray curls seemed to swirl around her head. Her eyes were red-rimmed; I could see that she'd been crying.

"But I think you've got a smudge, ducks," she said, pointing at my face in the rear-view mirror.

"What?"

I rather liked the way I looked these days. As I'd stopped eating so many sweets, I'd lost weight; my cheeks had narrowed and my jaw was sharper. I no longer wore a childish crew cut, though my hair wasn't as long as Elvis Presley's yet. In the mirror, I didn't see any smudge.

Miss Gilly licked her forefinger and rubbed my cheek beside my ear. "There," she said.

"That's a sideburn."

"Good heavens! Like one of those motorcyclists in the cinema."

I glared at the dashboard.

Miss Gilly sat back, still gazing at me. Her fur coat seemed to have grayed along with her hair. "Well, we mustn't use up our afternoon just sitting here!" she said, and fumbled with the key in the ignition.

As the car rolled away, I saw some of my old partners in crime standing beside the school driveway, and ducked down behind the window—I wasn't eager to have them spot me with my ex-nanny. I was immediately ashamed of myself for this thought.

"Are you going to take your car to Florida?" I asked in a cheerful voice that sounded fake.

"No, I'll have to get rid of it, poor thing." She sighed. "We're all going to fly in an aeroplane. I've never been in one. I'm petrified, I don't mind telling you."

"It's not so scary." I took one of her cigarettes, lit it, and blew smoke out of the side of my mouth. She'd given up smoking, but always left a pack on the dashboard for me. "You can look down on the clouds," I said. "They're like fields of white cotton candy."

"You always were such an imaginative child."

"No, that's what it looked like when we flew to Haiti—" I shut my mouth tight.

"I've bought us one of those almond coffee rings you like so much," she said quickly. "We'll have it with our tea."

I glanced at the paper bag on the back seat. The cake's familiar sweet scent filled the car, which had begun to seem smaller than usual and overheated. "That'll be great," I said, and rolled down the window.

At the bottom of the driveway, where she usually stopped to leave me off, she took a deep breath and swung the wheel hard. The Hudson lunged up the hill. She drove very slowly as if navigating a mined landscape. The lawn was strewn with dark leaves; through the bare tree branches the house flickered in streaks of pale white beneath the leaden gray sky.

"It looks like winter'll be here soon," Miss Gilly said. "D'you remember the snowmen we used to make?"

"Uh huh." I gripped the door handle to keep from sinking. Too late. I pictured the lawn coated with sugary powder; the scene was dimly lit, like a glass globe you shake to make the snow swirl around in the liquid. I was inside, a small child in a snowsuit running breathlessly beside a figure in a furry hood; together we rolled a big white ball over the lawn as the flakes spun around us.

She glanced at me. "Does it make you sad to remember?"

I shifted my position, sitting up straighter. "I'm fine."

"Of course you are," she said. "Mind you don't make a mess of your trousers, though." She pointed to the cigarette ashes on my knees.

I brushed them off furiously.

When she pulled into the gravel area behind the garage, I jumped out before the car had come to a complete stop. "Be right back," I called over my shoulder.

Several months ago, I'd been given a nearly full-grown, fluffy golden retriever. I liked him, though he still whimpered and cringed like a puppy. I'd began training him out of book— to sit, stay, lie down, heel, and in general to behave in a more grown-up way.

Now I ran to the pen behind the toolshed to let the dog out. When he spotted me, he got a frantic smiling expression on his face. He bounded out of the pen's gate, then made whimpering sounds until I commanded him to SIT! in the sharp decisive tone that my dog training book said to use. He sat. I petted his head awkwardly.

Miss Gilly stood beside the car holding the coffee cake bag by the top. "You never told me you had a dog, Jerry!"

"Mother gave him to me. A while ago."

Miss Gilly's nose wrinkled. "Oh."

"He's a good dog," I said. "I mean, mostly."

"I'm sure he is, dear."

The dog lay down and began edging along the gravel toward her.

"What's his name, Jerry?"

"Prince Nicholas of Willowdale Farms—that's the name on his papers. But he's just called 'Prince.'"

"That's a nice name for him." She smiled. "What's he doing?" The dog was skidding up to her, retreating, skidding forward again.

"He's just high-strung. Purebred goldens are like that. They're supposed to get over it." I tried to hold the dog still.

Miss Gilly reached down slowly. Prince sniffed her hand, then licked her fingers. "He's sweet," she said.

The dog wagged his big plumed tail. Suddenly he lunged forward and burrowed into her skirt, thrusting his nose up between her legs. Gasping, Miss Gilly staggered backwards. The paper bag fell from her hand and hit the gravel with a crunch.

"Sorry—sorry!" I said, my face flushing. "I'm trying to train him." I yanked the dog sideways by the collar as he began to sniff the bag. "SIT, PRINCE!" He lay down in a heap of whimpering orange fluff.

Miss Gilly snatched up the coffee cake and held it against the front of her coat. "Nice doggy," she said.

"YOU BEHAVE!" I told him in my firmest voice. When we entered the house, the dog tried to follow, but I closed the door hard behind me, shutting out his whines.

"What time is your mother coming back?" Miss Gilly asked.

"About four-thirty," I said. "What was it you wanted to get here?"

She looked at her watch. "Oh, just something in the attic for you."

I almost asked her what that was but I didn't want to sound as if I was rushing her. She tugged down her suit jacket over the bulge of her stomach and walked into the hallway. I hoped she'd go straight on through the pantry to the kitchen, but she paused outside my old nursery.

"What's *this*?" She strode in, her coat churning at her ankles.

I used to jump when I heard that tone of voice; it meant that I'd better start cleaning up my toys right away. I half expected the room to rearrange itself: my bed materializing and skidding into the corner, my old play table ducking under the window where it belonged, pictures from English fairy tale books leaping up onto the walls. All those things were gone, now, of course. A maple table and four chairs took up most of the carpet space; on the walls were bright, tropical watercolors my parents and I had bought at the hotel in Haiti.

"We eat breakfast here now," I said.

She gave the pictures a wide berth. "D'you mean to say your mother's getting herself out of bed for breakfast these days?"

"Sure," I said, though it wasn't true—she had started sleep-

ing late again, perhaps hung over, I didn't know. I hurried
through the room.

What had been my closet was now a door opening into the
kitchen. "They must have just smashed out the back of it,"
Miss Gilly said. "You used to keep all your stuffed animals
there—right up to the ceiling."

I pictured them there again, the bears and bunnies smiling
down from the shelves.

"There never was enough space in these little rooms," she
said. "Imagine, keeping a child in the old servant's quarters,
like some sort of dark secret!"

"I used to think I was," I said.

"Well, we made the best of it. We made it nice and cozy,
didn't we?"

"Uh huh." My voice sounded alarmingly breathless. How
old was I?

Pulling in her coat, she walked through the back of the closet.
The kitchen, with its scrubbed counters, sparkled like a cave of
white ice—the cleaning woman had come and gone. Miss
Gilly turned on the oven. "I know you always like your coffee cake heated," she said. Looking around, she took off her
coat and held it against her for a moment, then hung it on a
hook on the back of the door. "Right. Fetch me one of those
pie plates, would you, dear? They're in the cabinet next to the
fridge."

But they weren't there. The floor seemed slippery under
my feet as I searched the shelves. My mother had moved the
pie plates, I discovered, to the cupboard over the sink. Miss
Gilly put the coffee ring on a tin plate, and together we pushed
broken-off almonds back into it until it looked like a glazed
wreath. She slid it into the oven.

"What's that woman done with our teapot?" Miss Gilly
rifled through a cabinet over the stove. "I reckon she uses
tea-bags now, doesn't she?"

"I saved the pot," I said, and squatted down to pull out
a drawer near the sink.

"Good boy." She took the old round china pot from me
in both hands and beamed at it. I handed her a packet of
loose tea I'd also saved.

"More than a year old, it must be," she said, sniffing it.

"Is it okay?"

"Certainly." She spooned some into the pot. "Good tea never gets stale."

She watched the kettle boil on the stove and filled the pot. Then she stood still, her knuckles pressed against her lips.

"What's the matter, Miss Gilly?"

"Where can we go?" she asked in a wobbly voice.

"The living room?"

"No, no. That's for guests."

The clock on the wall hummed faintly. I stood off-balance with my hand on the doorknob. I didn't want to suggest the kitchen; she'd often complained of having to eat here as if she were a scullery maid. The new breakfast nook seemed wrong, too.

"I don't belong anywhere anymore, do I?" she asked.

Now I was my real age again, or older, and in the strange role of trying to help someone who had once done everything she could to help me. "How about the dining room?" I said.

"Oh, yes!" Her cheeks puffed out into a smile again. "Remember when we used to eat there while they were in Europe? We used to have some lovely times, didn't we?"

"Uh huh." I set about loading the tray, helping her to find sugar, spoons, strainer, napkins. She splashed milk into the teacups, filling mine almost halfway up as she'd always done. And for a while, we were mice at play while the cats were away, as she used to say. We talked about the radio shows we'd listened to when we slept in the downstairs rooms: *The Great Gildersleeve* and *Baby Snooks*. Relaxed, I sat with my feet resting on my father's chair. Miss Gilly, in my mother's chair, poured the tea. She set pieces of coffee cake on my plate with her fingers. I picked the sugared almonds off the top.

The air grew darker outside. I switched on the chandelier. Its glitter gave the room the insistently gay look of an amusement park lit up before nightfall. I usually ate piece after piece of cake until I was stuffed, but today the cake seemed hard to chew and too sweet. Miss Gilly kept sweeping crumbs from around her plate into her palm as if to conceal them. I glanced in the direction of the driveway each time she looked at her watch.

The sound I heard, though, wasn't a car but a whimpering from the terrace. I tried to ignore it. Finally I went to the win-

169

dow. The dog jumped up on his hind legs, smearing his muzzle against the glass.

"That look on his face reminds me of you," Miss Gilly said. "DOWN, PRINCE!"

"Poor thing, out there in the cold. I don't expect your mother lets you bring him into the house, does she?"

"The kennel man said he has to get used to the weather," I said. "If I let him in a lot, he won't be able to stand the winter."

Miss Gilly stood beside me listening to the high-pitched yelps. "Oh, just this once, Jerry. Who's to know?"

Frowning, I let the dog in through the terrace door. "SIT!" I commanded, and the dog did, more or less.

Miss Gilly turned sideways in her chair. Prince wagged his tail. "If you're good, you can have a nice piece of cake," she told him.

"I've been training him not to beg at the table—"

Seeing her lift a piece of coffee ring from her plate, he began to drag himself along the floor in a sitting position as if his back legs were paralyzed. He gobbled up the cake from Miss Gilly's fingers and snuggled against her leg.

"Poor little thing, he's starving," she said. The dog gazed up at her, his tongue hanging sideways from his mouth. "Lie down now, there's a good boy." And though I'd read that dogs could respond to only one person's voice, he immediately flopped down at her feet. I felt a sinking sensation and held the edge of the table.

"Funny, her buying you a dog when you're going away to prep school next year." Miss Gilly dipped a piece of coffee cake into her tea. "Perhaps it's so you'll have something you'll want to come home to."

"I think I'm going to a music school," I said, pushing myself up in my chair. "It's way out West."

"Well, good. Robert hated those stuffy New England places. D'you remember the lonely postcards he used to send? Where is he now?"

"He still sends postcards. He's back in the Air Force, in Alabama."

Miss Gilly shook her head slowly. "Too bad she didn't get a dog for your brother, years ago."

I set my cup down. It chattered like teeth in the saucer. "I don't want to come back without you or Robert here," I said suddenly.

170

"I know, dear." Miss Gilly rested her hand on my wrist. The reflected chandelier lights swam like raindrops on the table top. The only sound in the room was the steady thump thump of the dog's tail against my chair leg; its reverberations accumulated in my chest until I had to stand up fast.

Miss Gilly sighed. "We'd better start cleaning up."

As soon as she pushed her chair back, the dog scrambled to his feet, his paws slipping and skidding on the glossy hardwood. He followed us into the kitchen. Half the coffee ring was left on the plate, with the almonds plucked out of the glaze so that it looked naked and pockmarked. Miss Gilly put it back in its bag on the table. Then we washed the dishes and put them away.

"She'll never know anyone was here at all," Miss Gilly smiled conspiratorially at me.

I glanced at the clock. It was 4:00. I knelt down to replace the teapot beneath the sink, and felt strangely unsteady standing up. "What was it you wanted to get in the attic?" I asked.

She wiped her hands on the dishcloth. "A surprise," she said.

The dog leapt to his feet, skidded to the hall door, and tried to wedge it open with its nose.

"NO—STAY!" My voice nearly cracked.

"Be good, dear." Miss Gilly ruffled the dog's head. His feet went out from beneath him; he collapsed beside the refrigerator.

"I don't know what's wrong with him today!" I shut the hall door behind us.

"He's just upset. Puppies get like that."

"He's not a puppy!" The door shuddered against its frame; Prince was frantically pawing it on the other side. I rushed along the hall, fleeing the sound.

"Good heavens, what a change in this room!" Miss Gilly said, gasping for breath at the top of the attic stairs. "It always used to look like a storage bin. Someplace you'd store a child—"

"I fixed it up," I said, feeling much better in my own territory. On my bed was a new electric blanket tucked in neatly with Robert's baseball glove beside the pillow. Next to the bed hung a watercolor seascape with palm trees. I'd made the room's two long walls into a gallery of magazine pictures: baseball players, Civil War generals, old trains, jazz musicians. On my bureau stood the wooden horse—I wished now I'd put it away for the day. Miss Gilly picked up a photo of Tina, my girlfriend, from my desk.

"She's a great piano player," I said. "I'm teaching her jazz."

"That's nice, dear." She lay the frame face-down and peered around the room again. "The place even smells different. It used to stink of mothballs.... Right—that suitcase!" She began opening the closet doors and squinting inside. "You and Robert used to imagine there were secret passages under the eaves. Do you still hide under there with your flashlight?"

"Not much anymore," I said.

Squatting in front of an open door, she shoved away an old tuxedo and a ball gown hanging from a rod.

"What's in the suitcase you're looking for?" I asked.

She stood up slowly, holding her back. Then she smiled at me. "The eiderdown, dear."

I blinked. "You didn't take it with you?"

"No, I packed it that spring when the weather got warm. I've been putting off coming for it," she said. "D'you remember it?"

I stared deep into the closet. "The one on your bed downstairs."

"You always liked to pull the feathers out." She patted my cheek.

Feeling off-balance, I held onto the frame of the closet door. "I remember," I said.

"I won't be needing a down comforter—not in Florida." She cleared her throat. "So I thought I'd give it to you, Jerry."

"I don't—" I glanced toward the bed with the electric blanket covering it. Then I saw the look on her face. "Yes, I'd like it. Thank you."

She wiped her eyes. "But why can't I find it anywhere?" She opened another closet door and yanked some boxes out, then a stack of books, which fell over at her feet. In a few moments, the floor was in chaos: books, boxes, papers, and old clothes strewn onto the carpet with their hangers sticking out from their shoulders. I paced unsteadily among the debris, opening and closing my hands.

There was only one more closet to look into. Pulling open the door, she rocked back at the sight of a heavy-looking suitcase with wide fabric stripes. It looked vaguely familiar to me. "I know I put it in a case like this." Miss Gilly squatted down. "It was this very one, I know it was! I can picture that eiderdown!"

So could I, its silky cover printed with blue wildflowers, its corners coming to soft feathery points. Miss Gilly's fingers were trembling as she fumbled with the lock. I knelt beside her and tried it. The lock sprung open. Together, we lifted the lid. I let out my breath. The suitcase was empty.

She stood up, looking dazed. Suddenly she drew me to her. *"That woman threw out my eiderdown!"*

I staggered backwards. "I don't remember her doing it—"

"She did!" Miss Gilly's eyes swam with tears. "When something's lost its usefulness, it just gets. . . thrown out!"

Then I did recall my mother coming downstairs one day with armloads of blankets and quilts for the church rummage sale. We wouldn't be needing them any longer, she said, with the electric blankets on the beds. In the attic, I'd found the empty suitcase, and pushed it back into the closet. I didn't, of course, know what had been inside it. But my mother had. Now I was angry with her for not mentioning it to me. But not so angry, I suddenly knew, that I'd want to ask her about it later.

"Whatever are you going to do this winter, when it gets cold?" Miss Gilly threw her arms around my neck. "Oh, Jerry, I tried everything to make them let me stay with you!"

"I know—" My voice was shaky, but it didn't crack.

"We both tried so hard, didn't we?"

"Uh huh." I caught my balance against my desk as she began to totter. Holding her arm, I helped her move to my desk chair.

"Thank you—" She sat down with a bump.

"I'd like to have had it—the eiderdown," I said. "But—"

"But what, dear?" She pulled a tissue from her sleeve and reached up to wipe my cheeks. I stood still, though I could feel that my cheeks weren't wet; the tissue just rubbed against my skin.

I rested my hand lightly on her shoulder. "But having it

might have made things sadder, with you away," I said. "I'd rather just think of it, the way it was." I knew I was saying this to make her feel better, but my words felt true, as well. "I don't need it with me to remember you," I told her.

"Well, that's. . . ." Wiping her own cheeks with the tissue, she raised her face to me. "That's right, Jerry, isn't it?"

"Yes," I said, and stroked her hair.

As we walked into the kitchen, the dog began to quiver where he lay in the corner, searching our faces. Suddenly he scrambled up, feet skidding every which way, and came careening toward us.

"Nice doggy," Miss Gilly said, reaching out her hand. The dog licked her fingers frantically. Its tail thumped against the wall.

"*Damn!*" I looked down. The coffee cake bag, ripped open, lay on the floor near the fridge, surrounded by crumbs. "He ate up the whole thing."

"Oh, dear!" Miss Gilly frowned, but at the same time ruffled the dog's fluffy ears.

"Greedy—BAD DOG!" I shouted. He retreated, trying to wag his tail and tuck it between his back legs at the same time. I strode after him and whacked his rump.

"Jerry! He couldn't help it—he's just a puppy!" Miss Gilly said. "Anyway, we'd picked all the almonds out."

I caught my breath. "I guess it wouldn't have been much good without the almonds."

From the hall doorway, the dog smiled hopefully at me, his tongue hanging out.

"You won't be hard on him, will you?" Miss Gilly asked.

"No." I was suddenly glad the coffee ring was gone. Throwing it out later would have been very hard to do. "He'll be fine."

"That's good."

We cleaned up the crumbs together. Then I took Miss Gilly's coat down from the hook and helped her into it. We walked slowly outside. A chilly wind had come up, shifting leaves around on the grass. In the driveway, Miss Gilly hugged me for a long time, and I held her tight. When I finally stepped back, the skin of my face tingled.

"Thank you—for the coffee cake—and everything," I managed to say.

"Oh, Jerry, you don't have to thank me. . . ." She lay the palm of her hand along my cheek, then took a wobbly step backwards. "I'll write you as soon as I get to Florida."

"I'll write you too, Miss Gilly."

The dog came skidding up, letting out a yelp. Then he raced off in an orange blur across the lawn.

Miss Gilly's face seemed to collapse, lines appearing beside her eyes and mouth. "He won't get onto the road and chase cars, will he?"

I shook my head. "I trained him—he never chases cars."

She gave me one more hug, her face leaving a dampness on my skin. Then she opened the car door and heaved herself into the front seat. The engine started up. She lowered the window.

"Good-bye, dear! Good-bye—"

"Good-bye, Miss Gilly!" I pressed my lips together tight.

I watched the Hudson vanish behind some bushes. The air went still. The car reappeared at the bottom of the driveway moving slowly past the trees, and I waved, knowing she was turning to look up the hill one last time. The car rolled onto the road. Suddenly I spotted a patch of orange streaking after it.

"*No!*" I screamed. "COME BACK!" I broke into a run. At the bottom of the hill the ground dropped out from beneath me. I pitched forward, sprawling onto the lawn. My face hit the ground hard. I felt a kind of crack in the air. For a few moments I seemed to lose consciousness. Then I was lying on my side with my knees squeezed against my chest, my eyes shut tight. My mouth was caked with dirt; my throat hurt as if I'd been screaming into the earth. I had been sobbing; my cheeks were wet and raw.

I heard a high-pitched whimpering sound nearby, like an echo, and raised my head. The dog scuttled backward. His tongue drooped out of the side of his rueful smile. Then he lay down, his eyes level with mine. I reached out. Wagging his tale, he dragged himself along the grass toward me on his stomach.

I walked up the hill with the dog. The hum of car engines faded on the road. A wind rustled in the trees. The house stood empty before me, frozen inside a toy glass globe, where a heavy viscous liquid was about to freeze and imprison me in it forever.

Then the opposite happened. The ground seemed to shift, as if a giant hand were giving the globe a shake. No blizzard of fake snowflakes erupted; instead, leaves swirled up around me. The dog barked happily; he ran back and forth, chasing them. Like an explosion of startled birds they fluttered, careened in circles, fell and rose in delirious silence.

I gazed up, recalling the cracking noise I'd heard before—like a glass wall breaking. Currents of cool air streamed in through the opening. I took long deep breaths. My tears dried. I stumbled forward, then got my balance, feeling the ground firm beneath my feet.

The storm stopped. The leaves dropped peacefully to the grass. The air was clear and still.

The bare trees, the gray lawn, the old, white, lifeless house were outlined against the sky like a landscape in a faded monochrome photograph.

- THIRTEEN -

The smoking biplane swoops into the searchlight beam. Its wings tilt and twist—now it is skimming the clouds on its back—now hurtling through them, nose down, gaining speed. The ailerons vibrate like chattering teeth beneath the wings—the entire fusilage shudders—the plane dives faster and faster down a vertical shaft of sky. The earth leaps up to meet it in an explosion of mud and metal. For a precarious second, the plane's tail remains in the air, then collapses, already blazing. Red flames leap out of the motor; a fountain of smoke paints the air black.

I sit pinned in the bombadier's seat, salty blood rising in my throat, my eyes peppered with fumes. I catch a glimpse of the pilot writhing out of the cockpit, and heave my upper body forward, my arms outstretched toward my rescuer. . . .

Snarled wires and metal bury my legs in the pilot's seat. Gulping smoke, I try to stand but flop over the side of the fusilage, my feet pinned, my arms dangling uselessly. Turning my head, I cry out for the bombadier as he crawls through the blazing wreckage to save me. . .

Sweeping my beam down from a sky of boards and roofing nails, I can only watch the drama from above: a lighting technician in the rafters above the stage, still unsure who is rescuing whom, or from what.

When my parents were notified that Robert had again gone AWOL from the Air Force base in Alabama, the house became a combat zone. Late into the night my parents exchanged volleys of accusations across the second floor landing about whose fault Robert was. A box of my mother's face powder exploded against my father's door; floated down the staircase in an acrid gray-white cloud.

Weeks before, my mother, observing that I was reading a lot of Civil War books, had decided that the Gettysburg Military Park would be a good place for my father and me to take a trip.

177

"To get to know each other before it's too late," she said. Uneasy about spending so much time together after the incident in the dining room, we'd both found excuses not to go. Now my father ordered me to pack for the trip the next day. We were supposed to find refuge from one civil war on the battlefield of another one.

It felt good to leave Ridge Haven, but responding to my father's awkward attempts at conversation in the car was exhausting. Both of us got testy in the long silences. I asked if I could look for some music on the radio. "No!" he said. "Why *not?*" I demanded in a grating voice. "*No!*" he said again, gritting his teeth. I told him I wanted to lie down in the back seat, figuring he'd get madder and try to stop me, but he said, "Lie down wherever the hell you want."

I didn't lie down, I sat up in the back seat's corner just to spite him. He drove fast, as if he, too, were anxious to get far from home. The car careened out of Connecticut, roared through New Jersey, swerved around slowpoke vehicles on the back roads of Pennsylvania. The new countryside made me worry about Robert, whom I could picture wandering somewhere beside alien roadsides looking for a ride. Whenever we passed hitchhikers, I pressed my nose to the glass to get a look at them. My father glanced at them from the front seat, too, though he pretended not to.

Once, passing a solitary figure in a baseball hat, my father slowed the car. I cranked my window down, ready to shout my brother's name if the hitchhiker turned out to be him. I never did get a look at his face; as my father stomped on the accelerator, I was flung back against the seat, bumping my head.

I felt as if something had been jarred loose. "What's going to happen to Robert?" I asked suddenly.

My father gripped the steering wheel. "He could go to prison."

"Are you going to turn him in to the police if he comes home?"

"I'm a veteran. . . ." He wiped his forehead with his handkerchief. "I can't decide anything now. They'll have to find him—"

"They'll never find him." I narrowed my eyes, feeling a chill pass through me. "He knows how to disappear."

"Nobody just disappears."

"You probably wish he'd never come back." I rubbed the back of my head where it had struck the seat.

As we got closer to Gettysburg, the sun began to set, a bristly ball of flame that flew sideways behind the trees, shooting molten rays across the fields. A landscape from another century blended into the scene. It looked like old photos in my history books. In the distance, a haze the color of cannon smoke appeared. I saw the shapes of riflemen hiding behind tumbled-down stone walls. The scent of fertilizer on the breeze turned to the smell of galloping cavalry horses. I felt a reverberation in the air around me, an echo of thunder up ahead.

My father always planned things in advance, but for some reason he hadn't made reservations at the old white-columned inn where he wanted to stay in Gettysburg. He came down its steps shaking his head, and eventually we had to settle for a motel on the highway.

"At least it's clean," he said.

Neither of us said anything about how cramped the room was. A somber wood-grain pattern repeated itself in the wallpaper everywhere I looked. The window curtains smelled of cigar smoke, which I rather liked. But my father turned on the air conditioner, to freshen up the place, he said. The machine groaned, and soon the chilly air was giving me goose bumps. How was I going to survive three nights crowded in here with this man? I sat on the bed and immediately began to read.

My father showered, then shaved, thrusting his chin toward the mirror over the bureau. The electric razor buzzed a half-tone lower than the air conditioner; they sounded like two people humming with iron filings in their throats. The muscles in my father's arm rippled as he moved the razor up and down his cheek. I'd never watched him shave before; it was both embarrassing and interesting.

"You'd better get dressed for dinner." he said.

"I didn't pack any good clothes."

"What's in your bag?"

"Books, mostly." I braced myself for a lecture.

"You could wash, at least," he said, his mouth tightening.

"I'm not dirty," I told him. Then I snatched my bag from the bed, took it into the bathroom and shut the door.

The room had the alien smell of adult male sweat. I was sticky, but in the shower stall were flecks of my father's soapsuds that I didn't want to step in, so I washed at the sink. A skinny-armed kid stared at me in the mirror. I put on a clean T-shirt with my dungarees, washed the dirt from my sneakers as best I could, and put them on wet. Standing by the bathroom window, I saw a tall man who looked like my father crossing the highway. It *was* my father. He went into a phone booth outside a gas station. Why? I wondered. Didn't the phone in our room work? I ducked away from the window as he headed back across the road.

When I stepped out into the bedroom, my father had changed into fresh slacks and shirt and a seersucker sports jacket. He was pacing beside his bed with the room's phone receiver in his hand—talking to the Air Force in Washington, it sounded like. He'd been calling them every evening to see if they'd found Robert. I opened a book called *Lee's Cavalry*. My father cracked the phone receiver down. I didn't have to ask if there was any news.

"Listen, we're almost in Virginia, right?" I said. "That's pretty far south already. We could just keep going to Alabama."

"We can't drive all over the state looking for him. He's probably not even there still."

"He might be!"

"That's stupid—"

"It's not stupid!" I said, though I knew it was.

My father began tying his necktie—twice, three times, but the ends wouldn't come out even. He yanked it from his collar. "Do you want to go home, Jerrett?" he asked suddenly. "We can leave now and be there by midnight."

"I don't know." My voice sounded faint in comparison to the air conditioner's.

My father sat down hard on the bed. "Listen, we're in a different place. Let's not bring everything from home with us, okay?"

"I'm cold," I said.

He switched off the air conditioner. I heard the sound of crickets chirping outside the window.

"I've always wanted to see Gettysburg," he said. "Pickett's charge—it was the turning point of the war. If the charge had broken through the lines, Lee might have won the battle. The Confederacy might have survived."

"Everybody knows that," I said.

"If Grant had been in command, he would have stopped Lee's retreat. The war would have ended here, instead of dragging on."

I'd read the biographies of both generals. Lee was elusive and brave and heroic; Grant was crude, methodical, businesslike. "Grant wouldn't have caught Lee," I said.

My father glanced at my book. "Maybe not," he conceded.

We went out to look for some dinner.

The roadside was hot and dusty, but my father wanted to walk; we both could use the exercise, he said. He was sure he'd seen a nice restaurant just around the bend in the highway.

Near the motel was a strange-looking rounded cinder-block building. I turned to stare at it as I walked past. On top, a rickety neon sign shouted into the twilight at red intervals: SEE THE BATTLEFIELD DIORAMA! The building's doorway was sunken beneath ground level, and on either side, life-sized cardboard figures of Civil War soldiers—blue and gray—stood holding what looked like real rifles.

"What's a diorama?" I asked, squatting down to try to see inside.

"A tourist trap." My father didn't slow his pace.

I lingered behind, gazing at the place. Trucks roared by, rocking the air with big gusts of wind. My father's feet began to drag. When he turned to tell me to keep up, his forehead was spotted with perspiration and his cheekbones looked more caved-in than usual. He looked sixty years old—his actual age—not like the man who chopped down trees and won tennis tournaments. I walked several steps behind him.

"It can't be much farther," he said, breathing hard.

Suddenly I had the feeling that the restaurant he thought he'd seen didn't exist, at least not on this highway. Around the next bend were more billboards and gas stations, but no restaurant. My father shielded his eyes from the onrushing headlights and forged ahead. Finally we spotted a chrome-sided building shaped like a railroad car. I'd seen these diners before but had never eaten in one—my parents ate out only at inns or at the country club.

"I'm hungry," I said in a low voice.

My father wiped his forehead. "All right."

It was the sort of place I was sure he wouldn't like. There

were shiny booths instead of tables; cartoons were taped to the wall above the cash register. Grease and onions sizzled, giving off thrilling scents unknown at our house. I sat in a booth beside a window, pretending that I was on a moving train as I gazed out at the neon signs, their carnival colors looping along the highway. I wolfed down two hamburgers and a milk shake. My father ordered a chicken sandwich, which I expected he'd only pick at. But he ate it all, and even drank a milk shake. I glanced at him, realizing that I'd never seen him eating out without a necktie before.

When we started back, night had fallen; the air was swimming with hot exhaust fumes. We must have walked several miles altogether. By the time we got to the diorama, my father's shoulders were drooping.The building looked larger in the darkness, as if it had expanded while we'd been away. Red shadows splashed over its domed roof when the neon letters flickered on.

"Can't I see what this is?" I asked him.

Squinting at the cardboard soldiers, he looked even stiffer in his sports jacket than they did in their uniforms. His shoes were speckled with roadside dust; a long strand of gray hair fell over one eye.

"You don't have to come in," I said. "I've got money."

"All right, all right," he said.

We passed between the two soldiers. In the entrance, a burly old man in a hat sat at a battered desk chewing on a cigar. He smiled up at us like a leftover Halloween pumpkin. "Good evening, gentlemen," he said, pronouncing it "chentlemen."

I said, "Hello." My father stood still, as if not knowing what to do. Then he took out his wallet and paid the admission. We walked past a curtain into a dim, bare room. My heart sank to see how shabby the place looked. Would my father demand his money back? The walls were smoke-stained cinder-block; the ceiling was corrugated metal. A ring of bricks held down a cheesecloth that covered the floor. The diorama was just a shadowy crater that took up the whole room except for a rickety plank walkway around it.

On the far wall was a hand-written sign:
THE WORLD FAMOUS "BATTLEFIELD DIORAMA" OF GETTYSBURG WAS CREATED ENTIRELY BY JOHANNES SCHMIDT OF FRANKFURT, GERMANY * IT

TOOK 3 YEARS TO MAKE * OVER 5,000 PIECES ARE IN ITS CONSTRUCTION * OVER 600 BULBS PROVIDE ILLUMINATION FOR THE AMAZING BATTLE SCENES * THE NARRATION CAN BE FOLLOWED BY WATCHING CAREFULLY THE MOVEMENT OF THE LIGHTINGS * THE AUDIENCE IS REQUESTED TO REFRAIN FROM TALK DURING THE PROGRAM

I'd just finished reading when the room suddenly went dark. Then a pinpoint of light appeared along the bottom of the crater below me. The cheesecloth slid away. I heard guitars strumming like the country music that twanged in and out of my sleep from my bedside radio. An invisible voice from somewhere overhead spoke: "In July, 1863, Cheneral Robert E. Lee's army began its fatal assault. . . ." Miniature soldiers appeared among lifelike bushes, lit by tiny concealed spotlights high on the crater's walls. Gunshots crackled. Puffs of smoke floated above the landscape. I was sure that I could see regiments of soldiers clashing. Horses whinnied. Sabers clanged. The voice boomed above all the noise, describing troop movements, charges, retreats, and finally hushing as the landscape darkened at the end of the first day's battle. The air was dense with the smoky smell of gunpowder. I gripped the railing. From the movement in the wood, I could feel my father grabbing it, too.

The dreamlike music began again, far away, as if coming from many years ago. Again dawn broke, again the air shuddered with the sounds of battle. . . and finally darkened again.

On the third day, the South's last desperate attempt to penetrate Union lines began. The hillsides thundered, the air swirled with colored smoke. Lines of Confederate cavalry were driven back in a deafening finale of cannon fire. Twilight fell. . . rifle flashes grew fewer and fewer. . . then the landscape faded into utter blackness. From deep inside the dark came the sad slow notes of a bugle playing Taps.

Silence. Night seemed to pass. Then dawn magically lit up the rim of the crater. Now I could see the entire field. There were thousands of foot soldiers and cavalry spread out among miniature trees, stone walls, farmhouses. They had been there all along, but I'd only seen some of them at a time. I watched regiment after fallen regiment being brought back to life by the sunrise.

183

"It's completely clear!" My father leaned over the railing and tugged at my sleeve, never taking his eyes off the pit.

Someone moved. There on the other side of the crater, sitting on a high stool, was the strange old man who had greeted us at the door. He still had his hat and cigar. His eyes beamed at us like tiny bulbs. He must have been the Johannes Schmidt from the sign.

"You enchoyed the program?" he asked.

"My brother and I used to have toy soldiers like these," I said.

"Ah, Civil War soldiers?" The man asked.

"First World War ones. We had planes, too."

My father turned toward me. "I never knew that."

"It's true," I said. "Robert and I took turns flying them, under the eaves in the attic."

He shook his head and smiled.

"And you, sir?" the man asked. "How did you like it?"

My father gazed down into the diorama. "I used to get this kind of aerial view when I flew over the lines in France." He lifted his hands slowly from the railing. "Everything was so clear then!"

"You may stay as long as you want." The old man smiled down on his figures from above the crater like God perched on a stool above the world.

"Were you in the first war?" my father asked him, and it occurred to me that he and the man might have fought on opposite sides of the lines, perhaps bombing each other's positions. "You're a veteran?"

The man nodded slowly. "But now... only of this war." He pointed at the diorama.

Johannes Schmidt, it turned out, was a retired engineer; he said he'd wanted to build something that would express his gratitude to his adopted country. If, in the world outside the building, someone had told my father about a man who spent three years of his life wiring up toy soldiers on a plywood landscape, my father would have dismissed him as a crank. That night, though, he was so impressed with Mr. Schmidt that he hired him to give us a tour of the battlefield the next day.

At the motel, my father and I stayed up late going over a plan of the park together. It was easier to talk with a map spread out in front of us. The next day we walked through the battlefield with our guide. He carried a cane with a carved head. I kept trying to get a look at it under his gnarled hand as he walked vigorously over the uneven ground, speaking of the skirmishes as if he'd been in them himself. The green fields buzzed with warmth in the bright sunlight—it was late in the autumn, but Pennsylvania was warmer than Connecticut.

Heroic monuments stood in clearings: bronze soldiers shot silent rifles into the woods from their pedestals and waved swords at the fluffy white clouds. My favorite was a lone young soldier with a wide-brimmed hat and a pack on his back who stood searching the fields from a rise near the parking lot. To me, the whole battlefield seemed a reproduction of the diorama instead of the other way around. As Mr. Schmidt pointed out the overgrown trenches and mossy knolls that had been strategic positions in the battle, I visualized lines of tin soldiers rushing over a floodlit landscape.

By the end of the third day of battlefield tours, though, my memory of the magical diorama was fading, and the Civil War was starting to get realer to me. I walked along a grassy field where Pickett's charge had been repulsed and the Confederate army had been driven back into the South forever. Running my fingers along the rough stones of a wall that retreating rebel soldiers must have stumbled over, I wondered what it had all been for, this attempt to preserve a doomed kind of life. I pictured the Confederacy as a big white house on a hill where my mother was waiting behind her bedroom curtains. A gang of soldiers who looked like my father's tennis cronies overran the house; my father led the charge up the stairs to the landing, where he hauled my mother out from behind her door and put a stop to her dreamy discontent forever.

The afternoon was humid with sadness. It wasn't just my mother's world that had been invaded; my brother's empty room was also laid waste. I pictured his records strewn on the carpet—he'd smashed them himself rather than leave them for the marauders to find. Silence rang in the house; his music was gone, forgotten. Now he was in perpetual retreat, being pushed further and further south until his energy gave out, his flashlight batteries dead in the darkness where he was hiding.

At the end of the third day, the battlefield tour was finished. Mr. Schmidt turned down our offer of a ride to town. He wanted to walk, he said. Puffing on his cigar, he lifted the tip of his cane in the air to wave good-bye, and strode off into the woods. My father and I watched him, feeling stunned by his sudden disappearance.

"I didn't have a chance to pay him!" my father said.

He'd decided to leave a check off at the diorama later, and we got back into the car. I felt lost without the old man. His enthusiastic lectures had given me something to look forward to each day. My father and I couldn't go over the battlefield map anymore. It was too early to sleep when we arrived back at the motel. What were we going to do? We both avoided mentioning the trip home tomorrow.

My father took a deck of cards out of his bag and began to shuffle them. A veteran of thousands of club-car poker games, he could make the cards flutter like bird wings between his hands.

"How do you do that?" I asked.

"Your grandfather showed me once. He could do magic things with cards," my father said. "The trick is to bend them just so...." He positioned my hands around the cards. When I relaxed my grip, they flipped all over the floor. I expected him to get exasperated the way he did when he tried to teach me tennis strokes, but he just helped me pick up the cards.

I practiced over and over, and when I could shuffle without spraying cards, I dealt twenty or so games of gin rummy, and actually won about half of them. Then, my mind suddenly feeling overloaded, I said I wanted to go for a walk. My father didn't object. I figured that being with me had worn him out and he needed some time alone as much as I did.

On my way outdoors, I passed through a big empty room full of folding chairs. A piano stood against one wall. I brushed my fingers along its keys; the ripple of notes startled me, and I left quickly. Escaping the motel, I ran all the way to the diner and bought a pack of Camels. Then I came back and sat in the car in the parking lot. I opened all the windows. The evening was jittery with neon. The highway traffic gave off a high-pitched hum that rose to a roar when trucks rumbled by, knocking out of their way invisible barrels of air that I could feel buffeting the car as I smoked.

My hand stopped midway to my mouth. Standing in the middle of the road, a tall solitary figure swayed in place as cars careened around him. It was my father. He rushed through the traffic. When I saw him again, he was standing inside the illu-minated phone booth on the other side. I'd never asked him why he didn't use the phone in the room, and still had no idea. I stashed my cigarettes under the seat and started across the highway.

Keeping to the shadows, I approached the booth from the side. My father pressed the receiver to his ear. A big grin made the lines in his cheeks rise. I heard laughter from behind the glass like no sound I'd heard from him before.

Then there was a long silence. The smile faded. His eyes opened wider. He gripped the side of his face with his fingers and looked about to scream—another father I'd never seen at home.

I heard words: "*Laura—no!*"

He stood up straight, his hair almost touching the bulb in the ceiling. He dropped the receiver; it bounced on its cord and hung limp. He didn't move.

"Hey!" I shouted at him.

He didn't look at me or move at all. I waited. Trucks flashed by. I tiptoed closer. "Hey! Hey!" I yelled, as if I were throwing things at him but always missing. "*Dad!*" I screamed, banging my fists against my sides, but his eyes never even twitched in my direction.

Suddenly, as if propelled from behind by an enormous gust of wind, I charged the phone booth. My foot shot out against the glass. The impact reverberated up my leg. I heard a shat-tering sound. Slivers of glass lay at my father's feet.

A strange sound came from inside—a roar of pain. Then my father was out the door, grabbing me as I tried to run toward the road.

"What're you *doing*?" he shouted.

"What were *you* doing?" I screamed back at him.

He shook me by my shirt. My head bobbed, my vision blur-ring. I grabbed his wrist and shook back, shutting my eyes. I felt myself being half-dragged across one lane of the highway. We stood stranded on the median strip as headlights slashed by. I was so dizzy I would have pitched forward into the oncoming traffic if he hadn't been holding me up. Then he shoved me for-ward and we were both stumble-running across the road. The gravel of the parking lot tilted beneath my feet. I caught my bal-ance, my heart slamming.

"What the hell's—the matter with you—?" My father
gasped. "You—broke—that—"

"Are you going to turn me in to the police?" I shouted,
blinking hard. "Why don't you? Go ahead!"

He stooped over to catch his breath. Strands of hair hung
from his brow. One shoe was partly off his foot. His breath
came out in hoarse, dry sobs.

The trucks rumbled by on the highway. I took a step toward
him. "Who did you call?"

He stood up and wiped his face with both hands. Through
a gap in his fingers, I saw tear-soaked lashes part to reveal a
shiny, rolling eyeball, and I began to understand why he kept
his face so expressionless at home.

"Everything—happens—at once," he whispered. "I don't
know—what to do."

"You don't?"

"I don't mean—about that booth. I'm glad you—" He
coughed. "I might have stayed—in there forever—"

"Hey, Dad...." I cleared my throat. "I got an idea. Let's
go to the diorama again!"

"What?" He gaped at me.

"Don't you remember?" I asked. "You liked it!"

I could almost smell the puffs of colored smoke and hear
the explosions of tiny cannons again. I needed to stand in the
darkness holding the rail beside him again, to watch the pictures
flicker to life before me. "Let's *go!*" I took off around the corner of the motel toward the cinder-block building. Behind me,
his footsteps sounded hesitant on the gravel at first, then he was
moving almost as fast as I was.

But now the building looked different. No red neon letters
pulsed on its roof—the sign was extinguished. The doorway
was dark; the place looked covered with shadowy dust as if it
hadn't been open in years.

I tried to turn the door knob. It wouldn't turn.

My father stumbled down the stairs and grabbed the knob.
"It can't be locked—" He twisted it one way, then the other.
"*Goddamn* it!"

We walked around the side of the building, but there
weren't any windows to peer into. The cardboard soldiers
guarding the door looked shabby and faded, wires drooping
from their empty hands; the rifles were gone.

188

"It was a stupid idea," I said.

"No," he said. "It was a good idea."

We started back toward the motel, our feet scuffing in the dirt. It seemed to take all his strength to open the glass door to our corridor. I couldn't face the cramped room right away, and told him I wanted to walk around some more. He said he'd pack for the trip home.

Feeling shaky, I wandered through hallways until I found myself in the nearly dark room full of folding chairs. The glow from the highway shone through dusty Venetian blinds and made stripes along the floor at the far end of the room. The air smelled of stale smoke, but I liked the semi-darkness; I felt as if this place had been waiting for me all evening. The piano was almost hidden in shadow but I sensed where it was and walked right to it. Sitting down on the bench, I began to play.

At first I played the tunes from the diorama's Civil War music. Then melodies and base lines I'd nearly forgotten I knew began to fly out of the piano—as if touching the keys had released a switch deep inside me. I recognized the songs I'd listened to with Robert years before: "Night Train Blues," "Cow Cow Boogie," "Pine Top's Boogie"—all the titles that I'd repeated to myself drifting off to sleep at night. I pictured the sheet music I'd once written out for these songs; now my fingers knew where to find them in the dark.

A chair creaked behind me. I stopped in the middle of a bar; the music dissolved in the darkness. Without turning around, I knew that my father was in the room.

"Go ahead," he said.

I started playing again. The sound was ragged, but I didn't care. The notes thumped and rippled. The tunes were in me, and I'd always be able to hear them when I needed them. I played faster, suddenly beginning to improvise. I was making up extensions of the melodies, new verses, completely new melodies—I was off on my own now, flying far out into the night. . . .

I wasn't aware of how long I played. Finally I stopped. Hearing the sound of breathing, I turned my head. My father was sitting in a strange pose—his legs splayed out, his arms hanging down at his sides. I felt as if I'd somehow left him behind.

"Are you asleep?" I whispered.

"No." The chair creaked. He stood up unsteadily. "I used to hear music like that from Robert's room," he said, his voice hushed. "All the nights I yelled at him to turn it down, turn it off—" His eyes glittered in the flash of a car headlight. "I never heard it—the way you played it."

"Neither did I," I said.

He took a stiff step toward me. I braced myself, not knowing what to expect. "It sounded good," he said.

He started walking back and forth across the stripes on the floor beside the window. The stripes stuck to his clothing. Then he pushed through the door and held it open for me. His hand brushed my shoulder as I passed in front of him.

"You can lie down in back if you want and get some sleep," my father said, as we loaded the car. He'd decided not to wait until morning before starting the drive home—he was too restless to stay cooped up in the motel room, he said.

"I don't think I could sleep," I said, and sat in the front seat beside him.

He started the engine, and we pulled out onto the highway. Neither of us had spoken of taking a last look at the battlefield, but when we came to the park entrance, he turned the car as if we'd planned it all along.

The headlight beams glided slowly over the grass, and behind them, shadows moved along stone walls like creeping infantrymen. I was sure I could orient myself by slipping my memory of the diorama over the landscape. As soon as the car stopped, I took off at a fast walk across the grass. I figured my father was right behind me.

But he wasn't. I turned and headed back toward what I thought was the parking lot, and found myself in a sunken grassy clearing. I was miles, it seemed, from anywhere familiar. The battlefield hummed with a stillness that I could feel against my skin. Wet grass shone silver in the gauzy moonlight.

Groping my way over the rutted ground, I suddenly skidded down a slope and landed on my side. I was in a trench. The night lay like a black roof on the top of the walls. Staring up, I saw stars in it, and remembered the tips of roofing nails caught in the beam of Robert's flashlight.

But this was a real trench. I could feel the presence of young men who had crouched here, hiding from exploding shells. Some had died here. I recalled photographs I'd seen of corpses piled in trenches, legs entangled, mouths stuck open. The ground where I stood had been soaked with their blood. I crawled on my hands and knees up what must have been an earthen fortification. At the top, I was surrounded by shadowy outlines of more ditches as far as I could see. The silence was immensely deep: the ringing aftershock of an explosion. I inhaled the chilling scent of damp earth.

"Dad?" My voice sounded hoarse. There was something I needed to ask him. Hearing a sound behind me, I turned around fast.

"Jerrett?" My father stood up on the slope of the hill. "I thought you'd fallen down a foxhole."

I let out all my breath. "I sort of did."

He sat down on the grass beside me. "I came looking for you, then I got lost, myself."

"I thought I'd know my way around."

He nodded. "There's no old man to turn on the lights."

Slipping on the grass, we climbed an embankment. At the top, I stopped short. Silhouetted soldiers stood at intervals aiming long rifles. Cavalryman charged straight for me on gigantic horses. I tried to speak. My arm rose in the air, pointing.

"Monuments," my father said.

They all turned into statues on pedestals. I laughed in the dark.

Again the deep silence was over everything. The frozen figures around us looked sad, abandoned, damned. They had to stay here, year after year, while everyone else, for whom the war was long over, got to go home.

"I don't think anybody's supposed to be here at night," my father said. "There's a reason for that."

"Dad?" I asked. "Could Robert be dead?"

"No!" He cleared his throat. "No, he's okay."

"He's just hiding for a while," I said. "He knows how."

"That's right," my father said. "He knows a lot about that."

We stumbled on over the uneven ground, bumping into each other. Once he started to skid into a trench, but I caught his arm and held it tight. A little ways on, he took hold of my shoulder just as I was about to stumble over a boulder.

"Careful!"

"Okay," I said.

"What's that?" He pointed to a small rounded shape on the lumpy horizon.

"It looks familiar."

Keeping it in sight, we made our way toward it in as straight a line as possible. The shape turned to a hat, a head, shoulders—the statue I'd seen days before of the soldier with a pack on his back. My father paused, resting his hand on its elbow. Coming up beside him, I felt asphalt under my feet, and turned to see the car, shiny in the faint moonlight.

"We're back!" I said.

"We've been walking in a circle," my father said.

Driving out of the parking lot, we passed the solitary bronze soldier standing beside the asphalt. The car slowed. I twisted around in my seat to look at him. As we drove away, he faded into the dark landscape behind us.

I turned forward again and saw my father's face. He was still staring into the rearview mirror.

- FOURTEEN -

It's a beautiful old machine, long and gleaming white, with an elegant running board and a spare tire set into the front fender like a silver moon half-sunk into a rising ocean wave. Perched on the radiator cap is a statue of a naked figure, wings swept back. The front seat is a glassed-in compartment for a chauffeur.

It's winter, 1940. Wearing a smart uniform with a jacket and cap, I drive Mrs. Miller, my employer, along the water to the cottage where she's been going with Mr. Langley since 1924. All very discreet, of course. He's got to protect his "position in the community," as I've heard him say. Sometimes they forget to switch off the speaking tube between the back seat and the front.

Lately, she's been spending hours wandering around her apartment in New York listening to records of operas with slowly expiring heroines in them: *La Boheme, Adriana Lecouvreur, La Traviata.* About the only times she goes out in the city—besides when she sees Mr. Langley—is to volunteer at the children's hospital. She loads up the back seat with stuffed animals on her way over there, and dabs her eyes with a handkerchief all the way back. When she and her husband were first married, she set up a big nursery in their apartment. It never got any use. She was a glamourpuss in those days—lots of fiery red hair, jewelry twinkling all over her, nice round behind and bosom—but Mr. Miller was more interested in the Market.

She's gotten plumper over the years, but not Mr. Langley. Fit and angular in his dark suit and silver tie, he strides along Wall Street from his office as briskly as always. His watch-chain's tight across his vest. His hair's gone gray, but he hasn't lost any of it. Though he's always polite with me, he never smiles—not until he climbs into the back seat with her and clicks the door shut behind him.

Sometimes they get carried away before they reach the cottage. I hear the curtains slide over the side windows and the glass partition behind me. She's all over him with high-pitched

193

squeals like a little girl pulling open birthday-party favors. He's a musical grunter; he keeps the back seat thumping mile after mile, Henry Hudson Parkway to Cross County to Merritt Parkway, right through the toll booths. The collector gives me a look; he must feel the vibrations. Then as we drive along a back road, the car's full of whispering and zippering-up. I catch a glimpse of them in the rearview mirror through a crack in the curtains behind me. Her eyes are rolled back as if she's seeing visions of angels flicker on the ceiling. He's adjusting his watch chain over his vest.

Today they don't go into the cottage when I stop the car. She reminds him he's promised her a decision—she's been wanting him to leave his wife for years. He's told her he has to wait till the wife's more "stable." He's afraid she'll do something strange if he takes off, and everyone will think it was his fault.

I remember his wife. Back in the '20s, I used to drive her and Mrs. Miller to Macys, Bloomingdale's, Lord & Taylor. Mrs. Langley wasn't happy until she'd filled nearly the whole back seat with hatboxes and packages. She was always bursting with ideas about books; she must have saved them up for her pal. They were like a sparrow and a toucan, the two of them: Marian Langley twittering and bobbing in her gray suit and pearls, Laura Miller nodding and preening her feathers.

Then suddenly the excursions stopped. Mrs. Miller told me it was because the Langleys were moving to Connecticut, but I'm not so sure of that. I missed Mrs. Langley; she always had a smile for me. And without her, Mrs. Miller seemed to lose the will to shop.

"Marian's got everything she needs in Ridge Haven," Mrs. Miller is saying now in the back seat. She always speaks the name of the town as if it's coated with vinegar. "You can give her an allowance for Robert, and hire a gardener to keep the place going."

"I've planted the last of the trees. They're growing up like weeds." He sighs. "Yes, I think the time has come, Laura."

What's this? I can't let this happen!

"So you've really decided?" Mrs. Miller leans into his lap.

"Yes." He smiles. "*Yes.*"

I can't believe what I'm hearing. I've broken out in a sweat. I hear happy sighs and clothes rubbing together in the back seat.

194

"Dean, let's go away—today!"

Silence. He pounds the seat. "Damn."

"What?"

"The cruise tickets. They're already ordered."

"You can cancel them, can't you?"

"They'll be in this afternoon's mail. If Marian gets them, and then I suddenly tell her the cruise is off. . . ."

Mrs. Miller sniffles. "Oh, God!"

"She's been planning this trip for months." He looks stricken. "I hate to think what she might do, she's capable of such craziness—"

I clench my teeth. There's barely enough air in my glass compartment to breathe, but I don't dare move to open the window. If he doesn't go on the cruise with his wife. . . well, I feel as if my very life's at stake. Which—considering what needs to happen on that ship—it is.

"What time does the mail come?" Mrs. Miller asks.

"About five. I usually pick it up from the mailbox if I get home before supper. If I don't, Marian gets it."

"We've got time, Dean! It's only four. You could take the tickets out of the mailbox and say the cruise has been cancelled. Give her a few days to calm down, and then tell her."

"Yes. That'd work."

I sit up suddenly—the speaking tube is clicking.

"We're going directly to Ridge Haven," Mrs. Miller tells me, "but not to the train station this time. I'll give you directions. And, oh—please hurry!"

I pull away from the cottage, my mind racing. I know a stretch of road near Greenwich where there isn't a house for several miles—that's the route I take. I roll down the window, gulp the cold air and the sharp scent of snow-laden pines. A long stone wall flickers by me like a corrugated snake. I'm aware of the smooth hum of the engine, the feel of this beautiful old machine as it clings loyally to the curves.

Here's that long stretch of road. Nothing around but dark frozen woods. I slow for a turn. And then my target identifies itself before me: a single boulder just beyond a patch of shimmering white ice.

I slow to twenty-five miles per hour. . . twenty. . . fifteen. . . .
At the edge of the ice, I ease my foot onto the brake pedal. The car begins to slide. I steer slowly into the skid. The boulder

drops below the level of the hood. Gripping the steering wheel, I absorb the impact with my chest.

Something bumps against the back of my seat. Not Mrs. Miller, I hope. The engine's hum has stopped. All is silent... except a faint silver hiss in the air. Smiling, I watch the spray fall against the windshield. The winged hood-ornament has sprung a magnificent geyser.

"Back in a flash," I tell them, setting out to go for help. Then I take more than an hour to stroll through the woods, find a house, have a long cup of coffee with the maid, and finally telephone a towing service. By the time I return to the car to wait for the truck, night has fallen.

Mr. Langley has stopped looking at his watch. "When I get back from the cruise, Laura, there'll be nothing to stop us," he tells her.

I smile.

"All right, darling," she says with a catch in her voice.

The spray has made a lovely pattern of frozen drops on the windshield. In the front seat, I settle back and watch the darkness roll in toward me like dancing ocean waves.

After I got back from Gettysburg, school was as alien a place as home. During lunch period I sat against the wall of the music room listening to Tina play the piano. She smiled at me during the difficult passages as if my presence were helping her through them. For some reason, I felt as if I'd already said good-bye to her, though we wouldn't graduate for more than six months. I imagined running into her somewhere years later and telling her how much she and her music had always cheered me up.

I sometimes cut classes and lay flat in the tall grass, out of sight, near the place Miss Gilly had parked her car on Tuesdays. Across a field, dwarf deer grazed among some birch trees beyond a nearly invisible wire fence. Did they know, I wondered, that they were never going to grow any bigger, that they were destined to spend their entire lives in this little artificial grove that had been so beautifully landscaped for them?

I looked forward to Fridays—a weekend of mindless yard work awaited me. That Friday seemed no different from others. I carried Tina's briefcase to her bus and kissed her, perhaps longer than usual, before getting on my own bus. I must have dozed on the ride home. I remember stumbling down the aisle when the bus stopped at my mailbox; the waiting engine made the floor vibrate under my feet.

I was still rubbing my eyes as I started up the hill toward the house. Then I halted, wide awake, my sneakers crunching on the gravel. Someone was sitting on the stone wall at the bottom of the front lawn. I veered across the field toward him. The man looked like no one I'd ever seen before. A beard darkened his jaw; he wore jeans and a worn brown leather jacket. And yet I knew who he was.

He stood up and called to me—"Jerry!"

I knew that voice. I broke into a run, my books dropping behind me in the long grass. It was Robert.

His arm went around my neck, hard and strong. I felt his wiry beard push into my forehead, a sensation that made me want to scream with laughter. I wrapped my arms around his waist and hung on tight.

"You're here!" I staggered back a step to look at him.

"Hard to believe," he said.

"I—I knew you'd come back!"

He grinned. "You've gotten big. You look great."

"So do you!" I blinked. "Is the beard—are you in disguise?"

Robert rubbed his chin. "It started out that way. Now I wouldn't feel right without it."

"You're not fat anymore."

"I worked it off."

"Where?"

"Alberta, Saskatchewan, other places out West. I did a lot of ranch work and clearing land for pipelines." He sat down on the stone wall again, his grin fading. "How've things been around here? Not so great, I guess—from your letters." They'd been forwarded to him from the address I'd sent them to; he said they were one of the main reasons he'd come home.

I sat down next to him. He rested one foot on the worn canvas knapsack he'd leaned against the wall. I liked the smell of his leather jacket. I talked fast, as if I expected him to turn into an empty space beside me before I'd told him everything—Miss Gilly's departure, the new school, even the Halloween vandalism. His steady gaze absorbed the agitation in my voice. He wasn't surprised or angry that I'd gotten in trouble. I told him how bitterly my parents had been arguing lately.

"What makes them fight so much?" I asked.

For the first time since I'd seen him, the tic appeared around his eyes. "I used to believe it was because of me, but I know better now."

"Did Dad beat you up?"

"Yeah, especially after that cocktail party. The one when the woman in the white fur showed up. He scared himself as much as he did me."

"But why did he do it?"

Robert looked up slowly from the ground. "Do you know about Mrs. Miller?" he asked.

"I think so. From the way Miss Gilly used to talk, I sort of figured it out. Is she the reason Dad missed so many trains?"

"Sure." Robert leaned back, glancing up the hill. "She was the woman at the party," he said. "Miss Gilly heard her talking with Dad about running away together. They were talking just up there." He stood up to point to the forsythia bushes beside the garage. I stood up with him. "Miss Gilly'd come out to get me in—I was tossing a ball against the toolshed. She told me what she'd heard. Then I did one of the stupidest things I've ever done."

My head was spinning from taking in so much information and trying to remember the party at the same time. I recalled the way Mrs. Miller had held her cigarette holder like a wand as she glided up the front walk. "What did you do?" I asked Robert.

"I told Mother what Miss Gilly had heard Dad and Mrs. Miller talking about."

"I remember I heard you speaking with Mother on the stairs. Just before her door slammed."

"I remember that slam." Robert winced. "Dad got to me the next morning. I went away to school early. The next thing I heard from home was that Mother had swallowed a bottle of sleeping pills."

"Miss Gilly told me about the pills." I glanced at the driveway where I'd seen the ambulance. "Was that the first you'd known about Mrs. Miller?" I asked.

"Oh, no. I used to sneak into Dad's room when I was little.

Just to get close to him. I'd hide in his closet. Once he found me, after he'd just gotten off the phone with her. That was why. . . ." Robert shook his head slowly. "Lord, it's strange to be back here!"

"Laura Miller." I'd never spoken the name to anyone. To say it out loud made her real. I was angry and sad and curious all at once.

"Dad left a few times more, and came back. He always chose his home and family. And his position here in town. To run off with another woman would have wrecked everything he'd worked for all his life. And in his way, maybe he cared about us." Robert sighed. "We'll find out. . . ."

"But he still saw Mrs. Miller?"

"Yeah. I suppose he could never give her up."

I suddenly couldn't talk about her anymore—I felt overloaded with the past. And there were things I wanted to know even more about. Robert and I sat down on the wall again. It was a chilly fall day, but the stones were still warm from the sun. I asked what Robert had been doing while he'd been away.

At first it seemed hard for him to speak, as if he, too, were saying some things out loud for the first time. "I passed the Air Force basic training, at last," he said. "But then I found out what I'd been in training for. . . ."

He'd learned, he told me, that he wasn't destined to be a heroic Air Force pilot. Or to be a paper-shuffling company clerk who got pounded with nightsticks in the MP van after blind-drunk rampages in town. He'd decided that if he was going to be a fuck-up, he'd at least be a free one. "So I jumped a freight train and took off," he said.

"You really rode the rails?" I remembered Wayne the radio Night Owl's hoboing stories.

Robert told me how it had really been. As he spoke, I pictured him riding in a boxcar—a real hobo, sitting with his boots beside him, the sooty wind blowing in his face as the towns flew by the open door. But there were no romantic tales being swapped, no lonesome night-owl harmonica tunes drifting through the night air. Men lay sprawled on splintery boards, belching cheap liquor fumes. One dark figure knelt over Robert, trying to yank the boots out of his hands. The man stabbed him in the side—Robert lifted his shirt to show the long scar. He knew that if he lost his boots, he'd be walking for

199

miles along railroad sidings with the gravel turning the soles of his feet bloody. So he had to hit the dark figure over and over until the man didn't fight back anymore. He'd learned to never, never take his boots off again in the dark.

He also learned the freedom of having no last name and no past. He had only one purpose now, to keep moving: slipping out of bars when they were raided, ducking into roadside meadows as police cars stopped to check hitchhikers. Finding work, he walked out into the mountains with a chain-saw to turn mile after mile of dark forest tunnel to a green sky-lit path. He slept dreamlessly under bunkhouse blankets, rising at dawn to gulp scalding coffee among other men with no last names.

He learned, too, about the craziness, as he called it. Sometimes it was the terror of being followed by ghosts—a frowning skeletal pilot and a tipsy weeping crone. Sometimes the craziness had to be soaked up with alcohol that made the specters back off, their accusations fading into the garble of voices around him. Sometimes the figures had to be screamed at, kicked, punched. Then he learned how a jail cell floor felt slamming up into his face.

Once he landed in a cell that reeked of despair and rubber walls and shook like a boxcar hurtling through the night. The maze of hospital corridors gradually became home; it mirrored the puzzle of passages inside his head. He learned that this echoing maze didn't end in a tunnel to vanish into, as he'd always thought. The maze emptied like a sewer pipe into a place that was just the mirror image of the hospital world: a place of ordinary streets, alleys, bridges, of people, noises, smells, a place that was simply life.

I began to see even then that this craziness was not so very foreign to me. I'd seen it in me during my Halloween rampage. I'd seen it in Robert when he'd smashed the car through the garage door. I'd noticed it when my mother had thrown the burnt chicken against the wall the night after my father left. I'd seen it in my father, as, stalled in honking traffic after picking me up at my friend's house, he'd rambled on about the shame that his own father—the original family hobo—had caused him.

Such craziness wasn't supposed to enter this quiet town, or this beautiful estate into which my father had tried to barricade himself and his family with lines of trees. The barricade had turned to a high prison wall that made even him feel trapped. Robert had cut a swath through it on his way out, giving me a wider view of the sky.

A gray car rolled up the driveway and pulled into the garage. Robert and I saw the kitchen lights go on, though the afternoon sun was still bright. My mother was home.

When Robert and I walked into the kitchen, she was unloading a bag of groceries. Her mouth flew open. A bottle of olives rolled off the counter and skidded along the floor. I'd never seen her embrace anyone like that, but as Robert wrapped his arms around her shoulders, she clung to him, her fingers digging into his back. She couldn't speak; all I heard were little gasping sounds. Robert helped her sit down at the table in the breakfast room. He pulled a chair up, and I sat at the end of the table.

"Are you—are you home for good, now?" she asked finally. Robert sighed. "Not for good."

"Are the military police after you?"

"Always."

She swallowed hard. "What will you do?"

"I'll stay for a while."

"But—how long?"

Robert pressed his fingernails, black with dirt, into the table-top. "Until they come for me," he said. "Then, we'll see."

My mother wiped her eyes with a napkin, and seemed to notice me for the first time. "You sent Jerrett postcards," she said. "You didn't send us any! We never knew where you were!" Her lips stretched wide at the corners. "You hurt me so, Robert!"

He nodded slowly. Then he looked steadily at her. "You hurt me. We all hurt each other."

"He—" My mother's eyes narrowed. I knew she was talking about my father. "He—"

"Yes." Robert rested his hand on her arm.

She dropped her head. I heard the hum of the clock in the kitchen.

"Why did you come, after all this time?" she asked.

"You gave up on me, didn't you?" Robert asked suddenly, and an angry wildness flashed in his eyes. "You gave up on me years ago."

"No, Robert!"

His hand tightened into a fist. "It always seemed that way."

"I gave up on myself." My mother shut her eyes. "I shouldn't have. I was scared...."

"Me, too." Robert sat back in his chair, facing the window. "Then I got even more scared of forgetting everything. That's what brought me back, I guess." He stared at my mother. "Do you understand that?"

"I'm going to try. I hope it's not too late," she said. Then she sat up straight. "Where's your suitcase?"

He pointed to the knapsack he'd dropped in the corner, and pulled a wallet from his back pocket. "That and six hundred dollars," he said.

"Do you—did you steal it?"

"I have, once or twice, when I had to," he said. "I worked for this money, though. I know how to work for what I need now."

She gazed into his face. "Do you want some food? Are you hungry?"

"Hungry...." Robert scratched his beard. His eyes were bloodshot, as if he hadn't slept for days. "Yeah, I'm hungry."

"We've got plenty—plenty of everything—" She turned toward the kitchen, and I saw for the first time the tears streaming down her cheeks.

My brother walked slowly around the house touching things as if each china ashtray or silver candlestick was a relic of some lost civilization preserved in a museum. I was beginning to think of them that way, myself. He took a shower, and while his clothes were in the washer, wore a pair of corduroys and a flannel shirt he found in the closet in his room. With his beard and long wet hair and flat stomach, he didn't look like the brother I'd watched shuffle off to the Air Force so long ago. He no longer moved as if he was about to make way, smiling apologetically, for anyone who stepped in front of him. His tic was almost gone. But he looked exhausted. My mother kept asking him if he didn't want to take a nap and he kept saying no; then at one point, he went into the basement, turned on the television, and fell asleep on the sofa. I sat in a wicker chair beside him watching the shows with the sound turned off.

I fell asleep, too. I woke to hear rumbling voices above the ceiling. Running up the stairs, I found my father standing beside the living room fireplace.

"You can't keep it, Robert," he said. He sounded adamant, as if he were telling Robert he couldn't keep a filthy stray animal he'd brought home. "That's all there is to it."

"Don't lean—please!" My mother, standing in the middle of the carpet, pointed to the mantelpiece. Carved wooden grapes, vines, and leaves twined along its edge; once it had crashed to the floor when Robert had rested his arm on it, and had cost over a thousand dollars to have repaired. My father stepped away from the mantelpiece, his elbow still sticking out at his side as if not knowing where to settle. He hadn't changed out of his dark business suit and silver necktie. His watch-chain drooped across his vest.

"Your opinion of my beard...." Robert, sitting forward on the sofa, gazed up into his face. "I realize it can't harm me."

"It's mad to be talking about something like this, Dean." My mother shook her head. "It's not as if we're going to take him to the club for Sunday lunch—as if nothing had happened."

"Only bums and—and beatniks look like that," my father said. "Is that what you are now?"

Robert looked around the room, his eyes narrowing. "I hoped I could just be who I am here. Here. But maybe that's crazy." Then his head snapped back, his mouth open. He screamed at the ceiling: "*Shit!* I'd forgotten how awful it could feel!"

His voice seemed to knock flakes of ceiling plaster onto my parents' heads. Their faces froze in shock. They stared at the carpet, the walls, everywhere but at Robert. I felt trembly, myself, I watched him.

"He needs his beard for a disguise," I said finally. "If the MP's recognize him, they'll beat him up and take him away."

My father turned to me. "Listen, Jerrett, your brother and I need to talk—"

"*Please* don't lean on the mantelpiece—" My mother pressed her fingers against her forehead.

My father moved away from the fireplace and sat down hard in an armchair. "All right, the beard's not the issue—it's just the shock of seeing you looking so different. What matters—well, I don't see how we—you can't expect us to hide you indefinitely!"

Robert turned his head slowly toward him. "You'd turn me in?"

"You're putting me in a terrible position!" My father

203

cleared his throat. "It's a legal matter. And I have a loyalty to the Air Force—"

"We're not turning him in!" my mother said. "We're not."

"Marian, this is too important a decision—"

"Too important for me to have any say in it?"

"Too important to get so emotional about. We can't lose all track of what's. . . right."

"What's right," she said, "is that our son's come back to us."

"I know, I know." My father suddenly stood up. "I can't have dinner in this suit," he said, and strode out of the room.

My mother sat on the sofa and picked up her glass from the coffee table. "Do you want a drink?" she asked Robert.

"I'm leaving it alone these days," he said. "Jerry wrote me that you were, too."

"You wrote him that?" she asked me.

I nodded. "Yeah."

"Oh, dear." She stared at the floor. "I only started again a while ago. And only after five o'clock."

"But it sneaks up, doesn't it?" Robert said.

"The question is, which sneaks up faster, the drinks, or whatever it is they're supposed to chase away."

"I think they get to be the same thing." Robert said.

My mother swirled her ice cubes in her glass. "I didn't know you knew about that."

"There's a lot you never knew about me," he said. "We've got a few days to learn things."

"If the cops come, you could hide under the eaves in the attic," I said to Robert. "Like that time—"

"Jerrett—" My mother looked up.

Robert turned to me. "Thanks, pal. But I've spent too much time in places like that."

My mother wanted to know what he meant. Then he told her about the jail cells and the mental hospital, in less detail than he'd told me but fully enough to produce sharp intakes of breath from her. As he finished, my father walked in wearing his dinner clothes—flannel slacks and a sports jacket. He'd forgotten to change his silver tie.

"Dean." My mother stood up. "I know how we can get Robert off! We can get a psychiatrist to talk to the Air Force—"

"What the hell are you talking about, Marian?" My father stopped halfway across the carpet. "It's out of the question!"

"You don't know what's happened. Robert—" She turned to him. "Tell him—please!"

Robert shook his head. "I don't want you to get me off. Forget it."

"I think we should have dinner, a nice family dinner." My father turned toward the door. "We don't have to decide anything tonight."

Dinner was like a strange underwater dream or a play set inside a huge fish tank. My father made baritone gurgling sounds, my mother made higher pitched ones, Robert nodded like some sort of branch coral. The grinning Toby mugs, a school of thick-lipped poisonous fish hovering along the wall, nibbled at the tension that floated by like algae. Manta-like again, I blended into the flickery darkness out of candle range.

My father wanted to catch Robert up on the activities of his friends whose fathers he knew. Names of people Robert had known kept bubbling up, bursting against the ceiling. Food was passed slowly; the room was awash with politeness. When dinner was over, the last bite of partially defrosted cake eaten, a silence settled over the room like the shadow of an ocean liner passing overhead, its engines stalled.

My father lined up his placemat along the table's edge. "Well...." He looked up. "Maybe you'd like to take a walk, Robert. You'd be surprised how the yard's changed."

"Dean, he's tired. He's not interested tonight." My mother started to gather in the plates.

"Why shouldn't he be interested? It's his home, isn't it?"

Robert gave me a glance and stood up, pulling his leather jacket off the back of his chair. I watched him follow my father outside.

For the next few nights, he and my father went for walks. They didn't talk about much, Robert said. I had the feeling he was waiting for my father to say some special thing to him, and when he did, Robert would be able to leave again. I dreaded this terribly, though I also feared that the longer he stayed, the more danger he was in of being caught. People must have seen him on his way to Ridge Haven.

I began helping my mother with the dishes after dinner, something I didn't usually do, but it seemed appropriate now. One night, I was putting some glasses away when the telephone rang in the hall. The jangling sound startled me, as it always did—what if it was the military police calling? My mother, her hands soapy, asked me to get it.

Picking up the phone, I heard a high indistinct voice like a tiny animal trapped inside the receiver. I loosened my grip, as if that would help the sound get out.

"...Dean?"

"My father's outdoors," I said, relieved that it wasn't the Air Force. "Who is this, please?"

"Oh—Jerrett, it's you." There was a pause. I heard faint music in the background. "How's your turtle?"

"What?" I frowned. "Who is this?"

"You met me years ago, at a party...." I heard a long breath. "We had a talk. There was... a model airplane, and a turtle."

"Mrs. Miller." I said. I sat down hard on the chair my mother kept beside the phone. I felt as if I should hang up, but the small, high voice kept me intrigued, as if Mrs. Miller had turned into a pretty red-haired young girl. I pictured her with a soft white fur over her shoulders. "How are you?" I managed to say.

"Not very well, I'm afraid...." Another long breath, like sandpaper being pulled along a ribbon. "But I'm glad...we got a chance to meet that time."

"Me too, I guess." I peered through the window beside the terrace door. "I don't know where my father is right now."

I heard a sigh. "It's hard... to keep my head up to talk."

"Are you sick or something?"

"They let me go home from the hospital, there was nothing more...." Her voice grew faint, and I had to press the receiver hard against my ear to hear. "It would be lovely, if he could come see me. Tonight...."

"Does my father know where you are?"

"Yes, he does. I'm sorry to call. Just tell him... please tell him I haven't got much time."

"All right." I heard the slow breathing. Then it faded. I could picture the phone slipping from her fingers onto a pillow. The dial tone's sudden buzz made me pull the receiver away from my ear fast.

I started out the terrace door. Fog was rolling in from the woods. Two figures approached. They walked side by side, their footsteps silent in the wet grass. I thought the bent-over figure was Robert, remembering his old walk, but then I saw it was my father, and that Robert, walking taller, was slowing his pace so as not to leave my father behind.

"I believe you have some homework, young man," my father said when he spotted me in the doorway.

"I need to talk to Robert," I said.

"He'll still be here tomorrow." My father patted my shoulder, an uncharacteristic gesture.

I went to the attic and took out my books. But as soon as I heard Robert's footsteps on the stairs, I went down to his room. He was sitting at his desk, the glow from the lamp shining in his face.

"Someone called for Dad," I said, and sat down on his bed. "It was Mrs. Miller."

"No kidding—she called here?"

"A little while ago."

Robert turned in his chair. "I met her once," he said.

"Where?"

"In New York. Miss Gilly called me when Mother was in the hospital, and I went from school to New York to tell Dad— at Mrs. Miller's apartment," Robert said. "I expected to hate her. But I just felt bad for her, in spite of everything. No easy job for anyone, being in love with Dad."

"You think she's really in love with him?"

Robert nodded.

"What about him—does he love her?"

"I guess. It's always hard to know what he feels. It's probably just as hard for him to know as for anyone else."

I shifted my position. "She's sick. I think she's about to die. She said she didn't have much time."

"Damn!"

"You know, I heard him talking to her on the phone once— when we were on that trip to Gettysburg. He suddenly got upset. He made a terrible noise. Maybe it was because she told him she was sick."

"It must have been serious, if he carried on like that." Robert walked to the window. "Did she ask for him to come see her tonight?"

"Yeah. I didn't want to tell him." I watched Robert turn around. "I thought I might start yelling it at him," I said.

"Maybe I'd better do it."

"What about Mother?" I glanced in the direction of her room. "How are we going to keep her from finding out? She's going to flip."

Robert headed for the door. "She's not the one I'm worried about."

I went up to my room and burrowed under the eaves, not sure what I was looking for. I took out the carton of toy soldiers, the ones with which Robert and I had populated the battlefields of World War I France. I forgot all about the time. Then all of a sudden the carpet looked like a dusty field strewn with tiny corpses. No amount of arranging men in formations could make them look heroic any more. I kicked them all over the floor. Then I hurried down the attic stairs.

The house was nearly dark. Where was everyone? I felt as if I'd woken after a long sleep. My father's room was empty. My mother's door was shut. No sounds of movement came from inside. I checked my watch; it was past midnight. I went downstairs to the living room. Robert was sprawled on the sofa in his jeans and old shirt. He still didn't want to sleep in his own room, but he was closer to it than the basement where he'd been sleeping all week.

The moonlight streamed through the windows and made the place look like a big tank drained of water—or an empty stage set. In the dining room, the candlesticks stood on the table like left-behind props. I hurried toward the garage.

My father's car was gone. He'd been in such a hurry to leave that he'd left the garage door open, something he never did. This man who never did anything on impulse, who never revealed himself capable of a whisper of passion—he must have driven away in the middle of the night to be with Laura Miller.

208

- FIFTEEN -

Dean Langley walks into the apartment in New York. Mrs. Miller's ancient chauffeur whispers to him in the hall. He points him toward Laura's bedroom. Then he puts a recording of the final act of *La Traviata* on the phonograph. The music swells through the apartment. He sits in an antique chair just outside the bed chamber, watching.

The door opens onto an opera set, and there is the lovely courtesan sprawled across an enormous four-postered bed. She is lit from above, stage left, bathed in a sunset glow that flows magically through the bed's silken canopy. The red velvet curtains are closed behind her. Her robe is trimmed in white fur, open at her throat; her arm trails toward the carpet. As her lover approaches, she raises her head, and her hennaed hair floods over her shoulders. Her lips open in a happy gasp.

Dean kneels beside the bed, his shadow bending on the floor behind him. The darkness billows in the corners of the room, giving off a low hum.

I leave my chair. Casting no shadow myself, I stand in the doorway, my white hair falling over my forehead. I light the stub of a cigar and whistle an old cowboy song:

Eyes like the setting stars, cheeks like a rose
Laura, she's a pretty girl, God almighty knows

The smoke from my cigar drifts across the room, blending with the lady's perfume. I know from the way Dean twitches his nose that he smells the smoke. I grin.

What are they whispering to each other? Are they recalling their afternoons in Westchester County in the 1920's and '30s and '40s, and their '50s rides in the belly of the new white-finned whale as I drove them to Connecticut?

I used to stop in the park behind the station where his "late trains" arrived. Kids rode by on their bicycles and gaped at the car. In the back seat, she lay her plump hand on his arm as she listened to him. His silver hair was combed back from his forehead. He talked about his slowing tennis game, about the reorganization of the church vestry. She chatted about her nieces and the problems of settling her husband's estate. The lovers

209

pressed their cheeks together. He patted the back of her hand as he got out.

I whistle through my teeth.

He is holding her hand now, sitting beside her on the bed. Her fingers cannot twine delicately around his; her knuckles are swollen with arthritis. His own hand is bony and liver-spotted; it takes its warmth from hers. He gazes down at her, lines appearing in his cheeks. Her jowls sag when she smiles.

As she tries to push closer to him, her robe falls open, and a soft pink globe flops beside her on the sheet. He cups it from beneath, the palm of his hand remembering when it was firm and round and thrust high into the air as she arched her back beneath him.

She is too weak to cover herself. Her eyes close with embarrassment. Leaning over, he touches his lips to her breast. Then with perfect politeness he tucks it back into her robe.

I stand over him now, my fatherly hand, even bonier than his, resting on his shoulder. He shudders. My necktie, stained with boarding house gravy, dangles from my collar. He grabs it, yanks it hard, but he cannot choke me. Then he just hangs on for dear life, pulling me down.

She gives us a girlish smile and gazes up at us. The orchestra swells, *con molte passione*. We are one man now, sitting on the side of her bed and swinging our heels, telling salesman stories to bring a smile to her lonely small-town face.

Blow some of that smoke my way, she says, I love the smell of a man's cigar...and I do, making her laugh. She sits up, holding the sheet to her chest, letting it fall open along her white thigh.

Something to remember me by, she says, and reaches under the bedclothes. The sheet whispers as her hand burrows between her legs. The orchestra's conga drums do a *merengue* flourish.

Here! Suddenly she lifts her hand in the air, opening her fingers wide in the glare of the spotlight.

Something flutters down through the perfumed air. I dive for it in the folds of her robe. It tickles the palm of my hand as it escapes. The laughter of its butterfly wings brushes my ear. I turn and see a tiny ghost of a shadow flit out of the red light to be absorbed in the darkness.

Now I lift my head slowly, and hear her last breath. . . sandpaper scraping slowly to the end of a long silk ribbon.

I rest my hand along her cheek. Her eyelashes flutter but her lids are too weak to rise. Leaning close to her, I cry

Oh, Laura, Laura.…

The living room was dark, the house silent. I saw the moon slip into view outside the window, its glow turning the top of the piano silver. My brother rolled over on the couch, his arm draped over his eyes as he began to snore. I walked around the rooms downstairs, periodically checking my watch. My father must have taken an hour and a half to reach New York; he could be there now. Or he could be heading back by this time. I had no idea why I was waiting for him.

At about three o'clock, I lay down on the bed in Miss Gilly's old room. Then, minutes later, it seemed, I was aware of a machine pulsing noisily nearby, its vibrations filling the air around me. I sat up on the bed. The room smelled of exhaust fumes. The engine sound was coming from the garage.

Opening the screen door from the corridor, I nearly walked into the grill of the Dodge, parked with its nose flush against the door frame. One of its headlights was broken. The car was empty. I heard a noise from outside and walked into the damp gray air. A tall figure slipped out the side door of the toolshed.

"Dad?" I called out.

He stopped for a moment, facing me, and I could see that he still had on his sports jacket and tie. The tie hung sideways at his open shirt collar. He was holding an axe over his shoulder like a rifle.

He strode across the lawn. Mist rose off the grass further down the hill. He seemed to be heading into it when he stopped beside the terrace, glaring at the big maple before him as if it had just moved to block his way. His arm rose; the axe head swished through the air and thunked into the tree.

The terrace door opened. Robert stepped out. My father strode on. I ran after him, slowing as Robert came onto the terrace.

"What's he doing?" Robert called.

"I don't know. He just got home."

"I heard the car." Robert peered down the lawn. My father moved in a lurching zig-zag pattern toward a group of birch

211

trees. Another chunk! sound. Then silence. Then a barrage of chops from closer by, behind the big pine tree.

My mother's window opened. "Dean!" she called out. Then she saw us below her. "He's trying to cut down the pine!" she shouted.

"Don't lean so far out!" Robert called.

"I'm coming downstairs—" Her head retreated inside.

Robert and I ran across the grass toward the sound of chopping. I saw some long feathery branches sway. One fell, and in the space it left, I saw my father's face, a streak of hair falling over his eyes.

"Over here!" I called to Robert.

Then my father was gone again. We lost him in the mist. The hills across the valley were outlined in a wavy line like a child's drawing on glowing gray paper. The dog barked from behind the toolshed. Then we heard the whack of the axe from the front yard and ran toward it. My father was flailing away at the oak by the flagstone walk.

My mother stood on the doorstep beneath the carriage lamp. "Can't you stop him?" she called to us, hugging her bathrobe against her throat.

Now my father started on the forsythia bush beside the driveway. Branches flew as the axe head swished back and forth. I'd never seen his face so clenched, his eyes so wildly unfocused. He lurched behind the bush. When Robert and I began to follow, he came out on the other side.

He was heading for my mother. I heard him breathing hard. My mother walked out to meet him, her bathrobe flapping around her ankles.

She stopped in front of him. "Please, Dean—*no!*"

He kept moving toward her, his axe dragging beside him.

"I'm sorry—I'm very sorry about Laura," she said, her voice quavery. "But you don't want to destroy everything, do you?"

Robert came around the forsythia bush behind my father. I cut sideways, gauging the distance between my parents, ready to run between them. My father lurched forward, his breath rasping in his throat, the axe rising in his hand.

My mother took a step backward. "Dean!—" she shouted.

He stopped several yards from her. His head hung down. Robert was a running blur behind him. The axe lowered. My father let it slip from his hand an instant before Robert dove into the middle of his back.

The two of them stumbled to the ground together, Robert's arms locked around my father's waist. My father's eyes were wide open when he hit the grass. I ran to him and fell onto his legs, holding him down.

He didn't stir. I sat up. Robert rolled away from him. Lying on his stomach, my father looked as if he'd fallen from a great height and hit the ground with a terrible thud.

My mother sank to one knee. "Dean?"

Struggling to my feet, I heard him groan. His arm moved. Robert sat up and saw it, too—my father was crawling across the grass on his hands and knees toward my mother. He raised himself up, then dropped again, his face in her lap. Her hand rested on his head. His shoulders rose and fell. He was sobbing.

I picked up the axe, my fingers trembling so hard I nearly dropped it. Robert and I took it to the toolshed. Then we went into the kitchen to put on some water for coffee.

In a while, my parents came in through the front door. We watched them pass in the hall. My father's flannel trousers were torn at the knee, pale flesh showing through. My mother, her nightgown trailing beneath the damp hem of her bathrobe, guided him by the arm. Low voices came from my father's room.

"Did you think he was going to hit her with the axe?" I asked Robert.

He stared at the glass dome bubbling on the coffee percolator. "There's times you have to make your move and think afterwards."

"He'd dropped the axe before you tackled him."

Robert took a deep breath. "I'm glad to know that."

I sat down at the kitchen table and drank a cup of coffee with him, though I usually had tea for breakfast. "Have you ever seen him cry before?" I asked.

"I didn't know he even had tear ducts," Robert said. "I used to think he never secreted any bodily fluids at all."

I kept shaking my head. I could still feel the sensation of the axe handle in the palm of my hand. It made the cup hard to hold.

After a long time I heard footsteps on the stairs again. Through the kitchen doorway we saw my parents in the hall. My mother had on a skirt and blouse outfit, with pearls. My father was dressed in his business suit, his briefcase in his hand. He opened the closet door, took out a raincoat, then hung it back up again. He must have noticed the sunlight streaming through the living room windows.

"Is he really going to the office?" I whispered to Robert.

"I doubt it—look."

He was heading toward the front door, not the garage. When I saw my parents again, out the kitchen window, he was no longer carrying his briefcase. They walked slowly up the flagstone walk to the oak tree, where my father touched the gash he had made in its trunk. He seemed to be stroking it. They walked along the driveway toward the forsythia bush. Branches lay strewn on the gravel. My father leaned over and gathered some up. My mother picked up a handful. They lay the branches in a little pile. Then they continued on across the front lawn.

We watched them moving slowly along, several feet apart but side by side. They vanished behind some cedar trees and reappeared in the bright slanting sunlight, their legs moving in unison in a kind of strolling lock-step. Sometimes they leaned in the same direction, as if the ground were slightly tilting beneath their feet. They stopped, and my father stared down the hill like a man gazing out to sea. My mother took his arm.

They seemed to be posed in a photograph. I stood at the window and squinted into the glare, focusing on them as sharply as I could, trying to keep them framed there in the window.

After taking my father back to his room, my mother came down wearing a blue suit jacket over her blouse, and started frying some bacon. She didn't try very hard to make me go to school. I scrambled some eggs in a bowl and Robert reheated the coffee. We arranged some orange juice, a plate of eggs and bacon on a tray. Robert took it upstairs to my father. My mother and I made up another tray and carried it into the dining room.

In a few minutes, Robert joined us. "Dad's pretty calm now," he said.

"Did you get him his bathrobe?" my mother asked. "He'll need it to sit up in bed. He was very chilled."

"I got it for him," Robert said.

"Where's your leather jacket?" she asked him.

"I'm all right." He smiled at her.

She glanced at me and, seeing that I had on a sweater, confronted the yellow mound of eggs on her plate. "I don't know if I can eat this."

"How are you feeling?" I asked.

She took a sip of coffee. "I ought to be relieved, I suppose. But I'm a little sad, now that Laura's... gone. We were friends years ago, believe it or not. We used to go shopping at Lord & Taylor." One corner of her lips rose in a faint smile. Her coffee cup made a fast clicking noise against her saucer; she let go of its handle, silencing it. "When I had you—" She looked at Robert. "Laura came to the hospital with flowers, and an orange teddy bear."

Robert put down his piece of bacon. "Amazing," he said. "I remember that bear."

"It must have been hard for her. She wanted children so badly." My mother lit a cigarette and sat back. "Her last illness was very painful, evidently."

"Was he there when she died?" I asked.

"Until she lost consciousness."

"Aren't you mad at him?" I squinted at her.

"Yes." She dropped her eyes. "Yes, I am...."

"Why are you staying with him?" Robert asked.

She lifted her head slowly. "I'm his wife," she said.

I remember what a strange day it was—the air clear and bright with sunlight while people tried to sleep or wandered around the house finding things to do. Robert and I went to his room to sort baseball cards. It was a relief to talk about baseball. I needed to tell him how awful it was that the Dodgers were leaving Brooklyn to go to California, a place so far away it might as well be on Mars. The idea that we could never again go to games in Brooklyn had me so choked up that I actually started to cry.

"It's not *fair*!" I insisted.

"I know," Robert said. "They used to tell me about how fair things were supposed to be. At that Country Day School, and prep school. They shouldn't do that to kids."

I told Robert about the school in Colorado. He thought it sounded like a good place for me. "It's not that far from California," he said.

My father came to dinner dressed in his usual slacks, sports jacket, white shirt and knit tie. Since Robert hadn't put on a clean shirt, I didn't either. I hoped my father would ask me to go change. I wanted to tell him I wasn't the only one around here that needed to do some changing. That was exactly how I was going to put it.

But he didn't seem to notice what I was wearing. I wondered what he'd have to say to us. As he unfolded his napkin, I waited for an apology, or at least an explanation for his behavior this morning—something to show us that he knew we were onto him.

"Smells like steak," he said, glancing toward the kitchen.

I looked at Robert. There was nothing to do but unfold our napkins.

My father ate more slowly than usual, and sometimes he stared out the window, his eyebrows looking so bushy and heavy that it must have been difficult for him to see out from beneath them.

I remember him sitting there at the table looking tired, old, but apparently thinking nothing at all. I watch him press his fork into a piece of meat, put it in his mouth. . . and now, for a split second, comes a shudder in his jaw which tells me that eating anything at this moment is causing him pain and nausea. Then, determinedly, he begins to chew. His jaw moves, his Adam's apple bulges as he forces the food down his throat.

And in that brief pause I see that this is all a performance, this eating. This is the way the man has gotten through most of his life: grinding his jaws and forcing himself to swallow everything he has worked so hard for, then reaching for more, whether he likes it or not. Now and then he gets to act outside of his role. And very occasionally he gets caught out there. But that's not significant. The long-haul performance is what counts.

I see, too, that the act is more for him than for anyone else. He believes that he has no choice but to keep it up—look what happened this morning when he suddenly forgot all his training.

I scream at him though my eyes: I know what you're doing! You're acting it! You've always been doing it!

And he glances back at me in such a way as to slam my look away as if it were an easy backcourt lob. So what? You'll learn to do the same one day if you've got any brains. Meanwhile, eat your life and lump it.

And then his eyes go blank again. He takes a sip from his water glass to force down his grief along with the clotted meat collecting at the back of his throat. What is appalling is that, in a way, I admire his performance. He really does have what it takes to recoup and once again block all the chaos rising within him.

But he's so terribly lonely. I see him sitting at the table in the flickering glow of the candles, with four more candles blinking in the shiny mirror behind him, and again I see the man in a phone booth beside a roaring highway. He is still in his glass box. The air is thin and stale and hard to breathe in there. He hates living inside it as much as I hate to see him there, shut off from us. But he cannot get out now.

"We should take the car to the garage tomorrow," my mother said. "For that headlight."

He looked at her and nodded. "Yes."

"We'll take it in early, so you won't miss your train," she said.

He nodded again. "This is good, Marian," he said, pointing at the meat on his plate.

"I'm afraid it got a little overdone."

"I prefer it well done," he said. "How's yours?" He turned to me, then Robert.

We said that ours was fine.

I see the house as a big rickety stage set. I'm more of an observer now than a participant: a change I'm not sure I like. But it's not as if I have a choice about this any more.

The front wall of the house is cut away to reveal the various rooms, staircases, halls. Spotlights illuminate one room at a time where characters are talking, gesturing, moving about. From off-stage comes the occasional sound of a car starting, or a lawn mower droning. Sometimes there is the slap...slap of a

217

ball landing in baseball mitts. The ball's shadow arcs across the forest-green set behind the house, then two figures enter the kitchen through a screen door. A piano plays jazz with a hard, rumbling beat; it is cut off in the middle of a bar and the house goes dark again.

Sometimes two second floor rooms are lit at the same time. In one, a man pores over books with photographs of old airplanes in them. He looks up now and then, listening for something.

In the other room, a woman paces, lights cigarettes, sits on a chaise lounge and tries to read. She too stops moving from time to time, and listens.

Across the house, a very dim light comes on to reveal a bearded young man staring out a window. He does not read or smoke or pace. All his movement is in his eyes as he listens.

The light goes on in the attic. A boy sits on his bed and turns the knobs of an old wooden radio, its orange dial aglow. He is very restless, just marking time in this place. Now his hand stops moving. He, too, is listening, waiting.

Am I sitting too high above the set, or is no one speaking out loud? Now I begin to hear murmurs, everyday intonations whose meanings I can fill in: Don't forget your history book....We're invited for cocktails this Friday, have we got anything planned?... Time to feed the dog, you can give it those scraps from last night...Where's my raincoat?... The meat's a little too well done, I'm afraid....

I can see from their facial expressions and gestures that the players are throwing themselves into this production as if their lives depended on it. They seem hopelessly miscast in their roles, and it's hard to watch them struggling on without a script to work with. But if I leave I might miss something. And I know now that I'd regret that terribly.

Then what everyone seemed to have been listening for, happened. Strange cars rolled up the driveway, two of them. They stopped at the end of the walk. Men in military uniforms got out. Two stayed with the cars, looking around the yard. The other two knocked on the front door.

My mother, who hadn't seen them, was heading along the hall toward the door when I stopped her. "Military police," I whispered.

Her face went pale. I pulled her around the bottom of the stairs—I'd caught sight of a figure peering through the window beside the door. It was of opaque faux-antique glass; the man probably hadn't seen anything but a blur. From the pen behind the toolshed came the frantic barking of the dog. With each bark, my mother flinched.

"I'll go tell Robert," I whispered.

"I'll have to tell your father."

"What's he going to do?"

"I don't know." She gripped the stair railing. "He's hardly thought about anything else but this since Robert came home."

Upstairs, I pushed open the door to Robert's room. He stood far back from the window, staring down past the curtains at the drive.

I stopped a few feet from him.

"I saw," he said. Suddenly he turned toward the doorway.

My father stood there, looking exhausted. He lifted his eyes from the floor and stared at Robert.

"Don't tell the police he's here!" I blurted. "Don't do it!"

My father's mouth opened; I could see that he wanted to speak, but then the doorbell buzzed downstairs. He turned sharply. His shoulders straightened. We heard his footsteps going down the stairs.

"You can get out Dad's window," I whispered.

"I know. But I need to hear what he's going to say." Robert rested his hand on my shoulder.

"Dean?" That was my mother. From where we stood, we could see her leaning over the railing on the landing outside her room.

My father glanced up at her. Then he opened the front door.

"We're looking for your son, Mr. Langley."

"My son Robert?"

"We're sure he's in Ridge Haven now. He was seen a week ago."

"Oh?"

"Do you mind if we come in?" My father cleared his throat. I felt Robert's hand tighten on my shoulder. Outside the window, another car appeared on the driveway, a blue and white police cruiser.

"What do you want?" my father asked.

"We'd just like to look around, if you don't mind."

219

There was a long pause. I looked at Robert. His eyes narrowed.

We heard my father speak. "As a matter of fact, I do mind."

"Why is that, sir?"

"You'll have to excuse me," my father said. The door clicked shut.

Robert ruffled my hair. Then he rushed out of the room, nearly colliding with my father at the top of the stairs.

"Robert—"

My brother grabbed his arm. They shook hands fast. As Robert darted down the landing, my father reached out for him, his fingers brushing the back of his jacket.

My mother stepped away from the rail, her arms rising. Robert hugged her. I heard a faint cry as she buried her face against his chest. Then he was gone into my father's room.

I ducked between my parents and got there first. Robert had opened the window onto the garage roof. The dog's barking was suddenly louder. Robert climbed over the sill. I climbed down, too, and felt his hands steadying my legs as I dropped beside him. We slipped down the roof feet first as if sliding into a base.

He lay on his stomach, his legs dangling over the edge. "Can you hold onto my arm?"

"Yes." I dug my heels into the roof and grabbed his wrist. He let himself slowly down. His fingers dropped off the edge. I didn't want to release my grip, but I had to. His wrist slipped out of my hands. He was gone.

I squatted against the slope of the roof. The dog's barks grew faster and faster. With a crunch of gravel, the police car stopped just around the side of the garage. I saw Robert again: he'd landed in the flower bed and fallen forward onto the grass. He picked himself up.

"I'm okay!" He whispered up at me, grinning. Then he took off across the lawn.

I see him cutting around the terrace and disappearing under the plume-like branches of the pine. Some men stand at the corner of the driveway, looking toward the toolshed and the sound of the dog. But Robert is dashing along the side lawn on his way down the hill.

Flattening myself against the roof, I watch him move

behind the cedar trees. There are enough of them left to give him the cover he needs. The men beside the garage don't see him.

The grass glows in the sunlight; the lawn, open and empty, ripples as a breeze blows some leaves along its surface. Then Robert vaults over the stone wall like someone hopping a freight train, and I am with him, plunging into the woods.